PRAISE FOR TRISH JENSEN!

"Trish Jensen's writing is a giggle a minute…fast-paced, witty, and utterly captivating."
—*Romance Reviews Today*

"She's got a great comic touch and an ear for dialogue."
—*A Romance Reader Review*

STUCK WITH YOU

"This is a fun-filled romantic comedy that will definitely tickle your fancy."
—*Romantic Times*

"*Stuck With You* is a comic romp through the perils of love and lust. If you enjoy rapid-fire dialogue, sexual tension and comedic release, you won't want to miss this…"
—*Romance Reviews Today*

B E E P !

Leah scrambled backwards about as gracefully as a warthog and mumbled, "I'm sorry." She averted her gaze to anything but the man. She felt her cheeks go fire-truck red. Her breast had beeped at him.

And he'd obviously noticed, as his gaze honed right down on it. "Funny, I've never heard of a woman arming her body with a security alarm before."

"That was...ummm, my cell phone. I didn't have any room left in my purse," she said, coming up with about the lamest excuse ever utttered, but quick retorts had never been her strong suit.

He was either a real gentleman or a moron, because he just nodded. "Women have so much to carry around with them. I don't know how you do it."

Other *Love Spell* books by Trish Jensen:

AGAINST HIS WILL
STUCK WITH YOU

PHI BETA BIMBO

TRISH JENSEN

LOVE SPELL NEW YORK CITY

LOVE SPELL®

January 2005

Published by

Dorchester Publishing Co., Inc.
200 Madison Avenue
New York, NY 10016

ISBN 0-505-52585-2

The name "Love Spell" and its logo are trademarks of Dorchester
Publishing Co., Inc.

Printed in the United States of America.

Visit us on the web at www.dorchesterpub.com.

To Kate Seaver, an extraordinary editor, because she has to be a saint for putting up with me, and because she's a genius. Did I mention she's a saint? And to Leah Hultenschmidt for allowing me to steal her name and make her a bimbo when she's actually a very smart cookie. Dorchester rocks.

And to my nephew, Philip, who had the nerve to grow up. When you were one week old you slept on my chest. If you did that right now, I'd suffocate in a minute. The future is yours. And I don't doubt for a second that you're going to achieve all of your dreams. I can't wait to watch.

AUTHOR'S NOTE

There are days when I just want to stay in bed. This is usually accompanied by my dear friend and favorite author, Sandra Hill, calling me to insist I wake my lazy butt up. Writing isn't for sissies. And I'm a sissy. So it means the world to me that I have a friend who keeps reminding me not to be a sissy. She will call me (WAY too early) and say, "How about you write a book about this?" She was the one who encouraged me to write a book set at a dog spa, because I'm an animal freak. Thus, *Against His Will* was born.

Then one day she said, "Do I have a title for you!" And she threw it out. Phi Beta Bimbo. The problem was, she forced me to actually come up with a story to fit the title, and then made me write it myself. I hate when friends do that.

But I received enough mail from readers about *Against His Will* asking for Mark's story, I knew he had to be the hero in this one.

The funny thing is, Sandra pushed my buttons at the right times. And she kept on pushing. So my thanks to Sandra, for trying to keep me from being a sissy.

PHI BETA BIMBO

Chapter One

"Am I a sexpot, or what?"

"Or what."

Leah Smith laughed as she emerged from the Luscious Lingerie dressing room. "What do you think?" She thrust back her shoulders for maximum effect, straining the cotton threads of her cherry-red T-shirt. "Are these boobs or are these boobs?"

"I'd be really impressed," her brother, Steve, observed dryly, "if more than fifty percent of them were actually yours."

"Very funny," she said, eyeing his own 40Cs. "Considering yours are one hundred percent fa—"

"Hey, hey, hey, little sister," Steve said in his Stephanie voice—which Leah estimated to be about an octave lower than Bea Arthur's. He crossed his pantyhosed legs, winced slightly, then uncrossed them quickly and stood instead. "Not in public. You wouldn't want to ruin my image, now, would you?"

Leah rolled her eyes, strutted past him to the store mirror, and stared at herself. "Wow. I'm built."

"Literally."

1

She scowled, but didn't answer him. The same green eyes and mouse-brown hair stared back at her, but the sight of her artificially enhanced chest made her look foreign.

"Stephanie's" pumps clicked on the tile floor as he clanked up to her and took in her image over Leah's shoulder. "Kinda makes you feel a little wicked, eh?"

"Wicked's not what I'm going for." *Well, not completely, anyway.*

"Then you probably don't want them so pointy. Pointy definitely says 'wicked.'"

"What says 'bimbo'?"

"Cleavage. Lots of cleavage."

Leah glanced to her left and saw the store clerk eyeing them strangely. She could just imagine what the girl was thinking. "Back off, bro," she whispered over her shoulder. "People will talk."

Steve stepped back and glanced around. When he spotted the clerk, he gave her his best Stephanie smile. "Would you be a dear and bring us one of your Pump You Ups?"

Leah was almost positive she didn't want to know, but she asked anyway, "What in Hades is a Pump You Up?"

"You'll see."

"Sure," the girl said. "Any particular color?"

"Oh red, definitely red," Steve said.

The girl smiled and left.

"Doesn't she need to know what size?" Leah asked.

"No."

"Dare I ask why not?"

"It's all in the pump, toots."

"The pump," Leah said faintly. "This doesn't sound good."

"It's painless, I promise."

Leah glanced at her brother, dressed in his Stephanie

drag attire. It always amazed her how he fooled so many people with his female persona. Even with the wig and makeup and Donna Karan numbers, he still looked like Steve to her. How no one else had caught on all these years she couldn't fathom.

"Why are we Stephanie today?" she asked him.

"Board meeting," he said, scowling as he took in his appearance in the mirror. "God, I hate this getup."

"I thought you said it would be over soon."

"Three months, two days, and eighteen hours, but who's counting?"

"How are you going to do it?"

"Stephanie's going to send out a company-wide memo announcing a mandatory meeting. And then me, as me, will tell them all that their CEO has decided to seek new horizons, and has named me, her general manager, to take charge."

Leah turned from the mirror. "You hate this charade. The company's doing well. Why are you keeping it up?"

"Because I feel obligated to my backer. He wanted a woman in charge; he got a woman in charge. Once I pay him off, I'm free. No more Stephanie."

"I hope no one will fault you for the tiny deception if they find out the truth."

"Tiny?" Steve snorted. "Baby sister, I've been wearing drag for almost five years now, and I'm mighty sick of it."

Leah truly sympathized. Even though Steve had to don panty hose only on rare occasions, she knew how much he hated the ruse. So she quickly changed the subject. "Thanks again for letting me do my experiment at Just Peachy," Leah said.

He waved. "Anything for my kid sister. But tell me, why are you doing this again?"

"Pure research." *Sort of.*

"Doesn't sound very pure to me, brainiac. Or scientific. Besides, you already turned in your thesis."

"It's not meant to be scientific. It's more like a case study. The sociologist in me wants to test a theory." *Sort of.*

"Testing a theory is going under cover as a busty bimbo?" He looked pretty skeptical.

Leah shrugged, but didn't respond. If she were totally honest with her brother, she'd have to admit that part of her just wanted to see how the other half lived. Being a bookish, lackluster nerd had begun to grow old after twenty-eight years.

"What's the title of your masterpiece again?" Steve asked.

" 'An Ad Hoc Inquiry into the Contribution of Physical Presentation Toward Vocational Advancement Opportunities.' "

"Uh-huh. Translate that into English, please?"

Leah threw back her shoulders and faced the mirror once again. "Who gets the job? The busty bimbo or plain-Jane Leah."

"One of these days Gramps and I will be able to convince you that you're beautiful just as you are."

"Sure you will." *When hell hosts the Winter Olympics.*

"Thorndike will not hire the bimbo."

"Oh, I can almost guarantee he'll hire the bimbo."

"What's the bet?" Steve asked, waggling his Slap-on Nails. "My company hires only the best. Thorndike's not going to go for the busty-bimbo routine."

"I'm betting he will," Leah said, always ready to kick her brother's butt in any wager. "Name the stakes."

"Hmmm. All the laundry for one month?"

"Not a chance. I'm *not* washing your panty hose."

"Like I'd have a good time laundering your sweats.

4

You don't exactly come home in pristine condition after your morning torture."

She could argue, but she'd lose. "Okay, how about this? If I win, you go out on a date with the woman of my choosing."

"A blind date? I don't think so."

"You need to get a life, bro."

"Yeah, and you're just painting the town red. When was the last time you had a date?"

Leah was pretty sure it had still been the twentieth century, but enough about her. It was about time for Steve to find a good woman. He'd been working too hard for too long. Especially those times when he'd had to work in heels. "I win, I set you up."

"I win, I set *you* up. In fact, I know just the guy. He's doing some contract work for me at the office."

Leah hesitated only for a second, because she was fairly darn sure she'd win. She stuck out her hand. "Deal."

While Steve fidgeted with his girdle, Leah admired her bust in the mirror once more, strangely feeling like it changed her in some intrinsic way. "This being-built thing feels really different."

Steve frowned, looking like he wanted to argue her decision once again. But then he just shrugged his shoulders—which in Leah's opinion were way too wide for *anyone* to believe he was actually a woman. But he'd been fooling people for years now. People apparently saw what they wanted to see. And since Stephanie was supposed to be Steve's twin, people figured the resemblance made sense. At least, that was the only explanation Leah could figure.

"When do your interviews start?" he asked.

"The busty, blond bimbo's is Monday morning. I'm Monday afternoon."

Steve laughed. "Oh, jeez. Gramps is probably going to have a seizure. It's bad enough that his only grandson dresses in drag."

"He already knows about the plan," Leah said. "He's trying to be real twenty-first-century about it. Besides, he understands it's just an experiment."

"He probably heard Oprah— Oh, damn," Steve said, going stiff.

Leah followed his gaze to spot a gorgeous brunette entering the store. "Someone you know?"

"Unfortunately. That's the crook, Kate Bloom."

"Kate Bloom? The president of Apple Blossom Cosmetics, Kate Bloom?"

"The one and only," Steve said, his voice coming out in a low growl that would have passersby wondering what kind of steroids Stephanie Smith was ingesting.

"Uh-oh." Leah had heard plenty about Kate Bloom in the last few years. None of it flattering. "The competition."

"And the reason I just spent a fortune on a state-of-the-art security system. And why I had a setback paying off the loan. But soon this is all going to be over."

"A fortune on a security system. Why in the world?"

Another feral growl escaped his frowning lips. "That woman and Apple Blossom Cosmetics are just one too-small step behind us whenever we introduce new products."

Leah stared at her brother, whom she loved more than anyone else in the world, save Gramps. "You're not saying . . . she's stealing from you?" Indignation burrowed right up from her tummy to her throat. *No one,* and she meant *no one,* messed with the only family she had left.

"Damn straight," he said. "And I'm going to prove it, and then Kate Bloom and Apple Blossom are going down hard. I almost relish the image of her wearing very unflattering stripes."

Steve glanced away and began to pretend great interest in a display of tiger-print thongs. But in the mirror, Leah could watch the woman behind her, and she knew the second Ms. Bloom spotted him. The stunning lady hesitated a moment, then came strolling over with a grim smile on her face. "Well, hello, Stephanie."

With a nasty smile of his own, Steve turned. "Kate."

"I'd never have pictured you shopping at this store," the head of Apple Blossom Cosmetics said, her blue eyes shooting sparks. "Do they sell girdles here or something?"

"Taking time off from corporate espionage to get yourself some more edible underwear?" Steve countered.

"Ma'am," the sales associate said, unaware she was walking right into a minefield.

With a barely audible groan, Steve turned to the young girl. "Yes?"

She held up the glowing red item. "Here's your Pump You Up."

"Holy shit! Check out this babe!"

Mark Colson, founder and owner of Colson Complete Security Systems, Inc., glanced up from one of the five computer monitors in the small but efficient security office. "Hmm?"

"Check this out! This babe is *hot*."

Mark wasn't real thrilled that Just Peachy's new chief of security was into such unprofessional observations about employees and visitors to his company's offices. After all, the man couldn't be effective if he got sidetracked this easily. Not only that, Mark had recommended him for the job. But Mark would address the man's inappropriate comments in a moment. Right now he was just a little curious. In the few weeks they'd been testing the new security system Bernie Mills had never had an outburst like this one before.

Mark stood and strolled over to the third monitor, the one Bernie was transfixed to. It was labeled HUMAN RESOURCES.

Mark immediately understood why Bernie's tongue was hanging out. Standing beside Harold Thorndike's massive desk was Harold himself, and a Marilyn Monroe blonde with beamers out to there, and visible cleavage that could probably house a B-52.

Wowza! He sucked in a breath and silently paid homage to Mother Nature.

She was the epitome of the type of women he was drawn to these days—unless that killer body also contained a sneaky mind, high ambitions, and a steel heart.

His initial reaction was that she was fairly tall, but he revised that conclusion when Thorndike waved her into a seat and she crossed those luscious legs. That was when he noticed the bright red stilettos that probably added at least four inches to her stature. Between that and the highly teased hair, her height was deceptive. Without them she probably rang in at around five-foot-six.

She was slender. Almost too slender for that chest of hers. She wore a fitted red skirt and jacket—the kind of jacket that had only one button on it, at her waist. He sure hoped, for her sake, that the threads on that button were the extra-strength variety. Or maybe not.

The outfit—suit or not—was less than demure. Men would have a hard time keeping their minds on balance sheets around this woman.

Mark reached down and pressed a couple of keys,

pumping up the volume a few notches. "Go monitor lab two, Bernie."

Bernie made a barely audible smirking sound, which Mark ignored.

He sat down and typed commands into the keyboard, signaling the video camera hidden in the office to zoom in on the woman. He could argue that his FBI training taught him to catalog her features, but he wasn't into lying to himself as a rule. Any red-blooded man would take a minute to admire this woman. Below that teased blond look, she had a pretty, sloped, unlined forehead, brilliant eyes, and a pert nose. Her skin was soft-looking, and her neck was long and smooth, just the right kind for a man to bury his face in.

While she waited in silence, probably while Thorndike reviewed her résumé, he watched her fidget just a little, tugging on the bottom of her suit jacket, her foot jiggling nervously. That was when he noticed one of the sexiest things about her—and that was saying plenty, considering the rest of the package—a delicate gold bracelet encircling her left ankle.

Not that he'd never heard of ankle bracelets before; he'd just never seen a woman actually wearing one. Visions of chains encircling her hands and ankles danced through his head. He was so distracted by the enticing images that it took him a while to realize the interview had commenced, and he must have missed the opening pleasantries.

"It would seem, Ms. Devereaux, that you've worked in many, many places."

"Oh, yes, indeed," the woman said in a breathy voice that would have made Marilyn proud. "In my youth, mostly. I was trying to find my calling."

Mark snorted. "Couldn't hold down a job," he interpreted.

"Waitress. Hat-check girl. Aerobics instructor . . ." There was a pause right then, and Mark could just imagine the same thought flitting through Thorndike's mind that was crossing his own: How in the hell could she jump up and down without her breasts smacking her in the face?

". . . boat expo model—"

"That one came close to being my calling," Ms. Devereaux, did he say her name was?—chimed in.

"I see," Thorndike said in a voice that sounded strangely strangled. "Short-order cook."

"Too much grease."

"Flower delivery."

"Fun, but not much room for advancement."

"Ms. Devereaux, you *do* realize that this job involves a lot of typing and filing."

"Typing? Filing? Is that what administrative assistants do?"

This was the point where Mark, were he doing the interviewing, would force her to recite her ABCs.

"And answering the phones."

"I can do that!" she said with a breathy, triumphant squeal.

"Well, that's good. But the problem I'm having is that, although your résumé certainly shows you to have a varied background in the workforce, none of these jobs actually trained you for this position."

"I learn fast!" The woman leaned forward, probably giving Thorndike an eyeful. "And I really need this job, Mr. Thorndike. I'd be so grateful if you gave me a chance. You won't regret it."

"Well—" At that moment, Mr. Thorndike's phone buzzed. He picked it up and spoke softly into the receiver while Blondie squirmed some more in her chair. But Mark was an expert, in his opinion, of judging peo-

10

ple in stressful situations. After interrogating hundreds of crooks during his years with the FBI, he knew uncomfortable from guilty in a heartbeat.

This wasn't just a woman squirming because she'd squeezed herself into an outfit that was at least one size too small. This wasn't a woman who was worried about the impression she was making. This was a woman who had deception written all over that pretty little forehead of hers.

His senses began to tingle, and it wasn't from the face and body that wouldn't quit filling his field of vision.

Thorndike dropped the phone into its cradle and stood. "If you'll excuse me a moment, I have a matter to clear up. It won't take more than a minute."

"Take your time, sugar."

Mark rolled his eyes. The woman had just committed suicide. But once Thorndike stopped staring at her as if she'd beamed down from Mars, he cleared his throat, fidgeted with his tie, then marched out of the room.

Mark hit a few more buttons, and the camera zoomed in closer. If he wasn't mistaken, the woman had a bead of sweat running down her temple. She swiped it away.

At the same time she uncrossed her legs and kept adjusting the back of her skirt. Or what was underneath it.

Suddenly she began muttering under her breath. Too low. He adjusted the volume even more.

". . . damn idiot probably couldn't remember the color of my hair, much less my eyes," she grumbled, scratching at the moisture on her temple. While she scratched, that blond hair *moved* and he spied a flash of brown underneath, before she shook her head and adjusted her blond locks with a grimace.

The woman was wearing a wig.

She stood up and wiggled around, fussing with her butt area. "If Steve ever tries to talk me into thongs again, I'm killing him."

Her voice, he noticed, had lost the breathy quality. It was now almost gravelly with anger and disgust.

And intelligent sentence structure.

And she was wearing a thong. That information didn't exactly diverge from the persona she'd taken on, but he filed the information away just the same, merely because he could think about it later in greater detail.

"Whoever invented this equipment deserves to hang in it," she said, then began adjusting her cleavage.

Adjusting her cleavage?

Mark's eyes almost bugged out as her cleavage actually moved. Not in normal ways, either. Up, down, left, right—she was itching her way through a mound of what was supposed to be *her*, and it wasn't shifting naturally.

"Marilyn Monroe" was so uncomfortable that she stuck a pen down her jacket while muttering swear words a good girl probably wouldn't even know. This might not be a good girl, so that was understandable. Except *this* girl wasn't actually pronouncing them; she was spitting them out one letter at a time. And they were pretty complicated ones, too. Then at the end of each one, she kept saying, "Sorry, Gramps, I'll make dinner tonight."

Personally, if Mark got them right, he thought Gramps—whoever he was—*wasn't* who she should be apologizing to. Unless Gramps had a really, really strong link—straight to the Maker.

Mark was fixated on this woman. She wasn't anything like the bimbo he'd just heard being interviewed. She was *not* an idiot not even qualified to deliver newspapers.

He stared in fascination, as she kept digging into her cleavage with a pen, until a sudden *szzzzzzzzzzzzzzzzzzzzzzzzzzzt* sounded loudly through the speakers, and he watched a breast made in heaven deflate right before his very eyes.

The woman looked distressed. She couldn't be more disappointed than he was, seeing that a fantasy of his had just burst louder than that fake contraption that had his imagination running wild. But still, she appeared almost ready to cry.

He'd feel sorry for her, but he'd had it with fakes. There wasn't a chance in hell he'd waste a moment indulging in the desire to comfort the fake blond bimbo who looked like she'd just lost her best friend.

The woman wiped away tears, all the while scrambling through her purse. She began stuffing her deflated boob with tissues, mints, anything she could stick in there. She even used her cell phone to pad herself.

God, he wished he had her phone number.

She looked lumpy as hell when she was finished. And boy, she was finished. No way would this woman land the job. But he was landing her the moment she left the building.

His job was to ferret out the possible corporate spies Stephanie Smith felt certain were either already working here, or were trying to infiltrate the company. She was a prime candidate. A total imbreastinator, using cleavage to get the job done. How rude. What man could resist? She'd make the perfect spy.

With that in mind, Mark went out to meet Just Peachy's very first suspect.

Chapter Two

Leah wobbled out the front doors of Just Peachy's offices, muttering under her breath while trying to juggle a briefcase, her purse, and her stuffed breast. She was deep in thought, wondering whether Mr. Thorndike had noticed her slightly changed appearance when he'd returned, mulling over how to satisfyingly murder her brother, staring down at her shoes, willing them to keep her in a vertical position until she could make it to her car and kick them off, when she ran straight into a rock-hard wall. And to her horror, that wall set off the cell phone stuffed in her right breast, causing it to beep three times.

With an "Oomph" she glanced up sharply, only to realize the wall was a chest, and her nose reached right to the center of it. The chest was clad in a denim shirt, which smelled faintly of a combination of sandalwood and—strangely enough—plaster. An odd but not unpleasant mixture.

"Excuse me," a deep, almost amused voice said, and Leah risked raising her chin slowly up, up, up, while she took in a male throat, nice chin, full lips tilted in something of a smile, a nose that was somewhat thin, but with a small bump at the bridge, and then into a pair of the darkest blue eyes she'd ever seen. Almost black, really.

And those eyes were crinkled in a smile that matched his lips, but with a glint of something a bit cynical that said he'd seen a lot in his thirty-five or so years. Not all of it Mister Rogers happy.

To avoid the eyes she completed the trip up to his hair. Wavy brown with streaks of gold that bespoke time in the sun.

It suddenly occurred to Leah that her perusal had taken more than a couple of seconds, and she was still plastered to his torso, and if she wasn't careful, her second pump was going to burst from the pressure.

She scrambled backward about as gracefully as a warthog, and mumbled, "I'm sorry," as she averted her gaze to anything but the man. She felt her cheeks go fire-truck red. Her breast had beeped at him.

And he'd obviously noticed, as his gaze honed right down on it. "Funny, I've never heard of a woman arming her body with a security alarm before."

"That was . . . ummm, my cell phone. I didn't have any room left in my purse," she said, coming up with about the lamest excuse ever uttered, but quick retorts had never been her strong suit.

He was either a real gentleman or a moron, because he just nodded. "Women have so much to carry around with them. I don't know how you do it."

She voted for moron. Although a really cute one. If she were into dense stud muffins, she might stick around. "Well, if you'll excuse me," she said, and

moved to walk around him, concentrating on not top-
pling over on the damn shoes that were killing her.

"Wait!" he said, stepping right back in front of her
again. "I haven't seen you here before. Do you work
here?"

That was when Leah realized she'd forgotten to keep
up the bimbo pretense in the embarrassment of the moment, and if she *did* miraculously land this job, he
might be one of her colleagues. Although, considering
his attire, she felt sure he must be in maintenance or
something. No tie, denim shirt, and—after a quick
glance downward—jeans said he probably wasn't on
the board of directors.

She tried to think fast. She managed to meet his
eyes again, and batted her lashes at him. "I'm sorry
about being abrupt," she said, letting her voice go a
teensy bit breathier so he didn't notice the drastic
change right off the bat. Then again, if he bought the
beeping breast bit . . . "I was just so *mortified* at not
watching where I was going." *Oh, great, Leah, bimbos wouldn't know how to pronounce* mortified,
*much less know what it means. You suck at this sub-
terfuge business.*

To her surprise, he thrust out his hand. "Mark Colson."

She hesitated before taking it. Then she held hers
out, palm side down, and said, "Charmed, I'm sure,"
which managed not only to make her look like a
Southern-belle hussy, but to make her purse slide down
her wrist and drop to the brick walkway. It splattered
open and everything inside bounced out, which included her wallet, brush, lipstick, face powder, and
about a dozen condoms.

Now she had bleating breasts and a horny purse.

This was worse than anything she could possibly imagine.

Once again, the idiot didn't seem to see anything wrong with this picture—including the fact that she could have stashed about twelve cell phones in the damn purse, which would negate her earlier assertion that she had no room in her Air Force One–size purse for anything else.

Leah wasn't certain why she'd packed the purse full of condoms, except that Gramps had told her it would set the mood, according to *Sandra's Sex Tips*, a talk show he had embraced fully . . . philosophically, of course. According to Sandra, a woman should carry things that would make her feel naughty. Since Leah hadn't felt naughty in all of her twenty-eight years, she decided to take the advice to heart. So on the way to the interview she'd stopped at a drugstore and stocked up on king-size condoms.

Leah was considering suing Sandra at the moment.

Since all of those condoms were causing a shiny glare, lying on the sidewalk in the early-afternoon northern Virginia sun, she had the feeling even this dumb-as-a-dandelion handsome guy couldn't fail to notice them.

"Come prepared, do you?" he asked.

Once again, her spontaneity skills eluded her. "My gramps says they're good for a flat tire," she said. Inside she cringed, waiting for the cynical laughter, witty comeback, smart-aleck remark. She got none of those.

Instead he asked, "Do you blow them up yourself?" And he really sounded sincere, and still dumb as a stump.

Breathing a sigh of relief that his stellar body didn't

house a stellar brain to match, she gave him her best smile. She could handle this conversation. "I have good lungs."

It was a bad comeback. His eyes immediately reverted to her awfully un-balanced and sad-looking chest. She held her breath and tried to appear busty. When she was pretty certain she wouldn't be able to pull that off, she bent down to shovel her stuff back in her purse.

Another mistake. He bent to help her, which put his face right at a level with her one-sided cleavage. To the hunk's credit, he didn't ogle, just helped her gather her spilled belongings.

"You didn't answer me," he reminded her. "Do you work here?"

"Well, I'm hoping to," Leah said. "I just finished an interview. But I don't think I did very well." She chanced a glance at his face while she slowly stood. "How about you?"

"You could say that." He rose, too. "You still haven't told me your name."

Leah had to take a second to remember it. "I'm Candi Devereaux," she said, letting her voice get just a bit more breathy. "That's Candi with an i, not a y."

"Hello, Candi with an i," he said, and that slight grin was back. "It was very nice—and interesting—to run into you, so to speak."

"Thanks for your help," she said, wanting desperately to get away and get her own breasts back.

"Wait!" the clod said, taking her arm in a grip that wasn't punishing, but also was unrelenting. "I notice you're not wearing a wedding ring."

"Aren't you Mr. Observant?" she snapped, then nearly bit her tongue in half. Sticking to the script was proving difficult. A good actress she was not. And having foreign objects stuck down her jacket was making her testy.

Once again, her tone slipped right over his very tall head. "Does that mean you'd be free to have dinner with me?"

That question shocked her right down to her Pump You Up. "Pardon me?"

"Dinner. You know, meat, starch, vegetables."

"I don't think so. But thank you so much for asking."

"Why not?"

"I'm . . . busy."

"How do you know? I haven't picked a night."

"I'm busy most nights."

"If you don't want to go out with me, just say so. I won't be offended."

"I don't want to go out with you."

"Why not?"

Trying desperately to reprise her role as bimbo, Leah started batting her lashes at him, but recognized her mistake when her blue-tinted contact lenses began slipping around on her eyeballs. "Look, you seem nice. I'm just not interested."

"Are you involved with someone else?"

"No," she blurted before she thought it through. *Damn honesty.*

"Then why not have a free meal on me?"

This time she *did* think about it. Why not? Her social life was all but nonexistent, and the guy was definitely a looker. Dumb as a moon rock, but very easy on the eyes. And even though her thesis didn't include the effect of appearances in social situations, it would still be an interesting study. What would it be like to go out in public playing the part of a siren?

She shot him what she hoped passed for a coy smile. "How do I know you're not a convict or anything?"

He laughed, a low, rumbly sound that drummed in her belly. "Clean as a whistle, I swear. I'm just a poor working Joe who thinks you're pretty."

No one had ever told her she was pretty. Well, except for Gramps and Steve, but they were kind of required to say so. It sort of bit that she had to be disguised to finally receive that compliment, but it felt good, too. "Just dinner?"

"We could also take in a movie if you like. I'll even let you pick, and won't complain if you choose a chick flick. I'm real open-minded that way."

She could happily punch him in the gut for that one. What kind of Neanderthal used the words *chick flick*? But she just continued to smile at him. Through a somewhat clenched jaw she said, "Actually, I prefer suspense thrillers. Preferably with muscle-bound men."

She realized her mistake instantly, because he shot her a pleased smile. She wouldn't be surprised if he started flexing his biceps at her. The big clod.

"Perfect," he said, sliding sunglasses onto his nose. "When?"

"Next year?"

He grinned, which really annoyed her, because he was apparently too dumb to be insulted. "How about tomorrow night?"

"A Tuesday night? I don't know. I've got to work on my"—she stopped herself just in time from saying *bra*—"résumé."

He quirked a brow. "I thought you said you'd already interviewed."

"I'm not sure I did real well today," she said. Now

there was an understatement. She wouldn't hire herself to clean litter boxes.

"I'm sure you did just fine," the man assured her. He whipped up a killer smile. "Then how about Friday?"

This was about the dumbest idea she could possibly entertain. But there was that niggling desire to see how the public received Candi—with an i—Devereaux. "Well, I suppose I wouldn't mind getting a free meal. Where?" she asked, figuring that, the way he was dressed, wherever he took her would have a drive-through window.

Then she mentally gave herself a slap. Not only was that an unkind thought, it was pretty judgmental. Gramps would be so disappointed.

"I'll surprise you," he said with a wink.

Leah had never liked men who winked. To her it had always signaled shorthand for a person who *knew* he was full of bull. But somehow his wink was cute.

"That would be kind of difficult," she replied, "if I don't know where I'm going or how to dress."

"I'll pick you up."

Not in this lifetime. "I'm sorry," she said between gritted teeth. She had a terrible feeling this was going to be a disaster. "But I have a personal rule: I take my own car on first dates."

His eyes narrowed for just a minute, then cleared, and the twinkle reappeared. He nodded. "That's very smart of you."

She couldn't tell if his tongue was poking his cheek or not, but played it up, fluttering her hand. "Thank you. I don't hear that very often."

His lips twitched. "Okay, how about Clyde's at Tyson's Corner?"

Okay, Clyde's wasn't a fast-food joint by any stretch. It also wasn't the swankiest restaurant. Actually, it was almost a perfect choice. And considering it was known for being something of a pickup joint, it would give her lots of opportunity to observe reactions from men and women alike. "What time?"

"Seven?"

"It's a date, Mr. . . ."

"Colson. Mark Colson."

She tapped her chest. "Candi."

"With an i. I remember."

"Bam!"

Leah rolled her eyes as she closed the door to her grandfather's Great Falls home. Either Gramps was emulating his hero, Emeril, or he was watching a knock-'em-down talk show. Gramps had two passions: cooking and talk shows. And he revered Paul Prud-homme and Jerry Springer equally.

Leah loved Gramps more than just about anyone, save Steve. But the man who had basically raised her and her brother had some really strange ideas of what constituted entertainment.

She shucked her torturous shoes by the door and walked the mile-long trek into the kitchen. "Mmmm, smells good. What are we having?" she asked, stretching up on tiptoe to kiss his cheek.

"Thai chicken."

"Mmmm," she said again, beelining straight for the antacid tabs that prevented heartburn before it began. Somehow she hadn't inherited Gramps's iron stomach.

Leah glanced at the TV. A psychic was talking to some woman's dead great-aunt. "Why are you watching that, Gramps?"

23

"What, you'd prefer I watch soaps?"

"I'd prefer PBS. You could learn to paint or knit or be British."

Gramps—Edward James Smith to the IRS—grunted. "Why don't you just kill me now?"

Leah grinned and hugged him. "How was your day?"

"Joyce thinks I should get in touch with my inner woman, and Tamara thinks men are pigs."

Leah didn't have a clue who Joyce and Tamara were, but it would be a pretty good guess that they worked the talk-show circuit. "There are merits in both arguments, it seems to me."

"Speaking of getting in touch with my inner woman, why are your . . . is your chest . . . lopsided?"

"I unpumped."

"I don't want to know," Gramps said, turning back to the oven.

"It's all Steve's fault," she said.

Gramps ignored that, as always. He'd gotten used to Steve and Leah pointing fingers at each other whenever they found themselves in hot water. And he had the annoying habit of shrugging his shoulders and looking disappointed until the guilty one confessed.

Which was what he was doing now. And Leah folded like a badly built house of cards. "Okay, so I popped a balloon by mistake. But Steve's the one who told me to buy the contraption."

"Sally used to say that you have to love the real you first," Gramps opined.

"It's just an experiment, Gramps." Leah spied a huge thingamabob she'd never seen before resting on the counter. "What the heck is that?" she asked to change the subject. "It looks like a spaceship."

"Food dehydrator. I'm making jerky, dried bananas, and dried tomatoes all at once. Sherry the Shining Chef swears by it."

"Uh-huh. Well, I think I'll go change."

"Into yourself? Good. I like you better as you."

"Gramps, this disguise is just for fun." Leah shook her head and tried to figure out how to explain her compulsion. Gramps was such a forward-thinking man. Or he tried to be. But when he didn't like something, you knew about it. He bought weirdo kitchen tools and went mad concocting things. And that abomination in the corner of the kitchen—making *jerky,* for crying out loud—was proof she'd probably upset him big-time.

"It's an experiment. I swear. A social case study." *And I just want to feel wild for a while.*

"I don't like it; you're beautiful just as you are," he said, stirring the sauce in the pan furiously.

Which was why she didn't think she'd mention just yet that a complete stranger had asked her bimbo self out on a date. Worse, that she'd accepted. Gramps would be on the phone in a nanosecond ordering a solar-powered blender or something.

She hugged him once more. "I've got to go change. *Leah* has an interview this afternoon."

"You didn't say how the interview went."

"I'm a very bad sexpot."

"You're a very pretty brainy woman."

"You're a very sweet liar."

"Lord, no. You look so much like your mother. She was a beauty, all right."

Leah almost began to protest, but remembered that the first thing she'd done after driving out of Just

Peachy's parking lot was to tear off the blond wig and pop out the blue contact lenses. She smiled with pleasure. Although her real-life memories of her mother were fairly sketchy, Gramps kept tons of pictures of his only son and daughter-in-law all over the house. And though Leah didn't think she came close to the ethereal beauty that was her mother, the compliment always warmed her. "Can I do anything for you, Gramps?"

"You can tell me why two young, gorgeous kids still stick around with their grandfather."

Leah's heart flopped. "Are you sick of having us here?"

"No, I love having you here. But I don't want you two hanging out here just to keep an old man company."

"We hang out here because the rent's cheap."

"I always taught you to be practical."

"Yes, you did." Leah and Steve had made a decision a long time ago to stay with Gramps as long as possible. They were the only family he had left, and he was all they had left. The house was huge, so it wasn't like they were stepping over each other. But they were there if he needed them, and they had always needed him.

Not to mention, Gramps loved the home. It was where he had lived with Nanna for forty-five years, and where he'd raised his only son, and then his grandchildren. It held too many memories to move. At the same time, it was becoming too big of a burden for him to keep up on his own, even as vital as he was at almost seventy.

As long as they could, they were going to make certain he was able to stay in his home. But heaven forbid he ever thought they stayed for any reason other than love. He'd kick them out in a heartbeat.

26

"I adore you," Leah said, hugging him.

"You should. I'm the only sane person in this house," he said as he lifted the lid on his latest contraption to check on his jerky.

Chapter Three

Later that afternoon Mark happened to be gulping down his gourmet lunch—which consisted of a bologna sandwich and chips, with the obligatory apple his sister always packed for him—when another candidate for the secretarial job marched into the HR office.

People had been pretty much parading in and out of the man's office all day, so Mark barely glanced at the screen. But then he did a double take.

As flamboyant as Candi-with-an-i was, this woman exuded librarian prissiness. Her silky brown hair, held back in a painful-looking bun, stretched her temples. She wore a beige suit that defined demure. Her feet sported sensible brown shoes. She was about as exciting as a virus. And he was getting kind of turned on by her.

Which made absolutely no sense. He was definitely female-deprived. To be turned on by a woman who had LAST FEMALE VIRGIN ON EARTH stamped on that fore—

The forehead looked familiar.

Weird, he knew without a doubt he'd never met the woman.

But he looked her over more thoroughly. And a gold bracelet encircling her left ankle had him almost choking on his sandwich. Upon closer examination he also recognized that soft brown hair. He'd seen a glimpse of it earlier that morning, when a certain blond wig had slipped out of place.

He didn't know the chest, but he studied it for a bit just because his training said he should. Then he chanced a glance lower.

Oh, yes, he knew those legs. He'd ogled them on a screen just this morning, watched them wobble across a parking lot soon after, and had a date with them Friday.

Wow!

This was the same woman. He'd bet his 'vette on it.

Why would she be showing up at the HR guy's office under two different guises? And which was real? Or was either of them?

He tossed away the apple—figuring he could truthfully promise Shelley that duty had called, and he hadn't been able to eat it all—and punched the button that gave him access to sound. He shamelessly listened in.

"Ms. Smith," the human resources director said, "I'm totally impressed with your résumé. But I don't understand why you'd want to apply as an office worker when you're so highly overqualified."

"I'm looking to earn another Ph.D. I need to pay for it somehow. Trust me: I'll do well."

"I have no doubt. But I fear you might become bored."

"There's nothing boring about hard work, sir. Not when I have tuition payments due."

Same woman, different personas. Night and day. Bimbo versus scholar. Big chest—and he really resented that it was fake—versus a modest B-cup.

His instincts screamed at him. At best she was so desperate for the job she'd land it any way she could. At worst she was a spy, and not a very good one. And he was going to nail her—one way or another.

Ever since Heather, Mark had had a hard time trusting women. He realized it was almost ancient history, and he should be over it—and her—by now. Well, he was definitely over the woman. But the sour taste of her ultimate betrayal still lingered.

So knowing that this woman was playing some kind of game really irritated him. Yep, he was going to nail her, all right.

Leah made her way out to the parking lot, trying to assess her success in this most recent interview. Mr. Thorndike had been polite, but his skepticism beamed through loud and clear. She must have led a sheltered life, because she hadn't known there *was* such a thing as being overly qualified. Wasn't that a kind of reverse discrimination?

She glanced up when she heard footsteps approaching. There he was again. The hunk. What, was he the parking-lot patrol guard or something?

He was heading straight for her, and Leah sucked in a frantic breath. For some reason she was more apprehensive facing him as herself than she had been as the blond bombshell. Probably because she didn't want to see the uninterest in his expression as he checked out the real thing.

But as he approached, she noted the definite sparkle in his blue eyes. The same sparkle he'd had earlier this morning. Maybe he just twinkled all the time.

Leah tried to break eye contact and swerve to his left, but he just swerved right with her.

"Hi, there. Are you new, or just visiting?" he asked, planting himself firmly in front of her once again.

"Excuse me, but I don't talk to strangers," she responded in a voice that sounded prissy to her own ears. She tried to step around him, but the man was a mobile wall.

"Makes it kind of hard to make friends. You must be pretty lonely."

That was insulting enough—if not more than a little true—that she stopped glaring at his chest and tipped her head way back to glare into his twinkle. "If you don't mind—"

"For some reason you look familiar," he said, dimpling at her in a totally irritating and too-damn-cute way. "Have we met before?"

Uh-oh. "I'm sure we haven't," she said, figuring that wasn't a lie, since she wasn't *Leah* the last time he'd swooped down on her.

In a déjà vu move, he thrust out his hand. "Mark Colson."

She ignored the handshake. "Would you mind moving?"

"To where?"

"Right now, anywhere out of this hemisphere would be welcome, but a few feet to my left will do."

"Answer one question and I'll get out of your way."

Leah had to physically stop herself from asking him if he made a habit of accosting women in parking lots. "Is there a reason I should feel obligated to answer any question from someone I don't even know?"

"To be polite?"

"Miss Manners I am not."

32

He grinned at that. "Look, I'm not accosting you or anything. I just saw you coming out and thought you were pretty."

"Right." Now she knew he wasn't just dumb as a brick; he also had bad eyesight. Or was a terrible liar.

"And I'm not going to try any stupid pick-up lines, I swear. I was just curious whether you worked here, so I'd know if I might see you again sometime."

Hmmm, he actually sounded sincere. "Do *you* work here?"

"You could say that."

Same answer he gave her this morning. She didn't have a clue what that meant, but she let it pass, because one question to her brother and she'd have her answer. She shook her head. "I don't know if I'll be working here or not. I just interviewed for a job."

"Good luck. I hope you get it," he said, and actually stepped aside.

Leah was just dumb enough to be a little disappointed. The man had pounced on her as the bimbo, and was being polite to her real self. It was insulting, really.

But a thought occurred to her. What would it be like if he actually asked Leah out, as Leah? Would he treat her differently? It would be an interesting and informative experiment.

Unfortunately, it didn't look like he had any intention of asking mousy Leah out. But why would he when she'd been so rude to him?

Leah had begun this experiment because she'd wanted to be bold and different for once in her life. Did she really have to be a clueless blonde to accomplish that? Couldn't Leah get up the nerve to do something very unlike her?

33

She didn't know.

"Well, if you do get hired, I'll see you around," he said as he began to walk back toward the building.

Leah took one step toward her car, then stopped and whirled around. "Wait!"

Mr. Colson dutifully turned back to her, his eyebrows raised. "Yes, ma'am?"

She took a deep breath. "My name is Leah."

His smile was actually a combination of gentle and triumphant. "Nice to meet you, Leah. Pretty name. It fits you."

She tried not to let that make her feel just a wee bit flattered, but it wasn't working. Lord, she was pathetic. But that was going to stop right now. The new Leah was going to learn to take the bull by the horns.

"Would you like to have dinner sometime?" she asked, then held her breath. This could be truly mortifying. How did men do this all the time?

He hesitated for a second, and then grinned. "I'd like that a lot."

Then to test him a bit to see how fickle he was, and to see if he was just too polite to turn her down, she asked, "How about Friday night?"

Something sparked in his eyes, but then—a little too slowly—he frowned and shook his head. "I'm afraid I already have plans on Friday."

"Oh." Okay, so he wasn't going to dump the bimbo for her. Not surprising, but a little disappointing. "Okay, forget I mentioned it," she said, amazed at how much it actually hurt.

"I'm free Saturday," he said. "If you are."

Was he kidding? She hadn't had a date in years, and suddenly she was going on two in a row. She had to squelch a happy grin. "As a matter of fact, I am."

"Great. Shall I pick you up?"

Ooh, this could get sticky. "How about if you give me your address and I'll pick *you* up?"

"Stephanie Smith is stopping by tonight," Mark informed his sister, Shelley, who was busy peeling potatoes at the sink. He leaned over and gave her a quick kiss on the forehead, noting that today she had her Mickey Mouse sunglasses on. His favorites.

Shelley reached up and groped for his chin. When she found it, she grasped it, turned his head aside and gave him a peck on the cheek. "Who's Stephanie Smith? One of your bimbos?"

Mark could easily take offense at his sister's comment if it weren't pretty much true. Shelley heartily disapproved of most of the women he dated. And he couldn't actually blame her. Shelley might be legally blind, but she could sum up a person faster than anyone he'd ever known. "No, little sister, not one of my bimbos. She's the owner of Just Peachy Cosmetics, the job I'm doing now."

"Wow! The owner? A woman with brains? Marry her."

"Ha. I don't think so."

"Why, isn't she pretty enough for you?"

Mark didn't know how to answer that. Stephanie Smith was most definitely not his type. She wasn't ugly, but if there were female football teams, he'd bet she could try out. "She's . . . striking. Just not my type. And besides, she's coming here to discuss something pretty delicate. So you'll need to scram."

Having lived with him throughout his FBI days and now with the private security firm, Shelley understood delicate. She'd had to put up with lots of *scrams*.

She shrugged and said, "Okay."

"You're the best," Mark said, squeezing her shoulder.

"You'd better think so. I'm the only sane person in this household."

The doorbell rang about a half hour later, and out of curiosity Shelley wandered from the kitchen to the foyer of their Fairfax, Virginia, home. She lamented that her brother was never going to settle down with the right woman. Ever since his disastrous relationship with his girlfriend at Quantico, he'd had a string of women in his life whose accumulated IQs probably qualified them to pass second grade.

She understood his reluctance to get involved with brainy, ambitious females, but it was high time he got over it. The owner of a large, successful company sounded like a promising candidate.

"Hello, Stephanie, thanks for coming," Mark said.

"How could I resist with such an intriguing request?" an unfamiliar voice said. A very *low* unfamiliar voice.

"Stephanie, this is my sister, Shelley. She's the one who's about to scram."

Shelley moved toward them, holding out her hand. "How do you do?"

Ms. Smith took it briefly and rather limply. "Likewise. Wow, are you two twins? You look so much alike."

"That's an insult if I've ever heard one," Shelley said, laughing. "No, I'm *much* younger than this idiot."

"Two years," Mark said, his voice indignant. "Stephanie is a twin, which is probably why she asked. Her brother, Steve, is general manager at Just Peachy."

"Is that right?" Shelley said. "Well, before I skedaddle, why don't I show Stephanie to your office while you get some refreshments?"

"Good idea. What would you like, Stephanie?"

"What are you having?"

"Milwaukee's finest."

"That sounds lovely."

"Coming right up," Mark said, and Shelley listened to his footsteps head toward the kitchen. The moment he was gone, Shelley turned back in Stephanie's direction. "Does my brother know?" she asked, with a smile that she hoped conveyed that she meant no insult.

"Excuse me?"

"If you're a woman, I'm a race-car driver."

There was a long pause. "How . . . I mean, I thought Mark had mentioned that you're—"

"Vision-impaired. Yes, I am. It doesn't take working eyes to know you're packing a whole lot more under those skirts than panty hose."

Another stunned silence. "Ummm, I don't know what to say."

Shelley held up a hand. "No need to say anything. I'm not into judgments. Everyone has a right to his or her lifestyle."

"It's not what you think. There are reasons—"

"I'm sure. Seriously, it's not a problem at all. Really." She laughed. "No wonder you're not Mark's type."

"Mark knows?"

"If he does, he hasn't said anything to me. But he's used to keeping secrets. You know, the whole FBI thing." Shelley smiled ruefully.

"Well, if he does, he hasn't said anything to me, either."

"If he knew, he'd tell you." Shelley was sure of it.

"He hasn't said a word."

That news stunned Shelley. Very little got by her FBI spy brother. She boggled for a moment, then grinned. "Oh, wait till he hears this. I figured something out before he did. I'm never letting him live this one down."

"Listen, Shelley, is it possible to ask you to keep this a secret for just a while longer?"

Shelley stopped grinning. "I'm not real big on lying to my brother."

"It wouldn't be a lie. Well, not really. I mean, he believes one thing, and it's not going to hurt him in any way to keep on believing it for just a while longer. This is all going to be over shortly, thank God."

She cocked her head. The man had dropped his simpering voice, and his disgust over the ruse was evident in his tone. "Why are you doing it if you're . . . you know, not into it?"

"I don't have time to give the full answer right now. I know you don't know me, but I'm asking you to trust that I have good reasons."

One thing Shelley had always trusted—relied on, really—was her instincts. She believed him. "Okay, I'll keep mum."

He took her hand and shook it in a grip that was all male. "Thank you."

"You're welcome. So, let me guess, you and your twin brother, Steve, are one and the same?"

"Right again."

"We have our first suspect."

The longneck in Steve's hand froze halfway to his lips. "Are you serious?"

Mark, sitting behind the desk in his den, nodded grimly. "Not a sure thing, but a definite possibility."

"Who?" Steve asked, working hard to maintain his Stephanie voice when his mind was filled with a haze of anger. "An employee?" Steve prided himself on having handpicked the majority of his employees before he'd hired Thorndike to do the job, and it hurt like hell to think he'd placed his trust in someone who would betray him. He'd worked hard to create a fun and proud work environment, one where people were excited to show up each day, where he often had to force them to use their vacation time. Betrayal was unthinkable. But it was the only explanation for Kate Bloom's success in staying only one tiny step behind him in the new-products department.

Mark shook his head. "She's not an employee. At least not yet."

"She?" Somehow Steve had never considered a female traitor.

"It's a woman who applied for a job today. Twice."

"Excuse me?"

"Your human resources director held job interviews most of the day."

"That I know."

"One woman, in two different getups and bearing two different résumés, applied twice."

Steve considered himself pretty smart, but right now he was feeling a little stupid. "Huh? Why would someone do that?"

"To make sure she gets the job one way or the other?"

"Okay, did you get the names?"

"Yes."

"Then I'll make sure Thorndike doesn't hire her."

Mark shook his head. "On the contrary; hire her. Both of her."

39

He was getting dumber by the moment. "Huh?" he said again.

"The best way to keep an eye on potential enemies is to have them right where you can see them at all times. I say you hire her and I'll catch her."

Steve thought about that. He wasn't ex-FBI, but Mark's logic made sense. He pulled a yellow pad from his briefcase. "The problem is, I don't really have two jobs to fill."

Mark twirled a pen around as he thought about that. "How about hiring them both part-time for the same position? Tell them—that is, her—it's a trial period."

The haze suddenly cleared. One woman. Two different disguises. Applying for the same job. Leah. Steve had to force himself not to laugh.

"And let me tell you," Mark said, "I'm going above and beyond on this one, Stephanie. I've got a date with both of her."

"A date?"

"Yes. I figured I'd get her into a more personal setting and see just what she's up to."

Steve opened his mouth to tell Colson about Leah's "experiment" but then closed it quickly. This could prove interesting. After all, when he'd made the bet with Leah over which of her personas would get hired, he'd had Colson in mind as the man she'd have to go on a date with. Not only that, but if he had Thorndike hire both of her, she wouldn't exactly win the bet. Neither would he, of course, but they could call it a draw.

Oh, she'd probably lop off his head if she learned that Steve had intervened in the hiring decision, but in the meantime she'd be able to see how employees interacted with her as the two different females. And she'd be dating, too.

It was a win-win situation as far as he could tell. He nodded as if he'd just thought it through and made up his mind. "Give me the two names."

Chapter Four

"So how'd it go?" Steve asked Leah two days later, as he walked into her study.

She glanced up from her computer screen, frowning. "I got the job."

"So why do you look close to tears? That's great!"

"*Both* of me got the job."

Steve went for the bewildered look. She was definitely going to kill him before this experiment was over. "Excuse me?"

"Thorndike hired both of me part-time. A 'trial period,' he called it." She snorted in disgust. "Leah gets the morning shift. Probably because Thorndike is thinking the bimbo doesn't wake up until noon. Candi works the late shift."

"That's perfect!"

"Yeah, how's that?"

"You get to continue to observe how people interact with both of you. Isn't that what you were looking for?"

She perked up a little at that. "That's true! And come to think of it, Leah can fix all of Candi's mistakes, so I won't be hurting Just Peachy in any way."

"There you go."

She sat silent for a moment, and Steve knew that look. The cogs in her head were wheeling around double-time. Finally she crossed her arms. "You didn't have anything to do with Thorndike's decision, did you, big brother?"

Steve scowled at her for effect. "You mean cheat on our bet? I'm insulted."

"But are you guilty?"

As charged. "If you think I have the time to tinker around in Thorndike's business, you have no appreciation for what I do at my own company, brat. Not to mention I'm a little too busy trying to ferret out a corporate spy."

Leah grimaced and dropped her arms from her chest. "I'm sorry. It just seems so *weird.*"

Steve refrained from commenting that her own experiment was a little less than sane, because she'd probably remind him of the Stephanie thing. "I'm telling you, Thorndike's good. He's probably hedging his bets."

"Could be."

Steve turned to go, but she stopped him. He turned back. "Yeah?"

"Do you know Mark Colson?"

He pretended to mull that over. "Name rings a bell. Why?"

"Doesn't he work for you?"

Definitely. And he's expensive, to boot. "Possibly. I try to remember everyone, but we have a lot of employees, toots. Why do you ask?"

"He seems to hang around your parking lot a great deal. Is he the handyman or something?"

"Oh, sure, that's right. He's kind of a jack-of-all-trades. Does a little of this, a little of that."

"He does a lot of hitting on females."

Steve went for consternation this time. At this rate he could join the Screen Actors Guild. "Meaning what?"

"I have a date with him."

He shot her a look of pure astonishment. "You? A date? Let me mark this down in my calendar."

"Mark this down, you turkey. *Both* of us have a date with him."

"You and me? Really, Leah, I'm not into that."

"No, dummy, Leah and Candi."

Steve laughed, and this time he didn't even have to fake it. "This is going to be fun."

Mark's eyes nearly bugged out of his head cartoon-style when Candi-with-an-i walked through the door of the restaurant.

She was sporting a red leather miniskirt that could have revealed the knees on a Chihuahua, black fishnet stockings that begged a man to peel them off, and a ribbed black top that defied description, unless there was a line of clothing called "Cleavages 'R' Us."

Mark suddenly noticed that the restaurant had gone church quiet. He glanced around the room, and it was almost as if he were in a freeze frame. Waiters had stopped in midserve; patrons had halted in midchew. About half the men, including the maître d', practically had their tongues hanging out. At least half of the women were glaring menacingly at their male tablemates.

It would have been comical if he weren't so irritated. Actually, he couldn't quite pinpoint *why* he was irritated. Or with whom. And he instinctively knew he didn't want to find out.

Candi smiled sweetly at the stunned maître d' and

leaned forward to whisper in his ear. The man appeared ready to faint.

After a moment the host seemed to gather himself, and he waved vaguely in Mark's direction. Candi glanced at him, smiled, and winked, then sashayed toward his table, waggling her fingers at the men who suddenly sat up straighter as she approached.

He had to give her credit: the blond wig actually looked real. And it was styled in a pretty way today. Not teased up, but more of a Meg Ryan–in–*Sleepless in Seattle* way. But Mark couldn't help but think that silky brown suited her better. It didn't scream "pay attention to me" like the blond look did. Her real color sort of whispered "natural beauty."

Mark shook his head. When was the last time—or the first time, for that matter—that he had analyzed a woman's appearance so much? Well, okay, he knew pretty and sexy when he met her, but this was definitely weird, because he was more attracted to the other Candi. Well, Leah.

He was so busy worrying about his own mental health that he almost forgot to stand when she arrived at the table.

But he made it to his feet, successfully keeping the chair from falling backward by grabbing the back of it at the last second. He plastered a smile on his face, swallowing all of the aggravation over her runway-model entrance. "You look great. Thanks for coming."

She giggled. "Who turns down a free meal? That's a no-brainer."

Which was a good thing in Candi's case Mark thought, then remembered he was working with a fraud. "Good thinking." He held out her chair, and he could swear she wiggled her fanny before settling in.

Before he was even seated, a waiter—looking overly

eager—materialized. "Good evening. My name is Colin—"

"Colin! What a cute name! Will you be servicing us tonight?"

The man blushed straight down to his white shirt collar. "Ummm, yes, I'll be waiting on you."

Candi's eyes sparkled with humor, but she quickly recovered and resurrected the blank bimbo look. "Super!"

Mark's irritation was escalating exponentially. He figured that it was because he was the only person who realized this woman was fake from the tip of her blond wig to her overinflated breasts to the heels of her red stilettos. Was he the only one who saw through her?

Apparently every other man in the room was wishing he could see through her skintight top.

Colin, who seemed to have misplaced his tongue, pointed to each of their place settings with eyebrows raised in question. Mark made an educated guess that the man was asking if they'd like drinks. Even if that wasn't what the waiter was going for, Mark *needed* a drink.

"I'll have a draft. Domestic."

The waiter didn't even hear him. He was staring straight at Candi's chest, his pen poised over his pad.

"What can I bring you, miss?"

Candi, the fraud, smiled at the waiter. "What's that drink named after the child star? You know, the one with the curls?"

"Shirley Temple?" Colin suggested.

"Right!" she practically squealed. "Just add liquor to it."

The waiter might have seen the logistical stupidity in that if he weren't so interested in making her chest happy. "And you?" he asked Mark, much less enthusiastically.

This was going to be a long night. Mark had already ordered a draft, but since the guy obviously hadn't been paying attention, he swiftly changed his mind. "I'll have a Shirley Temple, too. But instead of ginger ale, substitute vodka, dump the cherry, and add an olive."

"Your sister is a menace to society."

Steve worked hard at glancing up casually as he watched Kate Bloom storm into his office. He set down his pen carefully, forced thoughts of strangling her with a long loofah sponge out of his mind, and plastered a wide smile on his face. "Problems?"

"She's accusing us of stealing from her!"

Steve sat back. Kate Bloom was so beautiful, his breath usually caught. But she was the enemy, and someone who would do anything to get ahead. "My sister doesn't make accusations lightly."

"She keeps it up and I'm filing a civil suit against her."

He barely stopped himself from snorting. "For what?"

She hesitated just long enough for Steve to observe that her mink-black hair was so shiny and thick, a man could get lost in it. Her eyes, even though gleaming with menace, were a sleepy blue. Her tailored suit was a pretty green. And she smelled fabulous, although that irritated him because he recognized the scent as one Apple Blossom had introduced two months after one Just Peachy launched. And they were *very, very* similar.

Finally she said, "Defamation of character?"

He sat back in his chair. "Can you defame a company's character?"

She waved. "Whatever. I'm sure my legal team will come up with something."

"How'd you get in here, anyway?" he asked.

She waved again. "That's not important."

"It is when my sister believes there are spies among us."

Kate plopped hands on hips. "Stephanie is delusional. You know that." She sighed and strolled farther into his office. "Steve, your sister might believe that Apple Blossom is doing something nefarious, but you and I have at least a marginal give and take. Can't you convince her that I am *not* stealing from Just Peachy?"

"I'd need a convincing argument. So far I don't have one."

"Give me an opening line."

"'Your sister is a menace to society' isn't my first choice."

"Can we talk?" She shrugged one shoulder, which Steve found incredibly sexy. "I can make my case."

An appealing idea came to him. He could have supper with a sexy woman and check up on Leah at the same time. "How about over dinner? Say, at Clyde's?"

"Don't look now, but one of your big-kahuna bosses has just walked through the door."

It had better not be Steve, Leah thought. He might be her big brother, but she was old enough that she didn't need him checking on her. He'd been doing a little too much of that ever since their parents had died. *If it's Steve, he's a dead man*.

"Jennifer?" she asked about her direct supervisor.

"Think higher."

"Bob Winthrop?" She hoped it was Jennifer's boss. She really did.

"Go up a couple of notches."

Steve is a dead man. "Jim Richards?" She prayed it was one of the vice presidents.

"You're not aiming high enough."

"Not Stephanie Smith?"

49

"Her twin brother."

A slow, painful death.

"And he's with Kate Bloom."

Leah almost blew a gasket. She remembered her bimboishness just in time. "Who's Kate Bloom?"

"The competition."

"Huh?"

"Never mind. Just brace up. They're coming this way."

Steve wasn't only dead; he was going to live through hell first.

But Leah was happily surprised when her brother and his nemesis passed by them without a word or glance. But what in the world was he doing with Kate Bloom? He hated that woman.

Leah tried to keep her attention on her date, but her curiosity was working overtime. She watched Steve and Kate get seated at a table two away from theirs, then turned back to Mark. "Rumor has it that he's just a lackey for his sister."

Mark, who'd been eyeing the two thoughtfully, abruptly turned back to her. "Rumor is wrong. He works his tail off for that company. His sister is damn lucky to have him."

Leah felt a little melting action going on in the vicinity of her chest. Mark Colson might be a snake, but he wasn't dim as a twenty-watt bulb, either, if he recognized how hard Steve worked.

She'd better watch it, or she just might begin to like the handyman.

Their drinks arrived, and the waiter just *barely* managed to deposit hers without diving into her cleavage. Leah was a little confounded. It was both flattering to be garnering so much attention for the first time in her life, and yet irritating, too, because the attention was purely superficial. If she'd come as herself, the waiter would probably be yawning as he offered her the cocktail.

But she just smiled brightly and worked to keep from kicking the man where it hurt.

"Are you ready to order?" the waiter asked her breasts.

"Her chest hasn't seen a menu yet," Mark said, sounding a lot more irritated than he really had the right to be.

Leah tried to giggle, but she had the feeling it came out more like a feral growl. She had an overwhelming urge to ask for a bib. "Yes, a menu, please."

"Oh, right, sure." Colin the waiter walked hastily away.

Leah glanced at Mark, who had thunder in his eyes. That made no sense, seeing as he probably asked her out for the same imbecilic reason the waiter was acting like an idiot.

She smiled lamely and brought her cocktail to her lips in a strange attempt to put *something* between her flesh and his eyeballs. "So, what exactly do you do for Just Peachy?"

He opened his mouth, but right then Kate Bloom strolled by their table, clearly headed toward the ladies' room.

Leah felt the need to "bump into" Ms. Bloom and find out what the heck she was doing with Leah's brother. She stood abruptly. "Excuse me. I need to . . . umm, powder my nose."

Even if he was a clod, he had the manners to stand. "Sure thing. I'll be right here."

Where else would he be? she had to wonder. But she just shot him a dazzling smile and waggled her fingers at him. "I'll be back in a jiffy, sugar."

* * *

Mark watched Leah strut her stuff toward the women's bathroom. No matter how good the view was, his eyes narrowed. A chance meeting with the enemy? He didn't think so. After Leah disappeared, he stood and strolled over to Steve Smith's table. "I think we have our traitor."

"What?"

"Did you see that woman who just hightailed it to the bathroom right behind Kate? She works for you."

"Is she one of the names you gave Stephanie?"

"Yes. And right now she's rendezvousing with the enemy in the ladies' can."

"Maybe she's feeling loyal toward Just Peachy and is hoping to get information out of Kate."

"Right. She's worked for you for exactly two days."

"Well, you're a charming guy. I'm sure you could finagle some information out of her."

"Charming, I'm not. But I'll definitely find out what she's all about."

"Stop short of torture," Steve said. "We don't want a lawsuit."

Mark grinned. "Damn, there goes plan B."

Steve's eyebrows shot up. "What's plan A?"

"Seducing it out of her."

For some reason Steve's skin suddenly went a little pasty. "Start with plan B."

Kate glanced in the restroom mirror as she attempted to fix the abomination that was her lips; she'd been chewing off her lipstick ever since deciding to have supper with Steve Smith.

Nothing fazed her. At least, nothing used to. She'd grown up in a household in which her parents insisted she demand the best of herself, and she could hold her own in any situation that confronted her.

But Steve and his sister Stephanie—particularly Stephanie—were proving to be a really, really bad situation. Not because of the accusations Stephanie was leveling at her and Apple Blossom. She could handle that, because she knew there was absolutely no truth to any of it. There was no way in hell she'd condone corporate espionage.

And she wasn't worried that Just Peachy could harm her company and her livelihood. She had too much faith in herself, her employees, and her products to be worried.

No, it was Stephanie Smith herself who unnerved Kate, and in a really strange way.

The woman was so aggravating, Kate wanted to kick her. But that wasn't unusual. There were a lot of people Kate would gladly kick. There were a lot of people Kate had had to kick. Kicking Stephanie would be a pleasure.

What had Kate biting her lips was that she got strangely excited by her sparring matches with the woman. Kate would meet Stephanie scathing remark for scathing remark, and walk away *stimulated*. Even when Stephanie managed to land the best parting shot, Kate would find herself grinning. Too strange.

And unnerving.

Worse, her pulse leaped whenever she found herself in the woman's company, although Stephanie had to be the sorriest excuse for a female she could imagine.

And one night in Las Vegas, after a day of meetings at a cosmetics CEO convention, and a particularly heated debate at the bar with Stephanie, Kate had wondered at her reaction to her nemesis. And in her wine-induced fuzziness, she'd actually asked herself if she was bisexual. There just didn't seem to be any other explanation for her physical reaction to this mammoth woman who made it her life's goal to drive Kate batty.

Of course, she'd scoffed at the thoughts the next morning once her mind had cleared. And she'd been desperately trying to scoff at it ever since.

Kate loved men. She'd never had a prurient thought about a woman in her life. So what was it with this deranged Amazon that affected her like this?

Her solace was that she found Stephanie's brother, Steve, *much* more attractive. Unfortunately for poor Steph, she looked a little too much like her handsome brother. But Steve was kind and reasonable, while Stephanie was infuriating and . . . exciting.

She was losing her mind.

Kate sucked in, then puckered her lips until she was satisfied she'd evened out the lipstick, then capped the tube and dropped it into her clutch purse.

In the mirror she watched a blonde breeze into the bathroom, then lowered her gaze to keep from shaking her head. Kate didn't understand women who painted themselves up like neon signs that read, *Check me out, sugar.* And if that wasn't a boob job, she'd give up her next paycheck.

The woman came straight to the mirror and began fluffing her hair. Kate ignored her while she washed her hands. She was drying them with a paper towel when their eyes met in the mirror.

The woman smiled at her, and then her jaw went slack for a second. "Hey, aren't you the lady who came in with Steve Smith?"

Oh, jeez. If Steve made time with women like this one, Kate's estimation of him just dropped several rungs. She smiled back. "Yes. You know Steve?"

"Know him? Honey, I work for him."

Kate had to keep from gaping. "You work for him?"

The woman waved airily, and Kate recognized the scent of Just Peachy's Don't Forget Me perfume wafting toward her.

"Well, I don't work for Mr. Smith himself, but for his company. I just got the job."

Kate turned from the towel dispenser. "Really? Are you enjoying it there?"

"So far, so good. Although today was a little stressful. I'm having a little trouble with the phone system. I cut off calls from two buyers. Oops! But they were real understanding about it."

The woman would be history within the next two weeks, Kate estimated. "So you've met Steve?"

"Oh, sure, he's real nice. He came by to welcome me personally."

For some reason, that irritated Kate, even though she made it a point to greet all of her new employees personally as well. "Did Stephanie stop by to welcome you, too?"

"You know Ms. Smith? Isn't she something?"

She's something, all right. Something vile and witchy and . . . exciting. "Yes, indeed, she sure is something."

"How do you know them?" the woman asked.

"We're in the same field."

"Field?" the woman repeated, screwing up her perfect skin.

"The same business," Kate said slowly. "We're all in cosmetics and personal body products."

"Oh, how fun! But doesn't that make you com . . . comp . . . you know, people who are not on the same side?"

"Competitors?"

"That's the word!" the blonde said, pointing at Kate's nose.

"Well, yes, but friendly competitors." *And my aunt Fanny drank only during holidays.*

The woman perused her closely and said, "You're very pretty. Do you wear only your company's products?"

Kate went still. "Why do you ask?"

"Oh, I don't know. It's just that the lipstick you're wearing looks a lot like Just Peachy's Wet 'n' Wild Red." The woman smiled and shrugged and turned to the door. Before opening it she looked over her shoulder. "You tell Mr. Smith that Candi says hi, okay?"

Kate stood there for a moment, trying to catch her breath. It *was* Just Peachy's lipstick. It was a guilty pleasure. She wondered if Steve had figured it out, too. Although she doubted it. Men had no eye for such things.

But as Kate gathered herself and headed to the door, a thought occurred to her: The woman named Candi hadn't done a thing in the bathroom but talk.

Chapter Five

Mark watched Candi/Leah emerge from the bathroom, and something fell out of the bottom of his stomach when he noticed that her fake sauciness had disappeared. As much as he'd pegged her for a fraud, he already mourned the loss of her trying.

He had to wonder what had happened in the bathroom that could possibly douse her spirit.

He stood as she approached and frowned at her. "What's wrong with you?"

She blinked, and her eyeballs almost turned into kaleidoscopes. Conjuring up a smile he knew was as real as her bustline, she sat down and gulped at least half of her Shirley Temple. "Bad toilet paper," she said.

Mark sat back. As much as he mistrusted her, knew she was a fake, wanted to bust her for spying on his client, he felt a primal need to make her feel better. "Did something happen to you in the bathroom? You look . . . I don't know . . . sort of sad all of a sudden."

He observed in fascination as she rallied. She whispered something to her lap he couldn't make out, then raised her head. The transformation back to Candi-with-an-i wasn't quite complete, but she was giving it the good old college try.

"I'm fine," she said, her smile not wobbling any longer, thank God. "I'm just hungry."

"Bad toilet paper does that to you every single time."

She laughed, and it was such a low, husky chuckle compared to her cutesy bimbo twitter that it hit him right below the belt. But he only smiled in response because, he didn't want to call attention to the fact that he'd noticed a difference in the two laughs. With any luck he'd get to hear the unconscious, sexy sound again.

She glanced at her menu for about thirty seconds, then closed it with a snap. Colin, the waiter, appeared instantly at her side. "Ready?"

She raised her eyebrows in question at Mark. He nodded. "You first."

"I'll have the trout amandine and the Caesar salad, please."

"Same for me," Mark said, although he'd originally planned to order the New York strip. But just in case she had an aversion to red meat, he didn't want to turn her off.

Which was a strange thought. What did he care? He sipped his martini and tried to regroup. He had to remember his ultimate goal. "So, what do you do for fun?" he asked when the waiter reluctantly took his leave.

"Me?"

He laughed. "I don't see anyone else here."

"Oh." She seemed to have to think about that. "Well, let's see. I like to . . . go shopping."

He almost laughed again. Apparently she had to come up with something typically bimboish. She actually had to work at it—which would be cute if she weren't a corporate spy.

The thought soured his stomach for some reason. He should be thrilled he was on a hot trail for his client. But suddenly he desperately wished there were another, more palatable explanation for this ruse of hers.

In his work for the FBI, he, along with his partner, Jake Donnelly, had tracked and nabbed plenty of white-collar criminals. He'd met and brought to justice some of the biggest scum in the United States. It was his forte. He never remembered regretting moving in for the kill before. That was, until a decision he'd made nearly got Jake and his now-wife, LeAnne, killed. That was when he decided to retire from the Bureau.

"What do you like to do?" Candi asked him.

He nearly missed the question, too lost in thought. *Nab bad girls and guys,* would probably not be an appropriate response. "Well, I like sports."

"Playing or watching?" she asked, seeming genuinely interested.

"Both." At least this much was true.

"Football?" she asked.

"My favorite." Again, no lie.

"Are you a Skins fan?"

He almost smiled. She was interested enough to forget to be dumb as a brick. "Of course. But I have a couple of favorite teams."

"Who else?"

"I grew up in Chicago, so I have a soft spot for the Bears."

She nodded, then patted his arm. "Poor you."

Mark grinned. "How about you? Do you like football?"

"Love it. I couldn't help it. My older brother played."

"Really? Where?"

She went still, and it occurred to Mark that she'd just revealed more than she had wanted or expected to. She erected the bimbo facade again and waved. "Here and there."

Disappointment shot through Mark, but it also rejuvenated his resolve. His job—and allegiance—was with Stephanie and Steve Smith.

Just then Colin showed up with their salads, and Candi dug in as if she hadn't eaten for a month. Mark let her enjoy her meal in silence. Plenty of time to grill her. He took a few perfunctory bites of his own salad and finished his drink. When the waiter returned to see if he'd like another, he shook his head. "Just more water, please."

When Candi pushed aside her salad, he conjured a smile. "How is it that a pretty woman like you hasn't been snatched up by now?" he asked.

She batted her lashes at him. "I haven't met anyone I'd like to be snatched by."

"Really? What type of guy do you go for?" He figured it was asking a little much to expect her to say, *Someone like you.*

Which was a good thing, because she didn't. "Old and rich," she said, then giggled.

If he didn't know she was trying to stay in character, that might have pissed him off a little. But he just smiled. "With a heart condition?"

Her jaw dropped open. "Of course not. I wouldn't wish ill on anyone."

Even in disguise she couldn't stand to be construed as bloodthirsty. Mark thought that was adorable.

She took a sip of water. "How about you? What type of woman do you go for?"

"Someone just like you."

She laughed. "Of course you'd say that."

"No, I mean it. You're pretty and fun."

Her eyes narrowed a little. "You wouldn't want someone more . . . educated? More . . . sophisticated?"

"Brainiacs are boring," he said, keeping a completely straight face with an effort.

"Is that right?" she said, all giggle gone.

He nodded, pretending not to notice. "Education is highly overrated, I think. All those letters after someone's name just seems . . . pretentious, you know?"

"I hadn't thought about that."

Colin arrived with the trout, and Candi-with-an-i attacked it with a vengeance. Mark cut into his, too, to give him something to do besides laugh. *Just wait until tomorrow night, babe.* He added, "And I'm not real big on dating women smarter than me."

"That definitely shrinks the available pool," she muttered.

"What?"

"This trout is delicious," she said.

"Yes, it is," he agreed with a grin. He could hardly wait.

Kate glanced over her shoulder at the floozy blonde and her date. "You see the woman over there? The blonde?"

Steve looked over at Leah. "Yes."

"She says she works for Just Peachy."

"Yes, she does. She just started this week."

"Oh."

"Why do you ask?"

"I was just wondering. She's . . . colorful."

Steve laughed. "If you only knew."

"Why would you hire someone like that?"

"Why wouldn't we?"

Kate waved, realizing she sounded like something of a snob. "No reason, I guess."

"So tell me, Ms. Bloom, why should we believe your company is squeaky-clean?"

She sat forward, for some reason almost desperate to make him—and his sister—believe her. "Because I'd never condone stealing a competitor's secrets."

"Maybe some of your chemists are doing it behind your back." She opened her mouth to retort, but he held up a hand. "You have to admit that your latest products have an eerie resemblance to those we'd previously introduced."

"But fundamentally they are not the same formula." She sighed and took a sip of wine. "Steve, I admit that I think Just Peachy products are good."

His eyes dropped to her lips. "Yes, they are."

Kate wasn't a blusher, but she felt her cheeks heating up. So he'd noticed. So what? She paid for the lipstick just like any other consumer. Nothing illegal about that. "The point is," she said, wishing she could hide her lips behind the cloth napkin in her lap, "Apple Blossom hasn't done anything illegal. I would swear to it."

He searched her face for she didn't know what. "I want to believe that, Kate. I really do."

"But you can't, because your sister doesn't believe it."

"Believe it or not, I'm capable of making up my own mind."

Now she'd insulted him. He was probably a little touchy about working for his sister. Many men might be threatened by that. Although she'd never seen signs of it in him before now. He actually seemed to care for the witch. She was his sister, so Kate supposed he sort of had to. Although she was a little confused by blind loyalty. She felt absolutely no affection for her brother, which probably said more about her than she cared to analyze. It was just that she didn't understand the guy. He seemed so aimless, still living at home with their mother at the age of thirty-two. He'd dabbled in dozens of different jobs, but never seemed to be able to stay at any one for a substantial length of time, citing boredom.

And Kate knew damn well that the money she sent home to her mother every month probably found its way into his pocket.

She was so deep in thought, she couldn't remember the last thing Steve said, or if she'd responded. She racked her brain, then suddenly remembered. She'd insulted him.

She laid a hand on his arm. "I'm sorry. I know you don't blindly follow Stephanie. In fact, rumor has it that you pretty much run the show."

He stared down at her hand, so Kate snatched it away. His skin had felt so warm and comforting, and although there wasn't a chance in hell that Steve and she would ever be anything but business rivals, she was heartened to know that a man had reached her on a primal level.

Stephanie Smith be damned.

Mark arrived home at a little after ten. Shelley was still up, sitting in her favorite reading chair, her fingers flying over the pages. Shelley could probably read faster with her fingers than most sighted people could read with their eyes. It never ceased to amaze him.

Her fingers went still and she marked her place. "You're home early," she said. "In fact, this might be a record."

He himself wasn't all that happy about it. He hadn't expected Candi/Leah to want to end the date almost immediately after the meal. He'd offered to take her dancing or for a nightcap somewhere, but she'd begged off, claiming, "I need my beauty sleep."

He'd been hoping to get a little more information out of her than he had, to pin her down a little, but after her initial obvious irritation over his comments about smart women, she'd slipped back into her bimbo routine and stayed there.

"Yeah, well, she's an early-to-bedder, I guess," he told Shelley.

She snorted her laughter. "And apparently not with you, huh, hotshot?"

He frowned. "You know I almost never sleep with a woman on the first date."

"Especially if she's not interested."

He didn't mention that part of him wanted to believe that Candi/Leah was too afraid to be caught with that contraption on her chest, to sleep with him even if she wanted to. But she sure didn't show any signs of wanting to. Even when he went to kiss her good night in the parking lot, she'd turned her head so his lips hit her cheek. Now *that* was a first. He'd never had a woman not even want to kiss him. And it wasn't good for his ego.

He'd actually had a good time with her, despite knowing she was a fake. It had been amusing to watch her try to keep up the bimbo performance, even though he knew for a fact that the woman had brains to spare.

And she obviously wasn't used to playing the role of airhead, because she was so bad at it. She'd used just about every cliché in the book when she felt the situation called for it. She was almost a parody, and consequently really fun to watch.

He could hardly wait until his date tomorrow night. He planned on pushing her buttons hard, and watching her honest reactions.

"So was this one a single-digit IQ, or did she manage to make it into the double digits?"

Mark would bet that Leah had a high IQ. "This one was double digits," he said.

"A step up! Miracles do come true."

"Hey!" Mark made no bones about the type of women he dated these days, and Shelley made no bones that she hated it, but she usually just pursed her lips and kept quiet, because she was well aware of his burning need not to get his heart broken all over again.

It was probably cowardly of him, but everybody coped with their demons in their own way and for now, this was where his comfort zone stood. Still, he was feeling a little insulted. "My date tomorrow night is a genius."

Shelley put aside her book. "Oh, really?"

"That's right."

"And exactly where did you meet this genius?"

"At my current job."

"Just Peachy?"

"Yes."

"Stephanie Smith?" she asked, and for some reason her lips twitched.

Mark had to keep from shuddering. "Umm, no. Someone else."

"I don't understand why you don't ask Stephanie out. She seems nice enough. And she's obviously successful if she can afford you."

"That's just it," he said, jumping on the opening. "I don't date my clients."

"But you're taking out one of the employees."

"But the employee isn't cutting my checks," he shot back, wondering what it was with Shelley that she was pushing Stephanie on him. He trusted Shelley's instincts, and understood why she'd taken to Stephanie, because she really was a nice lady. But . . . He shuddered again.

Shelley stood and stretched, yawning widely. "Well, maybe after you finish the assignment you can ask her out."

Mark opened his mouth, but she said, "Time for bed," saving him from a further excuse.

And she walked unerringly to the hall and down it toward her bedroom.

Stephanie Smith. *Ha!* He was sure someone, somewhere, would find her type attractive. And he liked Stephanie, so he hoped she'd find that somebody someday.

At the door to her room Shelley turned back. "Oh, by the way, Jake called tonight. I left his message on the kitchen counter."

Mark grinned. Jake, besides having been his partner at the Bureau for many years, was also Mark's best friend. Now *there* was a guy who'd lucked out in the female department. His wife, LeAnne, was gorgeous and sweet and smart. And she tolerated Mark, even though he'd nearly gotten her and Jake killed a couple of years ago.

He still felt a boatload of guilt over that, even though Jake and LeAnne had shrugged it off immediately. "But we *didn't* get killed, Mark," LeAnne kept telling him when he'd announced his decision to leave the Bureau.

A few years before, Jake and Mark were working a case of fraud. Jake had been taking a minivacation at a dog spa owned by LeAnne. Mark had made the mistake of believing it would be the perfect hideout for their star witness. Unfortunately, he hadn't realized that he and the witness were being tailed by thugs, and they followed him directly to the spa.

Then the thugs made the mistake of thinking LeAnne

was the witness, and tried to blow both her and Jake away. Jake and LeAnne had to go on the run, but because Jake and Mark's boss was working for the other side, the thugs were right behind them. Mark still shuddered to think what might have happened, all because of him. He'd have never forgiven himself. In fact, he pretty much *still* hadn't forgiven himself.

Although Mark didn't get to see Jake and LeAnne as much as he'd like, he still considered them his best friends in the world, save his sister.

In the kitchen he glanced at the number Shelley'd written down, and recognized immediately as the one for their house in southern Virginia, a huge, rambling country home with enough acres to handle their myriad dogs, and close enough to the pet spa that LeAnne owned.

Jake still worked for the FBI, now in the homicide division, so Mark guessed he was on vacation, helping LeAnne set up for the summer season.

Mark dialed the number, and LeAnne answered. "Hello, beautiful," he said. "What's the idiot want now?"

She laughed. "Hi. I'll let him tell you. One second; he's out tormenting Muffin."

Mark grinned. Muffin was Jake's butt-ugly English bulldog, but probably one of the most intelligent creatures Mark had ever dealt with. Muffin had an eerie way of knowing exactly what people were talking about. It was Muffin who had brought Jake and LeAnne together in the first place, so they both obviously worshiped him.

A few moments later Jake picked up the phone, sounding a little winded. "I'm going to kill that mutt one of these days," Jake muttered.

"Yeah, right. What's up?"

"We're pregnant."

Mark went still. Then he burst out laughing. He knew they had been trying for this for almost a year. "You dog! Congratulations."

The pride in Jake's voice was obvious. "Thanks. We're due in November."

"Sex?"

"Lots of it. Great work if you can get it."

Mark grinned, even if he *did* feel a twinge of envy. "Boy or girl, idiot."

"We don't know yet. We find out next week."

"Any preference?"

"LeAnne wants a boy; I want a girl."

"Do you two ever agree on anything?" Mark asked, still smiling.

"Sex. Lots of it."

Mark laughed. "Too much information, buddy. Give LeAnne a huge hug for me."

"One other thing," Jake said, his voice lowering. "I'm retiring."

That shocked Mark down to his toes. Jake was one of the best agents in the Bureau, and he loved his job. "Why?"

"I've got a growing family to think about now. I don't want to be gallivanting all over the country and miss watching my kids grow up. It's time."

"What will you do?" LeAnne was obscenely wealthy in her own right, but Mark knew Jake well enough to realize he would never be happy with a life of leisure.

"I'm not sure yet."

A thought occurred to Mark. "Go into partnership with me."

"Excuse me?"

"Become my partner. Business is booming. I could use the help."

"I appreciate that, buddy; I really do. But we want to stay down here full-time."

"Fine. We'll open up a branch office in Richmond."

There was a pause. "I don't need handouts."

"This is no handout, idiot. I really could use the help. And I've been thinking about opening satellite offices for a while now." That was absolutely true. He hadn't been thinking of Richmond, but then, he never thought he'd get Jake, either. He really missed working with the man.

"Let me talk it over with LeAnne," Jake said. "I'll call you soon."

"Good. And if you're even remotely thinking about it, come up to DC for a few days. I know you've been to my office, but I'd like you to see some of my handiwork."

"Show-off."

"That's me."

"Okay, I'll get back to you real soon."

"And Jake, I mean it. I would love to work together again. And I do need the help. I would have asked long ago except I thought they'd have to throw you out of there."

"You're not too bad for a conceited jerk. Thank you."

"Thank *you* for even considering it. I'm really excited. I'll be totally pissed if you turn me down to flip burgers somewhere."

Jake laughed. "There's a thought."

Mark smiled. "Congrats again, buddy."

They hung up, and Mark went to the fridge and pulled out a cold one. Slugging it down straight out of the bottle, he sat down and thought through the logistics. This could really work. And the thought of partnering with Jake again was fabulous.

He didn't know how long he sat, lost in thought, but just as he dumped the bottle into the recycle bin, his phone rang. He lunged for it quickly so as not to wake Shelley. "Yeah?"

"He'll be there the day after the doctor's visit," LeAnne said.

"I'm glad one of you has more sense than a worm."

"One of us has to. Thank you, Mark."

"My pleasure. And congrats again, lady."

"Thank you. We're pretty happy."

They said their good-byes, and Mark hung up, a goofy grin on his face. Jake, a father. Jake, his partner. Life was good.

If only he could find a woman as special as LeAnne, he might even consider taking the plunge himself someday.

And for some reason, as he headed to the bathroom to brush his teeth, a split-screen image of two gorgeous women—one a floozy blonde, the other a demure yet sexy brunette—flashed before his eyes.

His smile disappeared. "Don't even think about it, buddy."

Chapter Six

The next morning Leah sat glumly in the kitchen, sipping coffee, when Steve entered.

He was in an irritatingly good mood. "Mornin', sis."

"Yes, it is. Barely."

"What?"

"Morning. At least for another"—she checked her watch—"six minutes."

He shrugged cheerfully. "So sue me. I was out late."

"I'll say. Three fifteen, to be exact."

He poured himself a cup of coffee, then turned to her and leaned against the counter. His hair was still wet from the shower. "Since when do you keep tabs on me?"

"I wasn't keeping tabs. I just couldn't sleep."

"Bad date?"

"Horrendous."

"Why? I always thought Colson was a pretty decent guy."

"I thought you barely knew him."

The coffee mug stopped halfway to his lips. He flushed a little. "Well, it's just that . . . when you told me you had a date with him, I had to check him out."

"You checked him out?"

"Hey, you're my little sister."

"Who is perfectly capable of taking care of herself."

"Give me a break. You haven't been out on a date in God knows how long. And when you finally go on one, you look like . . . like . . ."

Leah's eyes narrowed. "Like what?" she asked ominously.

"Well, just not yourself." He waved. "So what was so bad about it? Did he try to get fresh? Because if he did—"

"No, not at all," she rushed to assure him. "In fact, he was almost *too* much of a gentleman."

"Excuse me?"

Leah shook her head. "It wasn't like I wanted him to get fresh exactly. But he could have at least acted like he was thinking about it." She rested her chin in her palm. "Even as a blond bombshell I can't spark any interest in a man."

"Oh, come on. I watched the other men in the restaurant. They were practically drooling."

"Old lechers and young boys. I mean a man like . . ."

"Colson?"

"Well, *like* him, not necessarily him."

"I'm not a huge expert, but he appears to be a fairly good-looking guy."

Oh, wasn't that the truth. The man was simply mouthwatering. She sipped some more coffee, trying to figure out what was really bothering her and how to explain it so Steve would understand. "There's just something not quite right about him."

"What do you mean?"

"I don't think he's what he appears to be."

"Excuse me?"

72

"Sometimes he acts dumb as dirt. But if you look in his eyes, there's intelligence there. It's like he's putting on an act."

Steve practically washed the floor with the coffee that came shooting out of his mouth. He grabbed a paper towel and wiped his mouth, then the floor. When he looked back up at her, his eyes were watering, but he was laughing. "Honey, do you hear yourself? Who were you last night?"

She had to concede that Steve had a point, but she was just grumpy enough to argue with him. "That's just an experiment," she said, her voice defensive.

"And yet you're willing to judge someone else who might be experimenting just like you?"

"Why would he be experimenting? I can almost guarantee the man isn't going for his Ph.D. in sociology."

"That isn't what this is all about, and you know it."

"I do?" She scowled at him. "Okay, so this is going a little far afield of scientific analysis. But that's how it started."

"And now you aren't liking the results."

No, she wasn't liking the results. But for the life of her, she couldn't figure out why. "I think I'm going to cancel my date with him tonight."

"Why? Don't you want to see how he treats the real you?"

She pointed a finger at Steve's nose. "You know what he told me last night?"

"What?"

"That he found brainiacs boring."

Steve laughed. "He was probably trying to make dumb Candi feel better."

"Maybe. Or maybe he does dislike intelligent women."

"Why would he ask Leah out if he did?"

73

She blushed. "Actually, I asked him out."

Steve blinked. "You've never asked a man out in your life."

"Experiment," they said in unison.

"I think you should go out with him. You might be surprised."

Unfortunately, she really *did* want to go out with the idiot. And if she was honest with herself, the experiment took a backseat to just spending time with him. He might be infuriating at moments, but in a stimulating way. The night hadn't been horrible because of him. Not really. It was more a function of her expectations. She'd expected him to flirt shamelessly and to try to put the moves on her. She wasn't about to allow that to happen, not with the Pump You Up pumping her up, but he could have at least tried.

"I don't know," she said.

Steve came and sat at the table, and once again Leah was amazed at how handsome her brother was. He was such a catch, she couldn't believe no one had claimed him before now.

And a bit of guilt seeped in, because she knew part of it was that he hadn't wanted to abandon her and Gramps.

"Leah," Steve said softly, "what's one night? It's not like you have anything more pressing to do. And if he was a perfect gentleman to a woman who all but had advertising on her chest, you can bet he's going to be on his best behavior for Leah, the lady."

That was what she was afraid of.

But enough of that. She didn't want to examine her emotions and behavior too thoroughly.

"So," she said, "let's talk about you."

He looked down into his mug. "Let's not."

"Oh, but I insist."

74

He frowned. "What about me?"

"How was *your* date?"

"It wasn't really a date. Just a sort of business meeting."

"Right."

"It was! Don't forget, she's the enemy." He took a breath and exhaled slowly. "I think."

"Oh, boy. She's gotten to you."

He shook his head. "I don't know. She seemed so sincere."

Leah thought back to the encounter in the restroom. "She's certainly beautiful."

"Is she?"

Leah laughed. "Last I checked, your eyesight was pretty good."

"Yeah, I guess she is."

"That wouldn't be coloring your thinking, would it?"

He sat up straight, indignation written all over his face. "You know me better than that."

She sat silent for a moment. "You want to hear something?"

"What?"

"I tried to get a pulse on her in the bathroom last night."

"And?"

"It was almost the worst part of the evening."

"Why?"

"Because she's so tall and elegant and beautiful. Not to mention successful. And there I was having to pretend I'm this idiot."

"She'll meet the real you someday."

Leah thought that comment was intriguing, because she couldn't see any reason why she and Kate Bloom would ever have a reason to make each other's acquaintance, unless . . .

"Did she say anything worth hearing?" Steve added.

"She pretty much despises you." At his pained expression she added, "I mean Stephanie. She doesn't like Stephanie."

"News flash, dear sister: *I'm* Stephanie."

"You are also Steve. And if she kept you out until the middle of the night, I'd say she likes Steve okay."

"Or she's just trying to sucker me."

"Only one way to find out."

"What's that?"

"Keep seeing her."

"Ha! The only reason she wanted to go out last night was to convince me that Apple Blossom is innocent."

Leah thought back to her encounter with Kate Bloom. Not that Leah was a perfect judge of character, but the woman hadn't seemed like the scheming type. Her eyes weren't shifty, and she didn't appear to have a coy bone in her body. She was too self-assured without being a snob about it. And this was the most interest Steve had shown in a woman that she could remember. She hated missed opportunities. And Steve needed a life.

"I'll tell you what," she said. "I'll keep my date with Colson if you ask Kate Bloom out again. At worst you'll be keeping the enemy in close sight. At best you'll find out she's not stealing a thing."

Steve hesitated. "Okay, it's a deal." In a gesture they'd had ever since they were kids, they hooked and snapped pinkies. Leah smiled. Steve smiled. And if her smile was any reflection of his, they both were happy with the agreement.

Which was scary and a little exciting all at once.

Just then Gramps strolled in from his usual morning walk. He looked at both of them, then crossed his arms. "This is the same expression you two wore when you were kids, and you were up to no good."

Steve and Leah donned their most innocent expressions.

"Didn't work then; isn't working now," Gramps said. "What kind of trouble are you two planning? Am I going to have to start raising bail?"

"He's been watching Court TV again," Steve said.

"We're not up to anything, Gramps," Leah said. "Have some coffee."

"Dr. Phil says—"

Steve and Leah both jumped to their feet.

"Gotta go," said Steve.

"Late for my run," said Leah.

"You think I won't get to the bottom of this, you're wrong. Communication is key."

"Mmm-hmmm," Leah said, sidling toward the doorway.

"Or you can stay and I'll make some blueberry pancakes."

Steve and Leah looked at each other. "That was low," said Steve.

"And effective," Leah griped.

They both sat back down. No one in his or her right mind would miss Gramps's blueberry pancakes.

Gramps grinned, then moved to the cupboard to pull out ingredients. "Okay, now let's take this from the top."

Mark had realized, as he began getting ready for Leah to pick him up, that he had to let Shelley in on what was going on. Otherwise she might slip and say something that would give him away.

Shelley, the most honest person he'd known in his life, had disapproved from the get-go. But she'd just pursed her lips and shook her head, muttering things he felt better off not interpreting.

When the doorbell rang—exactly on time—he couldn't beat Shelley to the door. His sister was on a mission.

As he finished dressing, in jeans and a Polo shirt, since Leah had told him casual was the name of the game, he heard his sister corral Leah into the living room and offer her a drink.

Although he couldn't make out Leah's exact words, he recognized the timbre of her voice. Instantly it reminded him of her husky laughter the previous night, and his blood began screaming through his veins.

Why did she have to be a fake? Was there any possible explanation that made sense? He really wanted to find out. And yet, he wasn't certain he wanted to know.

He belted his jeans, did one more quick swish of mouthwash, then headed out. The sight that greeted him nearly laid him low.

Leah was reading Braille.

Before she noticed his entrance, she looked at Shelley and laughed. "Does your brother know what you're reading?"

"Of course not. He's dumb as a stump." Her head turned toward him. "Hi, Stump."

Leah's had snapped toward the hallway, where he was lounging, deciding whether to kill Shelley in front of a witness or wait until later.

Leah was gorgeous—truly, purely gorgeous. As much as she looked like a bombshell in her bimbo persona, she looked like heaven as just plain Leah. And he was having trouble breathing. "You look great," he said when he finally found his voice.

She ducked her head. "Thank you."

"Exactly what is my sister reading?"

Leah hesitated, then said, "A treatise on the state of American culture."

Shelley snorted.

"So it's not *Moby Dick*?" Mark asked dryly.

Leah and Shelley broke into peals of laughter. Finally Shelley caught her breath. "Well, a different version."

He had the feeling the joke was on him. He also had the feeling he didn't really want to know.

Leah stood and handed the book back to Shelley. "By the way, Sandra Hill's my favorite author, too. Wait 'til you get to chapter seven."

Shelley's grin spoke volumes. "This girl's a keeper."

Mark was a little irritated they were speaking a foreign language he didn't recognize. "If my sister's through entertaining you, are you ready to go?"

"Wait!" Shelley said. "Tell me what Leah's wearing."

Leah looked horrified. "What?"

"I want to see what you're wearing. Mark, describe her outfit."

"Umm, I don't want to make her uncomfortable."

"No, that's okay," Leah said, her expression shifting to one of amusement. "Go ahead."

Her eyes were shining too much for his comfort. But God, they were gorgeous. And Shelley was looking belligerent.

"Well, she's wearing a skirt."

"Color?"

"Kind of green? Prettier than olive—sort of dusky green, though."

"And her top?"

Mark was getting hot throughout his entire body. He'd been describing things for Shelley all of his life. It had almost become a game. But she'd never demanded he do it in front of a stranger. Especially *about* the stranger in question.

"I don't think Leah wants me to—"

"Sure, I do."

"Thanks a bunch." He looked her over, which wasn't a real hardship. "Okay, it's a short-sleeved cotton top with a sort of seascape collage of greens and grays and blues."

"What color is her hair?" Shelley, who might be dead by midnight, asked.

"A sort of brown."

"Mouse brown," Leah said with a rueful laugh.

"No, it's not," Mark said. "It's more of a chestnut color."

"Eyes?" Shelley asked.

"Green."

Shelley was silent for a moment, then turned to where Leah was sitting. "You sound pretty."

"Trust me, I'm not."

"Yes, she is," Mark said.

"Okay," Shelley said, "you have my permission to go out with him tonight."

"Shell—"

"But don't try to take advantage of him. He's an easy mark."

Leah laughed. "I'll be very gentle."

"Don't go that far. But be home before Tuesday."

"I'm really sorry about that," Mark said as they headed out of the driveway.

"Sorry about what?"

"Shelley. She can be a little overbearing."

"She's adorable. And she loves you. What's wrong with that?"

"Well, if she made you uncomfortable . . ."

"No, she made *you* uncomfortable. I was fine." She laughed softly as she made a right turn. "Thanks for lying."

Mark's head snapped to his left. "You think I was lying?"

"Of course. But that's okay. It was really nice of you."

Mark took a few deep breaths before he spoke. "Leah, let me tell you something. I've been describing things to Shelley for twenty years. I've never lied to her yet. Not about what I see, anyway. She has to trust that I'll tell her the truth."

"I bet she figures out in a nanosecond when you're not telling the truth about your feelings."

She hit that one straight on the head. "How do you figure?"

"She's your sister. And she's so attuned to you. It makes sense."

Mark sat back, actually happy he wasn't behind the wheel because he was pretty floored. This ultrasensitive woman was the same one who'd tried to make him believe she was as shallow as a wading pond last night? "Shelley seemed to like you," he remarked.

"I liked her, too," she almost whispered.

"Where'd you learn Braille?"

"At an internship one summer between my sophomore and junior years of college."

"What was my sister reading?"

"If she isn't telling, neither am I."

"It was something racy, I take it."

"If you want to know, learn Braille."

They drove for a long way out of Fairfax in silence. Mark began wondering if Leah was taking him out to murder him when they cruised into a drive-in. Leah was taking him to a drive-in movie? Not to mention, the headliner was *Psycho*. He didn't know whether to be worried or not.

Once she paid and parked, she turned and smiled at him. "Best hot dogs ever. How would you like yours?"

Mark had had major plans for Leah tonight. None of

them were working out. First, they were having a blast with the movie; second, she was feeding him junk food at a wonderfully alarming rate.

He'd tried to pay for some of the food, but she wouldn't allow him to touch his wallet. She'd asked *him* out, she kept reminding him.

Third, she was beautiful in the most amazing way. She ate a hot dog like no one he'd ever known. She savored every bite as though it might be the last she'd ever taste. And she had to have everything, from chili to sauerkraut to onions, piled on it. Kissing her would be like kissing East German dirt, and he didn't care.

But the best part was that she truly got spooked by the movie, and kept moving closer to him. He hoped the equally spooky sequel was coming up next.

But he had to remember his goal, which was finding out what was behind all the disguise stuff. Was she spying on Just Peachy? And if so, why? Was she Apple Blossom's latest recruit to infiltrate their competition? Was she supposed to steal company secrets?

Mark owed his client the truth. He had to ferret out Leah's real identity, her real motive. And if she was guilty he'd have to turn her in to Stephanie and the cops in a heartbeat. It was his job.

He was beginning to hate his job.

"Let me ask you something," he asked her during intermission.

"Go for it," she said.

"Why are you working as a company dweeb when you're so smart?"

She pulled away from his arm around her shoulder. "I don't consider myself to be a dweeb."

"Okay, wrong word."

"Not to mention, there are no small jobs, just small

people. That company—*any* company—couldn't function without them."

He was a little taken aback by her ferocity, but also impressed, because he knew she meant every word. Which made everything about this situation even more puzzling.

"Where would the company be without you?" she asked. "Are you dispensable?"

"The company wouldn't go down without me," he said.

"But things wouldn't get done without you."

"Or someone else."

She nodded. "Okay, true. Why are you asking me this?"

He didn't know how to answer. But he tried anyway. "Because you're smart."

"Are you dumb?"

"I hope not."

"Is your work that much less important?"

"I like to think I earn my keep."

"There you go."

He not only couldn't argue that logic, he was dumbfounded she'd just turned the tables on him. So the only logical thing that came to mind in retaliation was to go for another hot dog. "I'm heading back for another dog. You?"

"No, thank you."

He was feeling very strange. And he wasn't quite sure how to handle it all. He began to head out, but she held on to his arm. "Please don't leave."

He could no more ignore her request than he could slit his own wrists. He was feeling very strange indeed. "I won't leave."

* * *

Leah didn't recognize herself. She'd shed her shoes, and her stockinged feet were lounging on the dashboard. The rest of her was hanging on to Mark Colson for dear life.

She'd always been a fan of scary movies, but she usually found herself hugging a stuffed animal. Right now she was hugging an animal, but he wasn't stuffed. He was alive and warm and letting her cling to him.

"I'm not really a sissy," she whispered.

"Yes, you are."

She tried to pull away, indignant and a little mortified. "I'm not."

"Yes, you are. Me, too. So keep holding on."

She was pretty sure he wasn't a sissy. And she was fairly certain that she was enjoying him a whole lot more than she did her stuffed bears. And she didn't care. It felt too good.

"I'm not a baby, either," she clarified.

"I am. So don't let go."

Leah was more than a little afraid that this hadn't been a good idea. She'd tried to think of something funky to do that was not a normal date. She'd wanted something out of the ordinary, that would prove to Mark Colson that she wasn't a boring brainiac. But now she had the feeling she was. Because asking him to a drive-in was probably the single most idiotic idea she'd ever had.

A hot woman would know how to pull it off. A risqué woman would take advantage of the situation. A mature woman would have taken him to the ballet or something. She was just plain Leah, and she was a sissy and a baby, and having shed her shoes on the floor didn't make her anything but shoeless.

She let him loose. She *liked* scary movies. She didn't

84

need to cling to him or anyone else. But she sure wished she had her teddy bear.

"You don't have to let go."

"I've seen this movie at least a dozen times," she said, almost ready to cry. And she didn't even know why. Probably because she was such a sorry excuse for a date, and she didn't want to be. She hadn't cared last night, because it really wasn't her. Tonight it mattered.

"That's the beauty of it."

"The beauty of what?" she asked, having been too busy feeling sorry for herself to remember the conversation.

"You can't see it too many times."

She dropped her legs from the dash and sat up straighter. "I can't do this any longer."

"Do what?"

"Pretend to be something I'm not."

He was silent for so long, she could cut the air with a butter knife.

"What do you mean?" he asked.

"I was trying to be different. Exciting. Not so boring. And the truth is, I'm boring. And a sissy."

He turned to her. "Leah, I'm not bored. And if you're a sissy, you're the prettiest sissy I've ever met."

She gulped down a sob, because it mattered too much to her that he was telling her the truth. A week ago she wouldn't have cared. At least she *thought* she wouldn't have cared.

"You said you didn't like brainy women."

The moment the words were out of her mouth, she wanted to shove them back in. He'd said that to her other half.

"When did I say that?" he asked.

"Candi told me this morning," she improvised.

85

"You know Candi?"

Leah took a deep breath. Then another. She'd never make a good spy. Or liar. And frankly, she was sick of trying. Maybe after tonight she'd come clean with him. "Of course I know Candi. She and I work the same job."

"You talk on weekends?"

"Why not?"

"You just don't seem like the buddy-buddy types."

"She . . . wanted to switch shifts with me this week."

"Oh. She told you about our . . . dinner?"

"Well, you can't blame women for exchanging notes when the same guy is going out with both of them." She had no idea whether that was actually true, since she'd never exchanged notes with anyone, but that was her story, and she was sticking to it.

He turned down the intercom all the way. "She and I didn't exactly hit it off, you know."

Leah didn't know whether to be offended or not. "Why? I think she's nice."

"Very nice," he said, nodding. "But not my type, I don't think."

"Why not?" She was now officially offended.

"I'm not into . . . I don't know . . . *loud,* you know?"

"Candi isn't loud, just maybe a little flamboyant."

"Okay, I'm not so much into flamboyant."

Now Leah was just getting ticked on Candi's behalf. Which made no sense whatsoever. Even *she* didn't like Candi that much. But who was he to make judgments? Besides, wasn't he the same guy who didn't care for brainiacs?

"Just what exactly is your type?" she asked, a little too irked to care that Norman Bates was causing mayhem up on the big screen.

He was silent for a moment. "I'm not sure. I just know her when I see her."

"How many times have you seen her?"

"Very seldom."

Leah resisted the urge to ask if he was seeing anything close to "her" right now. "Have you ever been married?"

His head jerked around. "No. Why do you ask?"

"Just wondering if you've ever seen a 'her' you were willing to say 'I do' with."

"No," he said, but that one word held a wealth of emotion. "I never said 'I do.' "

"Not even close?"

When he looked at her, his gaze was so dark it was almost scary. "Why are you asking me all of this?"

Leah kept herself from shrinking—or running screaming from the car. "I was just interested. Forget I asked."

He swiped a hand over his face. "I'm sorry. Touchy subject."

"And none of my business. Let's just watch the movie." Right now Norman Bates looked less menacing.

Leah wondered what can of worms she'd just opened. The man was obviously a fake in many ways, but whatever feelings she'd just unleashed were so obviously real. And close. And hurtful.

As much as she wanted to hear what was behind all of that anguish, she didn't think it was in her best interests to keep probing that wound.

But the truth was, she wanted to have him tell her what—or who—could possibly have hurt him that badly. Maybe that would give her some insight into why he was pretending to be something he wasn't. Or pretending not to be who he was.

She was truly confused by him. She was missing something important. And she didn't know what it was, which drove her batty.

Here was this handsome man who could act like a

moron in one sentence, and sound almost profound in the next. Here was a man who'd professed to be attracted to airhead bimbos one day, then denied the attraction the next.

Who was he? What was his game? She didn't know, and she didn't know if she wanted to know. And she didn't know if not knowing would make her crazy.

This was supposed to be an experiment. She had to keep that in mind. Just a delving into the real world after years in classrooms and libraries. A reality check.

Except, she realized, she'd entered the real world under false premises. She'd wanted to test whether appearances could be deceiving. And already she knew the answer was yes. And no.

Great.

She needed air, and she needed room. "Let's go to the snack bar, okay?"

He didn't seem to hear her for a moment, and it wasn't because he was lost in the film.

"Mark?"

"Hmmm?"

"Can we take a walk to the snack bar?"

"You change your mind about having another hot-dog?"

"No, I'm not hungry. I just want to stretch."

"Oh, then sure. Let's go for a walk."

Mark knew exactly one thing: He wanted to kiss Leah. As they strolled passt the snack bar and toward the deserted end of the drive-in, he felt a hunger in his gut that had nothing to do with food.

There was something so vulnerable about her. Maybe it was the way she *tried* to be tough. Well, not tough exactly. Just self-assured. She was smart in the most naive way.

The notion sounded strange even to himself. He'd met smart. He'd met not-so-smart. He'd met sophisticated. He'd met witchy. He'd met friendly. He'd met standoffish.

And, unfortunately, he'd met and fallen in love with self-centered.

He'd never met a Leah before. So book-smart. So unworldly. She didn't even know how to be dumb well.

And he wanted to kiss her.

His problem was ethics. He was lying to her. He wasn't what he'd been portraying himself as. Then again, she had an agenda, too, and he hadn't figured that out, either. He'd considered asking Jake to look into her background, but somehow he'd wanted to puzzle her out all by himself. Or get her to come clean all on her own.

And he wanted to kiss her.

They came to the chain-link fence at the perimeter of the drive-in and stopped. The halogen light several yards away lighted her face. And her lips. She was gazing up at him, a worried look in her eyes.

"What's wrong?" he asked. "Are you afraid of me?"

"Yes."

"I'm not going to hurt you, Leah."

"I know."

"Then what?"

"I want to kiss you."

"But?"

"I haven't been completely honest with you. It would be under false pretenses."

Finally she was going to spill her secrets. "Just tell me."

She hesitated for a second, then took a noisy breath. "I forgot to bring breath mints."

Chapter Seven

"I don't care about breath mints," Mark said, stepping closer to her.

"But I do."

"Be right back. Don't move."

He sprinted to the snack shop, bought peppermint gum, then ran back to Leah. He hadn't figured that leaving her alone for a few minutes would be a problem. He'd been wrong.

His heart dropped straight to his stomach at the sight of three men forming a triangle around a clearly frightened Leah. He approached slowly, assessing the situation.

"Come on, baby, let's have some sugar," said the man whose back was directly in front of him.

Mark's blood began pumping overtime. All of the old instincts kicked in, and he actually reached for the gun that had hugged his ribs for years. Of course, it wasn't there.

He stopped about five yards away and said, "Security. Anything wrong here?"

Leah held up her hand as if she were answering an

algebra question in class. The three thugs turned to him, and he was happy to see they weren't armed with anything but stupidity.

Mark pointed at her. "Yes, ma'am?"

She actually smiled. "I think these boys need to go out to recess, sir."

He glared at each man in turn. "You heard the lady. Time to take a break, boys."

The young thugs looked at each other, probably assessing their ability to go three on one. Mark brought his watch to his mouth. "I've got a three-one-nine on the west end. Bring in the backup."

The boys scattered like roaches when the lights came on.

Once they were gone, Mark took a huge, gulping breath. He'd just left a defenseless woman alone in a badly lit parking lot. All for the sake of a kiss. He was an idiot.

He moved to her. "You okay?"

Her laughter shook a little. "I'm okay."

"They didn't hurt you?"

"No." She glanced down at his wrist. "That's some walkie-talkie you have there." She raised her head. "Does it do anything?"

"Tells time."

Leah bent over, laughing. "I thought so. Oh, you're such a weasel."

He pulled her up, ignoring the weasel comment. "Seriously, are you okay?"

"I'm fine now. Thank you."

"But they scared you."

She straightened and opened her mouth, her demeanor full of feisty valor. But then she surprised him by throwing herself at him. "Yes, I was scared."

Mark felt a weird twitching sensation in his stomach,

part residual fear, part relief. In his years with the FBI he'd encountered many hairy situations. And he'd been scared. Anyone who professed not to be scared was a liar or a fool. But this wasn't exactly the same.

And having Leah leaning against him, holding him as if he were her savior, felt so right. Even if he'd done little more than scare away three cowards. He didn't have the willpower to push her away.

Her body, pressed into his, hit him in all the right places. Her arms wrapped around him and her hands pressed into his back. She didn't say anything, but her body said it all: She'd been more frightened than she cared to admit.

He tried to fight the fury, but he'd witnessed good people hurt too many times. How could humans do that to one another?

"Mark?" she mumbled against his chest.

"Yes?"

"Thank you."

"You said that already. And you should be cursing me. I was the one stupid enough to leave you alone, all for the sake of getting to kiss you."

She nuzzled his chest before lifting her face to his. "But I don't have any breath mints."

He stuck his hand in his pocket and pulled out the pack of gum. Unwrapping a piece, he said, "Chew fast." Then he stuck it in her mouth. She chomped like a chipmunk, actually groaning with pleasure.

"Spit it out," he commanded.

She obliged.

He spit out the piece he'd stuck in his mouth at the snack bar, then looked at her. "*Now* I'm kissing you."

"Okay."

"Okay? Really?"

"Would you like an engraved invitation?"

He smiled. " 'Okay' works for me." He gazed at her for one moment longer, then slowly lowered his lips to hers. Her response astonished him. She wrapped her hands around his neck and pressed his mouth into hers. But he pulled back and just stared at her for a heartbeat, then laid his lips over hers again, this time coaxing hers open so his tongue could invade her mouth.

She jerked back a little, which really made him stop short. He stepped away for a second, but didn't let go of her. "I'm sorry," he said, but wasn't certain what he was apologizing for.

"No, it's okay. I . . . just am out of practice."

"Let's go back to the car."

"Are we going to kiss more there?"

For the first time since high school he wanted to do a lot more than kiss in a car. But it was obvious she wasn't that schooled in car sex. In fact, it was obvious she wasn't schooled in much sex at all.

"Leah?"

"Yes?" she said, looking a little dazed and frazzled.

"Don't take offense at this."

"Okay."

"Are you . . . a virgin?"

She stared at him as if he were an alien. "A virgin? Am I that bad a kisser?"

"No! Not at all. You just seem . . . tentative."

"Well, I'm not. I went to college, you know."

What that had to do with the current discussion, he wasn't sure. But he nodded his head like he understood, because she seemed to think that explained everything. "I was just wondering."

"Well, I'm not." She looked at him. "Is that a good thing or a bad thing?"

He didn't know. If she wasn't a virgin, she was pretty damn close. He sighed. "Let's go."

"I disappointed you, didn't I?"

"No, Leah, I just don't have a clue what to do with you."

"Why?"

"Because you're beautiful and sweet and a liar."

The date had gone downhill from there. Leah had stomped back to the car and refused to speak to him on the ride home.

She dropped him off with a terse, "Out." Mark hadn't meant to hurt her or accuse her of being a liar. He was just so confused.

Worse, when he talked to Shelley about it, she walked out on him. So he sat in the living room, nursing a beer, and wondering why he was even on this planet.

Life in the FBI had given him a mission. It wasn't that he didn't feel he was doing good now. It was more that he didn't know what good he was doing. And that was the conundrum. He wanted to make a difference. He'd always wanted to make a difference. But it felt like every time he tried, he screwed up.

Take Leah, for instance. He'd been hoping to dig into her secrets. Instead he'd been so focused on her lips that he'd completely forgotten the original plan. It was a good thing he'd left the FBI. He might have been an average agent, but had he made a difference? Other than putting some thugs behind bars, what contribution had he really made to society?

And was he making a difference now? He helped people keep criminals away, but that just sent them elsewhere. And if Leah was a criminal—a bad one at that—how much good would it do to put her behind bars? In the big picture it seemed like a small matter indeed. Not that he was proving to be very adept at figuring out her secrets anyway. He almost didn't want to know if she was involved in something underhanded. He liked her too much, was too attracted to her.

He was so confused. And frustrated. And neither Leah nor Shelley was speaking to him.

He was heading for bed when the phone rang. His instincts kicked in. At this time of night, it was an emergency.

"Yeah?"

"Mark?"

Leah. His heart almost stopped. "Yes?"

"I forgive you."

"What?"

"Just listen. Okay, so I'm not all that experienced. I'm sorry for being so mad that you could tell."

She thought he'd called her a liar over her previous sex life. He could live with that.

"No need to be sorry. I shouldn't have said it."

"Forgive me for being mad?"

"Of course. I'd be mad, too."

"Here's the deal. I sort of was lying. But I want to fix it."

"Okay, how?"

"Want to have meaningless sex?"

Chapter Eight

"No," Mark nearly barked into the phone.

Leah leaned back against the wall, fully prepared to die of embarrassment. What had possessed her to issue such a bold invitation? It was clearly a fatal error. But on the drive home she'd been replaying the night's events over and over again in her mind. She'd convinced herself that Mark was actually attracted to her, that he'd actually wanted to make love to her. And she'd decided to take the plunge.

Big mistake.

She regrouped, striving for a chirpy response. "Okay, then. Have a nice night."

"Wait!" he practically shouted. "What I mean is, I'd rather have meaningful sex."

Leah hated to tell him, but she didn't know the difference. She *wasn't* a virgin, as he thought. But she also wasn't schooled in the intricacies of making love. She knew that she enjoyed the physical act. Even her first time hadn't been painful, as many of the girls in college had confided was the case for them. She didn't doubt their claims. It just hadn't been true for her.

97

So she understood the pleasure of sex. She just didn't quite get the meaningful part of it. She assumed Mark meant he wanted to care about the woman he was with. Which would be noble except his rejection meant he didn't give a damn about her.

"Leah?"

"I think I have to go now."

"No, wait. Please."

"Why? The conversation seems to be over."

"I'm saying yes."

"You just said no. And I feel like a fool."

"I didn't say no to you. I'm saying no to meaningless. And I definitely don't think you're a fool."

"I don't get it."

"Of course you don't."

Leah couldn't decide whether to be insulted or not. She preferred insulted to insulate her heart. She preferred not-insulted just to get a glimpse of him naked. Gramps would kill her. Or send her to Dr. Phil.

"Look, it was a dumb idea. I probably had too much to drink."

"You drank iced tea all night."

"Very intoxicating iced tea."

"Right. Maybe it fermented."

She laughed. "Seriously, Mark, I'm sorry for even putting you in this situation. It's completely my fault. I don't know what I was thinking. And I'm really embarrassed. So I'm going now, please."

"Where would you like to go?"

"Excuse me?"

"Can I come to your place?"

"Absolutely not. My brother and grandfather would kill me."

"We can't meet at mine unless you want Shelley listening in."

"Mark, I was temporarily insane. It was a horrible idea. Please forget this phone call ever took place."

"I don't want to forget it."

She sucked in a breath. "Please do."

"I didn't handle this well," he said. "What I'm saying, Leah, is that I'd love nothing more than to make love with you. But I'm not just a body, and neither are you."

Leah had to shake her head. Something was off here. Weren't men programmed to enjoy sex for sex's sake? It was usually the women who read more into it. So here she was offering him what men dreamed of—a no-strings-attached one-night stand—and he was rejecting it.

Rejecting her, more likely.

"Listen, I really shouldn't have called," she said, needing to hang up before she broke down in tears. "I have . . . stuff to do."

"Go out with me again," he said.

"I don't think that's a good idea."

"I think it's an excellent idea. I really enjoyed tonight."

She wanted to believe him. She *desperately* wanted to believe him. Which probably qualified her as the most pathetic creature on earth. "Let me think about it, okay?"

"Fine. Call me when you decide."

"I will."

Leah stomped through the house, up the stairs to Steve's room. She knocked, and when she heard a muffled, "Go away," she walked in.

"I need to talk," she said.

"Uh-oh. That is never good."

She sat down on the edge of his bed and gave him a shake. "Stick with me here and start earning your wise-big-brother status."

He scrubbed his face with his hands, then sat up, fluffed the pillows against the headboard, and leaned back. "I take it the date didn't go well."

"It was a disaster."

He went still. "He didn't do anything wrong, did he?"

"Yes. He rejected me."

"Excuse me?"

"I offered to sleep with him, and he said no."

Steve bit his lip, and Leah had the feeling he was trying to keep from laughing. "And this is bad why?" he asked.

"You think rejection is a good thing?"

"Leah, this was your first date with him."

"Technically, my second. And I'm pretty sure he'd have slept with me last night if I'd given him the chance."

Steve sat silent for a moment. "Did it ever occur to you," he said after a moment, "that the reason he turned down Leah is because he respects you more than Candi?"

"No, that hadn't occurred to me," she said. "What occurs to me is that he's more attracted to the blonde than plain old Leah."

Again, Steve paused before answering. "Well, then, that tells you something about him, right? You should be glad to be done with it."

"You men don't understand a thing."

"Hey! I'm as enlightened as the next person. It's women who don't make sense."

"We're the only thing keeping this planet going, buddy. If it were up to men, you'd have killed each other off a long time ago, and grasshoppers would rule the world."

"I'm not even going to question that logic."

"Good, because you'd lose." She shook his shoulder a little, just to make certain he was semiawake. "I'm mad."

"I wish I had an answer that would take your mind off of grasshoppers, but I don't. Are you saying you want me to do something about him?"

"Yes. Make him human."

"I mean, do you want me to fire him?"

Leah pulled back. "I would never ask you to do that to someone."

"I know you wouldn't."

"Then why would you even say that?"

"Because I want you to make sense."

Leah hated when Steve tried to pull psychological crap on her. She was well within her rights not to make sense. She'd just been cruelly rejected. Then again, she prided herself on being smart and logical. One little "no" shouldn't throw her into a mindless tizzy—no matter how much it hurt. "Okay, I'm sorry. I don't understand myself right now."

"Not a problem. Anything else I can't help you with?"

"Well, yes. Did you have fun with Kate?"

"I can't help you with that, either."

"Why not?"

"Because I did, and I don't like it."

"What's wrong with having fun with her?"

"I don't know any longer."

"She's beautiful. And she actually seems nice enough."

"She hates me."

"She hates Stephanie. She likes you."

Steve ran his forearm over his eyes. "Have you noticed what a sorry pair we are? We're expending an awful lot of energy to hide our true identities. Are we that uncomfortable with our true selves?"

Leah sat back at that. The implications hadn't struck her until now. They were both pretending to be people they were not. What did that say about them? She considered Steve the coolest guy on the planet. And she absolutely understood why he'd had to take on a different persona to achieve his goals. But what was she playing at? "What am I doing?"

"Testing a theory?"

She shook her head. "No. That was a convenient excuse. And what I'm learning is not making me happy."

Steve frowned at her. "Turn your back."

"Why?"

"I'm putting on my robe and we're going to talk."

"I just need to think."

"You'll think better with more knowledge. Turn your back."

A minute later they both padded down to the kitchen, and Steve made two glasses of chocolate milk. He sat down at the table with her, and Leah began to worry. He looked so serious.

"What is it?" she asked.

"Don't get mad, okay?"

"Get mad about what?"

"I thought it would be fun."

"What would be fun?"

"Drink your milk."

Okay, this was serious. When Steve demanded she drink her milk, he inevitably imparted bad news. She drank her milk because she knew he wouldn't say a word until he thought he'd drugged her with 2 percent and chocolate. "Okay, tell me."

"Colson thinks you're a spy."

"Excuse me?"

"He knows you and Candi are the same person. He thinks you've infiltrated the company as a spy."

Leah found it hard to breathe. Mark had known about her dual identity? He'd dated both of her just to keep tabs on her? "Meaningful sex" took on a whole new definition. To him it probably meant getting her to confess in the middle of an orgasm.

"Who is he?" she asked. "He's not your handyman, is he?"

"He's an independent contractor."

"Whom you've contracted to do what?"

"Install a security system and try to track down a spy."

"And I'm his suspect?"

"Well, you're one of several he's following. But you have to admit you make a good one."

She folded her arms over her chest, feeling suddenly chilled. "Why do I make a good one?"

"He caught on the very first day you showed up, honey."

"Why didn't you tell him who I am?"

Steve glugged down his own milk. "I kind of wanted it to play out. I wouldn't have let him arrest you or anything."

"How kind of you." Leah stood up and began pacing back and forth across the kitchen. "So the man went out with me because he thought I was a felon."

"Here's the funny part."

"I can hardly wait."

"Don't get mad."

"Oh, I wouldn't dream of it."

"I'm lucky I'm not dead, right?"

"The jury's out until I hear the funny part."

"He advised me to hire you. Both of you."

"You are so lucky I don't have a lethal weapon in my hands." She stopped in midpace. "Why did you do this?"

"Remember our bet?"

103

"You've lost that one, buckwheat."

He held up a finger. "Technically I didn't win, but I didn't lose, either."

She wanted a bat. Or a boxing glove. Anything. "You figure this how?"

"Both of you were hired."

What was the term for killing a sibling? Offhand she couldn't remember. But she didn't think there was a jury in the country who'd convict her for murder. This had to be a case of justifiable homicide if ever there was one. "I'm still waiting to be bent over with laughter."

"Well, the funny part is that if you lost—which technically you kind of did—Mark was the man I planned on hooking you up with. So, see, it sort of worked out."

What was the term for wiping out the entire male species? There had to be a name for it. She might even go down in history as the first woman to give it a try. "You'd better go back to bed. And lock your door. Otherwise, I won't be held responsible for my actions."

Steve stood up and backed away slowly. "You know I love you, right?"

"I know you and Mark made a fool of me."

He stopped at the doorway. "Hold on. I did not ask him to ask you out. He came up with that all on his own. I just let him pursue a possible lead."

"What's the term for killing a security specialist?"

"Homicide?"

"There you go. Works for me."

"Leah, what are you going to do?"

"Make sure he has every reason to believe I'm the mole."

"That might distract him from finding the real culprit. I'm paying him a lot of money to figure out what's going on."

"Lock your door, Steve."

"On my way."

Chapter Nine

Leah spent the rest of the night formulating a plan. Since she was fairly lousy at plotting revenge, she had to work at it.

There were so many reasons to be angry and hurt that she wasn't certain how to wrap her mind around all that had happened. Her little experiment was her fault, so she couldn't blame anyone but herself.

She wanted to strangle her brother, but unfortunately she loved him. And she recognized why he'd made the choices he had.

She could shoot Mark Colson straight through the heart, but not when it was apparent he'd gone above and beyond to try to ferret out a traitor. He should be working for the FBI or something. He'd be good at it.

Nope, it came down to her. She'd set this wheel in motion. She had no one to blame but herself.

It just hurt that Mark had dated her solely as part of a job assignment.

It would be so easy to hate him. She *should* hate him. And yet, she didn't quite know how to. Even if

107

everything he'd said and done had been fake, some of it felt real.

For someone with a Ph.D. in sociology, she sure didn't feel very smart. Should she trust her gut instinct and believe that he did really like her, or should she cut her losses and face the truth: that he'd only pretended to like her to get her to drop her guard.

Ugh! Men were so exasperating. Who could figure out their motivations? Even her brother had bought into a scheme because he wanted her to date. It hadn't seemed to occur to him that when both parties were acting under false pretenses, the relationship might suffer a little.

At eight in the morning, while she was taking a shower, inspiration struck. As a retaliation maneuver it was the perfect foil to all of Mark's and Steve's machinations. It was time to teach the men just how much smarter women were—especially when they worked together.

She hopped out, wrapped her hair in a towel and dressed herself in her oversize terry robe. Then she padded downstairs and grabbed the phone book.

"How do you feel about teaching the opposite sex a lesson?"

Kate sat up in bed and looked at the clock. Eight A.M. on a Sunday morning. And a lunatic was on the phone. "Excuse me?"

"Kate, you don't know me. Well, you do, but not really."

"Should I be calling the cops?"

"My name is Leah Smith. I'm Steve and . . . ummm . . . Stephanie's sister."

That jolted her awake more than a shot of caffeine. "Okay."

"We need to meet."

"And that would be why?"

"Because I like you, and you can help."

"Help do what?"

"Kick a couple of men where it hurts."

Kate brushed her hair from her face. "Why would I want to do that?"

"Because men are stupid as dirt."

Kate sat up straighter. "You really are Steve's sister?"

"I really am. I can tell you what he did in kindergarten that got him expelled for three days."

"Was it perverted?"

"No, that didn't come until the teenage years."

"I'm listening."

"Remember that blond ditz you met in the bathroom the other night at Clyde's?"

Kate had to sift through a foggy morning brain. "Yes, the one who works for Just Peachy?"

"That was me in costume, sister. And I'm bent on revenge against all men in the universe."

"Who, for example?"

"My brother Steve, for one."

"Okay, although I have to admit I like him more than anyone else in your family so far. What was with the blond-ditz routine?"

"Long story, but trust me, Steve needs to be kicked in the butt."

"I'm not against this notion."

"Feel like having fun?"

"If it doesn't include jail time, I'm in."

"Men suck."

"Tell me about it," Kate said, looking gorgeous, as always.

They were sitting at a Greek restaurant in Falls

Church. It was a stormy day, and Leah felt as though her hair and clothes had suffered inordinately as a result of the weather. Not so for Kate, whose hair was neatly swept up in a bun, and whose pants and blouse were perfectly pressed. Leah tried to leash in her envy, but it was too hard. "Do you mind if I'm honest enough to say I hate you?"

Kate stared at her. "I promise you, I have never spied on your sister or her company."

Leah needed time to remember she was supposed to have a sister. She had to laugh. "I don't mean that. I mean you're just so beautiful and put-together."

"Thank you!" Kate said, with a smile that could sell a million posters. "That's really nice."

"I wasn't being nice; I was being catty."

"You do that very well."

Leah laughed. "Okay, so you hate my sister. But I promise you she's okay."

"In what universe?"

Leah waved. "There has to be one out there. But this isn't about her. This is revenge on men."

"Who messed with you?"

"A guy who thinks I'm spying for you."

"Excuse me?"

"It's kind of a long story."

"I've got time."

Leah explained about her quasi-experiment. The more she talked, the more Kate smiled.

Leah finally took a breath. "I don't know why I'm telling you this, except I don't think you're trying to steal company secrets from Just Peachy."

"Believe me, Leah. If I ever thought we had a corporate spy in our organization, he or she would be in jail. I'd hand the person over to the authorities myself."

And Leah was convinced of Kate's sincerity. "It must be a female thing."

"Excuse me?"

"Females. We understand one another better. You're telling the truth."

Kate chuckled, then sipped her water. "Somehow your sister must have missed out on those female genes."

Wasn't that the truth? If Leah didn't love Steve so much, she'd spill the beans on him, too. But just on the off chance that she'd totally misread Kate, she didn't dare. In a couple of months they could all laugh about it.

Right.

"Anyway, since Mark believes I'm a spy, I'm going to lead him on a little goose chase."

"That's devious."

"Does he or does he not deserve it?"

Kate hesitated, then nodded. "Okay, I'm in. Do I get to neuter him first?"

"My job, but you're welcome to my brother, Steve."

Kate sat back. "I kind of like Steve. Why would I do that?"

"He let Mark believe I was a snitch for you."

Kate didn't even hesitate, bless her. "Let's get them. What's the plan?"

Mark stared at the computer that monitored Leah's work area. Of course, right now she was Candi in all her pumped-up-hair-and-chest glory. He had to admire her determination to pull this ruse off. But he also hated the getup. She was so much more attractive with her natural beauty.

And he couldn't believe he'd said no to her. Was he out of his friggin' mind? He had the horrible feeling that Leah wasn't giving him a second chance anytime soon.

111

He was mulling over his stupidity when a strange man approached Leah's desk. How'd the guy get past security? He made a note to ream the front desk out.

He turned up the sound.

The man leaned over Leah's desk and said, "Hiya, sugar."

"Well, hello, there, baby doll!" Leah said in that breathless voice that was beginning to irritate the hell out of Mark.

"Are we still on for tonight?" the man asked.

"You better believe it. I wouldn't miss it for the world."

Mark practically gaped. "Sugar" Candi was actually dating someone else?

The man, who in Mark's opinion wasn't all that attractive, casually dropped an envelope on Leah's desk. "Here's making sure you show up."

She made a big production of dropping the letter in her purse. "I'll be there, honey."

"You going to have good news for me?"

"The best."

Because he was monitoring a couple of other potential suspects, it was more than an hour before Mark could get away from the security office. But he was still hopping mad.

And he wasn't quite sure why. Well, he was, but he was having a hard time with it. He was mad that Leah was dating someone else.

He couldn't care less about Candi-with-an-i, but Leah was under there somewhere, and she was *dating another guy*. And the guy wasn't even that good-looking, either. A little too skinny, and Mark thought he walked like a girl.

Nonetheless, he had a meeting with Steve Smith, and he had to report all he knew so far.

Steve's secretary escorted him into the office, and after shaking the man's hand, Mark sat down and pulled out his notes. "A couple of things."

"Go ahead."

"Renfro is making copies of his notes."

"That's standard."

"But he takes them home with him."

"That's not standard, but maybe he's working overtime? He's one of our best chemists."

"I'm only relaying my observations. He looks awfully strange when he's making copies. It's just a gut feeling."

"Okay, I'll keep that in mind. And you've already done a background check on him, right?"

"He seems to be clean, except he just bought a new car that is a little bit out of his price range."

Steve grimaced, but nodded. "All right. Keep an eye on him. What else?"

"Genevieve in accounting. She's been making some strange moves lately."

"She's been with me forever. I can't believe she'd do anything wrong. And she doesn't have ready access to files about formulas."

"But that's what she's been doing. Going through files."

Steve sat back for a moment. "There might be a reason she's doing that. I'll ask Stephanie, but I think she has her looking into a few things."

"All right. Genevieve's probably okay. But I'm not ruling her out."

"I don't want you ruling anyone out. But I hate that anyone would be ruled in."

113

"I know." Mark understood too well the shock and disbelief of betrayal. The pain was remarkably intense.

"Anyone else?"

"Candi is dating somebody."

Steve actually laughed. "That would be you."

"No, she's dating someone else. And let me tell you, he looks pretty ugly."

"And this is suspicious why?"

"He handed her an envelope."

"Oh, well, let's go arrest them now."

"It sounds strange, I know. Except he wasn't her type at all."

"And what would her type be?"

"She liked me. Well, the Leah part of her liked me. The Candi part of her couldn't get away fast enough."

"What does this have to do with our spy?"

"I think that envelope might have been a payoff."

"Then by all means, let's go ask her."

"We can't do that. She has no idea who I am. She thinks I'm a handyman."

"Then go get your tool belt. I'm sure there's something seriously wrong in her office."

Mark would protest, except he was really irritated Leah had a date. *If* she had a date. He almost hoped that the man was actually an accomplice in crime, and not a love interest. Which just went to show what an idiot Mark was. Jake would be laughing his butt off right about now.

By the time Mark found and confiscated a tool belt and he and Steve made it to Leah's desk, she was gone and an intern was manning her desk.

"Candi's gone," the intern said. "But Leah should be here in about thirty minutes."

Mark hid his frustration as best he could.

And why he was frustrated, he couldn't say. Well, he probably could, but he didn't want to.

He didn't want Leah to be guilty. But he didn't want her Candi persona to be dating a dweeb, either. So he was torn between being attracted to a lying thief or being jealous of a guy who wanted his lying thief.

Yes, he was losing his mind.

The intercom sounded, with instructions for Steve to call the receptionist. Steve picked up the phone and dialed the three-digit code to the front desk. He said a few words, put down the phone, and grabbed Mark's arm, pulling him out into the hall.

"What?" Mark asked.

"There's a guy out front claiming to be FBI. Why would the FBI be here?"

Mark grinned. "Did the FBI guy give a name?"

"Donald? Something like that."

"Donnelly?"

"That's right. Do you know him?"

"I do. And now I have a plan."

Chapter Ten

Leah watched a man who could easily be a cover model approach her desk. He strode toward her with such authority, she was actually a little frightened.

"Can I help you?" she squeaked.

He whipped out a wallet-type thing and flipped it open. "Jake Donnelly, FBI."

She stared at his credentials and badge, then looked up at him. "Is there something wrong?"

"Do you know a man named Colson?"

"Mark?"

He flipped open a small writing pad. "Yes, he'd be the one."

Not as well as she wanted to, but . . . okay. "Yes, I know him. Why?"

"We suspect him of trafficking corporate secrets."

"You think Mark's a spy?"

"That's our contention, yes."

Leah stood up so abruptly her chair fell over. She didn't care. "Not a chance."

"Why is that, ma'am?"

"He's the one trying to—" She stopped herself just in time. She wasn't supposed to know his real role here.

"Trying to what, ma'am?"

Leah never prided herself on being quick on her feet. But she gave it a try. "Clean the toilets. He cleans the toilets."

"And he's only trying to do that?"

She shrugged her shoulders and raised her hands. "Who can ever really get a toilet perfectly clean?"

He gave her a hard stare that would have her confessing to murder in seconds. But then he nodded and said, "I think that about does it."

And as she gaped at him, he turned on his heel and left.

She had to get to Steve. And she had to get to Mark. They were both idiots, but they were *her* idiots, and no cocky, full-of-himself federal agent was messing with what was hers.

"She's not guilty of anything but being protective of you, pal," Jake said to Mark several minutes later in Steve's office.

Mark stood up. "You talked to her for all of thirty seconds."

"So?"

"You'd make a really lousy FBI guy."

Jake grinned and shrugged. "Probably. But she's only guilty of being a lousy liar. You clean toilets around here?"

"She thinks I'm a handyman."

For some strange reason, Steve had a coughing fit. Mark looked at him. "You okay?"

"Uh, sure," Steve said. "But I have to agree with Jake here. I don't think she has a spy bone in her body."

Mark glanced back and forth between the two of them, wondering exactly what he was missing. "You're both out of your minds. Watch a pro in action."

Jake shook his head. "I can't wait."

The moment Mark left the room, Steve stood up, grinning. "You're good."

Jake looked at him for a moment, then said, "What am I missing?"

"I don't know if I should tell you. You're his friend, after all."

"I am. But as long as you're not screwing him, tell me anyway."

"Leah isn't a spy. She's my sister. All she's doing is conducting an experiment."

"What kind of experiment?"

"She's working on her Ph.D."

"In what?"

"Sociology."

"Ohhh, sociology. She's one of *those* types."

"I'm afraid so."

Jake sat down and hooked his left ankle over his right thigh. "Why don't you just tell him?"

"Because he likes her, I think."

"Really? So allowing him to continue looking at her as a suspect is a good thing?"

"He keeps looking at her, doesn't he?"

"Depends. How does she feel about him?"

"She's mad as hell."

"And this is good because . . . ?"

"Because if she didn't like him, she wouldn't care."

Jake stared at him for a second, then burst out laughing. "Wait till LeAnne hears this." He leaned forward. "Do you really think there's potential here?"

"I'm counting on it."

"At the risk of Mark's being distracted away from the real culprit?"

"He's still being more than thorough, so I'm not too worried about that. Besides, I'm not so sure there *is* a real culprit any longer. I've . . . umm . . . had a talk with the woman who runs our competitor company, and she seems sincere about not having a mole in this organization."

"Oh, yeah, guilty competitors would come clean right away."

Steve loosened his tie a little. "Well, that's why I'm keeping Mark on the job. Just in case."

"Right. And to matchmake with your sister."

"Merely a side benefit."

"Devious. I think I like you."

"Thanks. I do what I can."

"Not to mention—and don't forget, this is purely an observation from an extremely happily married man— your sister is really pretty."

"Try telling her that."

Mark walked toward Leah's desk. She looked up and then stood rapidly. "Oh, I'm so glad you're here."

He stopped short. "You are?"

"I don't want to alarm you, but there was an FBI guy in here asking about you."

He went for a shocked look. "Why would the Fibbies be asking about me?"

"That's what I want to know. But just be careful."

"Who was this?"

She waved. "Some guy. But he looked really scary."

Mark had to work hard not to laugh. "Thanks for the warning."

"What do you think they want? I had the feeling he

120

thought you're . . . you know, a corporate spy or something."

"Me? A spy?"

"That's the impression I got."

"Do *you* think I'm a spy?"

"Of course not!"

Man, she was so beautiful, the little fraud. "Why not? Think I'm too dumb?"

"Of course not."

Mark was unnaturally happy about her ferocity. She was cute when she was defending him, even if she claimed he cleaned toilets for a living. "So, would you go out to dinner with me tonight?"

"I'm sitting here telling you the Feds are after you and all you care about is feeding your fool stomach?"

"What are they going to pin on a handyman?"

"Who knows? But I'm telling you, they're asking."

He shrugged. "I'd rather worry about my fool stomach. Dinner tonight?"

"I . . . can't."

"Why not?" He wanted to hear her say it. Her Candi persona had a date.

But all she said was, "I'm busy."

"Doing what?"

She glared at him. "I'm trying to remember when my private life became your business."

Now he was getting annoyed. "When you called me the other night, that's when."

"That was a mistake."

He was about to open his mouth when it suddenly smacked him in the head that they were being monitored. "I'll talk to you after work."

"I don't know what there is to talk about."

"Plenty, Leah. Plenty."

"Why don't you just go talk to Candi?"

That stopped him short. He leaned over her desk and whispered—for her ears only, he hoped—"Because I don't want Candi. I want you."

Leah had a couple of long hours to contemplate Mark's words. Fortunately, she had a lot of Candi mistakes to fix, so she wasn't just twiddling her thumbs. She also wasted some energy being mad at her brother because he wasn't returning her calls. And she desperately wanted to warn him about the FBI guy.

It was really strange how protective she'd felt when the man came in and began asking about Mark. She didn't think for a moment that Mark was guilty of anything. Well, except for lying to her about knowing she was also Candi. And lying to her about his actual role at Just Peachy. And for refusing to have sex with her.

Now that she thought about it, the man was a scumball.

Nonetheless, she didn't want to see anything bad happen to him.

Then again, the man was a scumball.

She had no doubt he'd witnessed Kate coming in, dressed as a man, making a date with her. She was acutely aware that she was being watched intently. But it still bugged her that even though Mark still believed she was a potential spy, she still kind of wanted him.

Well, more than kind of. More like a whole lot.

If he didn't consider her a spy, it would be more than a whole lot.

Her phone rang, and she stopped refiling papers, hoping Steve was finally available.

"It's me," Kate said, her voice low, as if she were afraid of a tap.

"Hi. What a day."

"Did you-know-who take the bait?"

Leah glanced around, wondering just where the camera and/or microphone was hidden. "That would be my best guess."

"Can't talk, hmm?"

"Right. Let me go take a walk to refresh my soul. Where can I reach you?"

"Call my cell phone." Kate gave her the number.

"Gotcha. Talk to you soon."

When Mark returned to Steve's office, Jake and Steve were laughing like they were old buds. This made Mark very nervous. Jake wasn't an easy man to get to know, and here he'd left him for all of ten minutes.

Something was up. "What's up?"

"Not a thing," Jake said. Which was a really bad sign.

Mark turned raised brows to Steve, who was suddenly studying his calendar intently. "Your turn. What's up?"

"Jake was just telling me about . . . umm—"

"Muffin," Jake said, just a little too quickly.

"Right," Steve said. "Muffin."

But his expression said he didn't know if Jake was talking bran or blueberry.

"Oh, Muffin," Mark said. "She's the cutest little cat, isn't she?"

"She sounds adorable."

Jake rolled his eyes. "We're busted, buddy. Muffin's my bulldog."

Mark sat down. "Okay, *now* tell me what's so funny."

Leah walked across the street to the park. She sat down on a bench and dialed the number Kate had given her.

"Hi," Kate said.

"We've got a situation here."

"What's that?"

123

Trish Jensen

"The FBI showed up. They're investigating Mark for some reason."

"Why?"

"They think he's the spy."

"Something's fishy."

"Why?"

"I'm not up to speed on law-enforcement rules, but I'm pretty sure the FBI doesn't get involved in cases unless they involve interstate crimes. These are local cosmetic firms, for crying out loud."

Leah hadn't thought of that. "You're right. Something stinks."

"Other than that, did they buy my suave-man routine?"

"I hate to tell you, but you're no Cary Grant."

"I work with what I have. But the point is, did Mark say anything?"

"He conveniently asked me out for tonight."

"What did you say?"

"I told him I'm otherwise occupied."

"Okay, here's the plan. Somehow let him know where we're going for supper."

"You mean you're going through with this?"

"Hey, I had fun. Let's see if he shows up. At worst we'll get dinner out of it."

"You are sneaky."

"Isn't it fun?"

"Extremely. But if you really want to fool anyone," Leah suggested, "you need some inserts."

"Inserts?"

"You want to look like a man in those pants or not?"

"You have *got* to be kidding me."

"I'm the disguise specialist around here. You frankly look like a eunuch."

"I don't mind."

124

"Candi would."

"I don't believe this. Where in the world would I get inserts?"

"Have you checked your sock drawer lately?"

Chapter Eleven

Leah reluctantly donned her Candi attire, and headed downstairs—only to meet Steve all decked out as Stephanie. She stopped short.

"Where have you been all day?"

"Busy, why?"

"Do you know we have the FBI traipsing around the office?"

"As a matter of fact, I do," Steve said, adjusting everything from his chest to his cheeks.

"Well, what are you going to do about it?"

"What do you mean?"

"They think Mark's a spy! You have to tell them different."

"Why? It's possible he is."

"He's working security for you, dipwad."

"So he says. The FBI thinks he might be greasing his palm on both sides, if you get my drift."

"I don't believe it."

"I don't either, but I'm not ruling anything out."

"Where are you going?" she asked. "And why Stephanie?"

"The Fed wants to meet Stephanie, esteemed leader, so I'm going to dinner with him and Mark. I believe the aim of the evening is a little spying on you."

"You have to be kidding me."

"Colson wants to keep an eye on you."

"Why?"

"Apparently he didn't like something he saw you doing today."

"I just made a date for supper with . . . an old buddy from college."

"Whatever."

"So once again you're horning in on my personal life."

"No, Colson and the Fed are. I'm just there so they can wine and dine Stephanie."

"Right."

Unfortunately, just then Gramps returned from the market. He looked at both of them and sighed. "What did I do to deserve this?"

Leah felt bad. She loved her grandfather with all her heart. She hated causing him distress. "Gramps, it's just—"

"I know, I know. An experiment. You know, Oprah would have a field day with this."

"We'll be sure to give her a call." Leah moved to him and gave him a kiss on the cheek. "See you later. I love you."

Before she left, she made an emergency call to Kate. "You really need to ratchet it up a notch. Company coming."

"I'm afraid of what you want me to ratchet up."

"I'm pumping it up. So should you."

Leah met Kate, who was bearing a jarring resemblance to Groucho Marx, in the parking lot of a Japanese restaurant in Fairfax. Although Kate had done an admirable job of trying to look as masculine as possible, Leah worried that she wouldn't stand up to close scrutiny. "No offense, but I wouldn't date you in a million years," Leah said.

"No offense, but I could deflate those boobs in a nanosecond."

"Just so we understand each other."

Leah laughed as they walked in, feeling a strange camaraderie with this woman who was supposed to be the enemy. She didn't think she was betraying Steve, but she wasn't quite sure where the line was that she could possibly cross by mistake.

The good news was, she had the feeling Steve was beginning to feel differently about Kate. The bad news was, Stephanie was here. With Mark. And that FBI guy.

"Oh, great," Kate said the moment she spotted them. "When I told you to let Mark know where you'd be, I didn't think he'd bring the witch along."

"And that's the Fed sitting with them. It's just one big happy party."

A smiling Japanese man met them. "A table for two?"

"Yes," Leah said. "As far away from that large table over there"—she nodded in Steve's direction—"as possible."

But before the man could assess the possibilities, Mark looked over at them, then said something to Steve. Steve stood up and wobbled his way over to them. He really should have learned to master heels.

"Miss Devereaux! How nice to see you. My brother tells me great things about your work."

"Thank you, Ms. Smith," she said through gritted

129

teeth. She really should have researched the word for killing a sibling, because she'd like to know what crime she'd be committing later tonight.

"I'd love to have you and your . . . date join us."

"No, thank you. We'd like to be alone." Leah turned back to the Japanese man. "How about that small corner table over there?"

The man nodded and bowed and then led them across the room.

"Why didn't you want to sit with them?" Kate asked after they were seated.

"No offense, but your disguise—as good as it might be—could be detected."

"And you make a lousy bimbo."

And besides, you hate my sister."

"*Kate* the competitor hates your sister. I'm just your dweeb date and potential partner in crime."

Leah glanced toward Steve's table, only to find a scowl on Mark's face as he looked the couple over. "Besides, the FBI guy makes me nervous."

"Why do you think the FBI guy is out with Mark and Stephanie?"

"I'm still a little sketchy on that." And that was the plain truth. She didn't understand the logic of these guys wanting to spend time spying on her and her "date" at all.

"I'm a little suspicious of the whole situation, unless the FBI guy is considering arresting me." Leah cocked her head in thought.

"Your sister is not going to let the guy do that."

"True. But I'm not so sure about Mark. He still suspects me."

"And now me," Kate said with glee.

A waiter appeared at their table, carrying a bottle of

champagne chilling on ice, and two flutes. "Compliments of the three men over there," he said.

"Well, wasn't that nice of them," Kate said, lowering her voice. "Whatever they're drinking, buy them a round on us."

Leah stared at her. "What do you think you're doing?"

"If they're trying to get us tipsy so we'll spill all of our secrets, it would be rude of us not to offer them the same."

Before their soups were even served, they'd traded drinks three times. Leah felt herself wobbling, and that was while she was sitting down.

Then the notes began to arrive with the champagne.

You are the wind beneath my wings. M, Leah received first.

She countered with, *You are the windbag beneath my feet. C.*

For the rest of the meal, the two tables were trading drinks back and forth, and the poor waiter was a frazzled wreck. By the time they were finished with their sushi, Leah was feeling the drinks, great irritation, and an overwhelming high that had only to do with the champagne, she was sure. "I think we'll need to order a cab."

"Good idea." She called the waiter over. "Another round for the boys. And then steal their car keys."

"You know, with all this alcohol swapping, we haven't had time to act suspicious," Leah noted.

"Let's pay the check, then go into the lounge for a nightcap. What do you want to bet they aren't far behind?"

"What if they see through your disguise up close?"

"At this point, who cares? That'll just make them all the more suspicious. Anyway, I've been in that lounge.

It's really dark. And if they can see straight at this point, we didn't do our job."

Leah shrugged. "What the heck?"

They paid up then stood, and Kate grabbed Leah's hand and led her on a path directly past Mark's table. "Thanks for the drinks, boys," she said. "And lady," she added, winking at Steve.

They entered the lounge and headed to another corner table. Leah was almost surprised she didn't topple over in her heels. Sober, she could barely navigate. Tipsy, she wasn't exactly the picture of grace.

They were barely seated when the men entered and took a table fairly close to theirs.

Leah held her breath as they sized up Kate. But all three of them were sort of squinting, so she probably didn't need to worry too much.

Kate smiled at Steve. "Candi has been telling me wonderful things about you and your company."

Steve stared at Kate for a minute, and the irony was almost overwhelmingly funny. Leah almost wanted to shout, *If there's anyone in this place who is who they say they are, please stand up.* She had a feeling lots of butts would still be seated.

Steve stood and held out a hand to Kate. "I'm so pleased to meet you. Any friend of Candi's is a friend of ours. And you are?"

"William . . . William Shakespeare."

Leah nearly peed her pants.

It took Steve a moment to find his voice. "Well, it's very nice to meet you, William. I take it your parents were literary."

"No. Why?"

"You know . . . Well, never mind. We'd love for you to join us."

"Candi, what do you think?"

What she thought couldn't be printed. But she shored up, because for some reason Mark looked gorgeous in khakis and a hunter-green polo shirt, and being near him appealed to her. Still . . .

"That's very nice of you, Ms. Smith. But I suspect you're in a *meeting*, and we wouldn't want to interrupt."

"You won't be interrupting. Please, be my guest."

"I'll be sending you a big, fat thank-you note later."

Steve swallowed, which just emphasized his Adam's apple, and once again Leah couldn't believe anyone would take him for anything but a man. But Kate was so busy trying desperately to look like a man herself that she didn't appear to notice.

If Leah wrote this story, not a single person would believe it.

Leah and Kate stood and approached the other table.

They nodded at the cocktail waiter, who looked like he wasn't sure what to do. He probably thought a drag-queen fight was about to ensue. And she pretty much figured their dining room antics had already made the rounds back in the break room.

Steve held out a chair for Leah, leaving Kate to fend for herself. It was obvious Kate was a little put-out—until she remembered she was a guy. What she obviously was missing was that Steve was a woman. At least tonight.

"Mark, you know Candi, right?" Steve said after sitting down.

"I do. Hello again, Candi."

Leah conjured a smile she wasn't exactly feeling, seeing that she knew darn well the man knew darn well that there was no such person as Candi. But she decided to go for it, if for no other reason than to make him squirm. "You never called me again, Mark, you bad boy."

Mark frowned and the FBI guy grinned. "I've . . . been busy."

"What girl hasn't heard that same old song?" she said. "I thought we had something special."

The FBI guy slapped a cocktail napkin to his mouth.

Steve cleared his throat, then said, "And this is William Shakespeare."

"Nice to meet you," Kate said, keeping her hands under her armpits in an apparent attempt not to let anyone see her hands.

"William Shakes—" Mark stopped and smiled. "Nice to meet you. I take it your parents were big into literature?"

"No. Why?"

Steve dumped Leah into her chair. "And this gentleman is Jake Donnelly."

Greetings over with, they all sat down.

"Drinks?" Steve asked, and Leah practically shouted, *Yes*. She wasn't a drinker as a rule, but staying tipsy held a certain appeal. This surreal situation called for a slightly dazed state.

The Jake guy said, "You work for Stephanie?"

"Yes," Leah said. "Part-time."

"Oh, that's probably why I didn't meet you today."

"Why? Are you coming to work for Just Peachy?"

"No, I'm trying to decide whether to arrest this guy," the man said, hiking a thumb at Mark.

"Over dinner?"

"You can tell a lot about a man by the food he orders."

"I see." Leah frantically waved at the waiter. "Just what is he supposed to have done?"

"Money laundering."

134

Mark shook his head. "I keep telling you, I'm innocent."

"You have to admit, you ordered the California-roll platter."

"That makes me guilty of what? Liking avocados?"

"No, liking California."

"Is that illegal?" Leah said. "I know it's dumb, but is it really illegal?"

"It tells me he has an affinity for California."

The strange thing was, the only person not gaping at the Fed was Steve. He was acting as though this were a perfectly sane conversation. Leah suddenly felt as if she were in an Abbott and Costello skit, only she had no idea who was on first.

"It seems to me there's a simple solution here," she finally said into the silence.

"What is that?"

She batted her lashes and tried not to lose a blue contact. "Let's ask him." She turned to Mark. "Where do you stand on the orange issue?"

To his credit, he kept a perfectly straight face. "I prefer the Florida variety."

She looked at the Fed. "There you go."

The man pulled out a small notebook. Again. "So he's also operating in Florida."

Okay, this was a joke, but she wasn't going to let it be on her. She turned to Steve. "Where do you stand on the orange issue?"

"I prefer papaya."

"Aha! Arrest this ma—er, woman! She's obviously a smuggler from Hawaii."

"I like salmon," Kate chimed in.

"So my date here is not only doing business in Washington, he's also a pinko."

135

The waiter took their drink orders and left for the bar. A somewhat uncomfortable silence followed while the guy named Jake continued making notes.

Right then the waiter returned with their drinks. Every single one of their group grabbed their glasses like lifelines.

Leah sat back. "Okay, what's the joke?" she asked Jake.

He looked up. "Joke?"

"You're about as FBI as a clown."

He set down his pad and pen. "I showed you my credentials."

"Right. I could probably buy one of those at the toy store."

"It doesn't pay to piss off a federal agent," Steve said.

"Find me one and I'll be sure to be polite."

Somehow the joke had been turned on Leah and Kate, and she couldn't figure out how. It had started out with her and Kate pretending to be partners in crime, which had pretty much fallen through after the second bottle of champagne.

It was supposed to be about the FBI guy checking up on her, but he'd been too much of a smart-aleck for that to be the case. And he certainly wasn't grilling Mark about nefarious schemes too darn hard.

Life was a little confusing. And the three men at the table were beginning to tick her off.

Jake looked at Steve. Flipping through his little notebook he said, "I thought you told me that Candi Devereaux was somewhat . . . Wait, let me find it. Here it is. 'Cranium-challenged.'"

Both Steve and Kate spit out their drinks. Leah would have tossed hers, but she couldn't decide which one of the lot of them she wanted to hit first. And it occurred to her that she really was supposed to be dumb.

Not for Steve or Kate or the scumbag Mark, but probably for the fake Fed. So she set down her drink slowly and asked, "What's a cranium?"

This time Mark practically choked, which right now wasn't upsetting her too badly. When he caught his breath he said, "You know, one of those big construction machines that move big things from one place to another."

She smiled sweetly at him. What was the word for murdering a jerk? *Justifiable homicide* fit, but that was two words. There had to be one that encompassed the act. "Well, you're right about that. I never learned to use one of those things."

"In all of your jobs over the years? I'm surprised."

And it hit her. Of course. He'd figured her out because he was monitoring Thorndike's office the day she applied for the job. How, she wasn't quite sure, because when she looked in the mirror, Leah and Candi didn't look a thing alike. But something must have tipped him off. And she wanted to know what it was. She also wanted to know who this Jake person was. If that was his real name.

"Mr. Colson, may I see you at the bar for a moment?"

"You're not helping him get away, are you?" said Jake, the good-looking jerk.

"Trust me, if he's doing something illegal, I'll testify against him myself."

"But honey bunch—" Kate started to say.

"Keep Stephanie company," Leah said, feeling it was the least of what Steve deserved. "We'll be back shortly."

Mark followed Leah to the bar, half-excited, half-worried about what she wanted.

She whirled on him so quickly, he almost rammed

into her and knocked her over. He had to grab her shoulders to keep her from landing on that very, very cute rear end.

"What gave me away?" she all but spit out at him.

"Excuse me?"

"Give it up, Colson. I know you know."

"Know what?"

"I have Mace and I know how to use it."

He backed up, laughing. "Down, boy."

"How'd you figure it out?"

He held out a stool for her and she sat. Then he shocked her by running his hand down her leg. He stuck a finger under her ankle bracelet and said, "This."

She stared down at it for a moment. "Damn, that was dumb."

"Well, in your defense, I don't think you're very experienced at this kind of thing."

"What kind of thing?"

"Espionage."

She plunked her hands on her hips. "Do you really think I'm guilty of that?"

"No. No offense, but anyone who'd hire you to spy for them would be pretty damn stupid."

"Thanks a bunch."

"Hey, that's a compliment."

"Oh, yeah, I'm flattered beyond belief."

"So why *are* you doing it?"

"Why are you pretending to be a handyman?"

"I never pretended that. You drew that conclusion, and I just chose to let you believe it."

She went still. "You're right. I made a snap judgment just on your appearance. I'm sorry."

"I came to a couple of conclusions myself that first day. No worries."

"Like what?"

"Like it's probably a bad idea to stick a pen down your jacket."

"Oh, my God, you saw that."

"The stuffing of the cell phone was inspired."

Her hands flew to her face. "You realize I can never look at you again."

He encircled her wrists and pulled. "Sure you can. But I'd rather you looked at me with green eyes and darker hair."

She still wouldn't look up at him. "I'm not a spy."

"Of course not. But what the hell are you doing?"

She swallowed hard and turned her head. "I was testing a theory."

"What theory is that?"

"The one that said these"—she waved a hand in front of her chest—"would help me get a job easier than this." She pointed at her temple.

"And you wanted to know this why?"

"I was writing my thesis. It was just a thought. A dumb one, I guess."

"Well, I have to admit you're a bad bimbo."

Finally she raised her eyes to his. "You asked me out because you thought I was a spy."

"Guilty."

"You weren't attracted to me at all."

"Not guilty. At least not to Candi."

She stared at him. "No way."

"Why is that so hard to believe? Do you really think this getup makes you more attractive?"

"Sexually? Yes."

"Who brainwashed you?"

Leah shook her head. "No one but me."

"Well, then you're dumber than I thought."

Just then Steve came over to the bar. "They're going to kick us out shortly. It's almost closing time."

"We'll be right there," Mark said. Then he took her shoulders. "What do you say if after we finish our drinks we ditch the others and go have coffee somewhere?"

"I'm on a date."

"Right. Tell Kate you'll call her real soon."

Her eyes went wide. "You knew?"

"Please. You two are so bad you'd get bonged off *The Gong Show.*"

He took her arm and started dragging her back to the table. Suddenly he wanted this night to be over as soon as possible.

Right before they hit the table, she stopped dead in her tracks. "Okay, as long as we're all coming clean, tell me, who is Jake Donnelly—if that *is* his real name, anyway?"

"Oh, he's definitely FBI."

Chapter Twelve

The rest of the evening didn't fare much better, even though Mark had kept his promise not to "out" Kate. But Leah was so busy disliking Jake for constantly insinuating that he was going to be hauling Mark off to the pokey at any moment, she had a hard time enjoying her drink.

Not to mention, there was something odd going on between Kate and Steve. It was like they were attracted to each other, which made no sense, because Steve looked like Nanook of the North in lipstick, and Kate looked positively twitchy in that mustache.

One thing she knew for sure: She wanted to spend time with Mark later tonight. Just as soon as she deflated her bra.

It was hard to imagine that he really preferred her as herself than as Candi, but she believed him. She wasn't quite sure why, but she did. It might be the dumbest assessment she'd ever made, but so be it. She'd live with the consequences.

In between sips of his drink, Steve kept glancing over at her with a worried look in his eyes. He should be worried. He was in deep trouble. And he had a lot of explaining to do.

Then again, all she had to do was look over at Mark, blissfully unconcerned about the FBI threat, and she couldn't fire up too much indignation. Whatever his reasons, she wasn't all that unhappy with the results.

She just wished she could take off the damn bra already.

"So what do you do for the FBI?" Kate asked Jake.

"Fraud," he said, looking at her pointedly.

Kate's skin went pasty, and she dug back into her cocktail.

"What do you do, Mr. Shakespeare?" Jake asked.

"I'm in insurance."

"Is that how you and Candi met?"

"He wrote my auto insurance policy," Leah said, giving a loving squeeze to Kate's forearm. "He was happy to do it, even after the . . . *incident*. Isn't he sweet?"

"Did I mention I investigate fraud?" Jake said.

When the evening came to a blessed end, and Leah and Mark said their good-nights to Jake, Steve, and Kate, Mark turned to her. "Let's go somewhere and talk."

Talking was okay. She could do that. It wasn't number one on her priority list with him, however. Nonetheless, it was a start. "Where?"

"Your place is out, right?"

"Yes."

"Well, Shelley's at mine, but she knows when to disappear."

"She doesn't have to disappear if we're just going to talk. It's her house, too."

"She'll disappear."

"Good."

* * *

Mark's house was only five minutes from the restaurant. It was a neat ranch in a nice area of Fairfax.

Leah knew how to get there, but she followed him anyway and pulled up behind him.

"I like your place," she said as they walked up to the front door.

"Thanks. I bought it from a friend."

He unlocked the door and gestured for her to go in ahead of him. The first thing she noticed was that the place smelled like cookies. The second was that Shelley was sitting on a navy couch, reading a book in Braille.

"Hiya, bro," Shelley said, putting the book aside. "Hi, Leah."

"Hi," Leah said, but looked up at Mark in amazement.

"Tell her how you knew," Mark said, grinning.

"Oh, please," Shelley said, as if it were a cakewalk. "Two sets of feet. You aren't alone. You unlocked the door, then allowed the person to precede you into the house. Obviously a woman. You haven't dated seriously in two years until recently. And you never shut up about her. Hi, Leah."

"Hi," Leah managed to squeak out again.

"My sister has a big mouth," Mark said, appearing a little flushed.

Shelley shrugged. "You asked." She bookmarked what she'd been reading and stood. "Cookies, anyone?"

"No, thank you," Leah said.

"You look tired," Mark said.

Shelley sighed. "Night."

"You don't have to go!" Leah said.

"Yes, she does."

"I'll go read in my bedroom. Leah, if you need me, just yell. I'm mean with a cane."

Leah laughed softly. "Thanks, I'll keep that in mind."

She marveled as she watched Shelley maneuver her

way around the furniture, wave at them, then disappear down a dark hallway. Leah had a weird impulse to run and turn on the lights for her, but realized the absurdity of that. Shelley could take care of herself, and she certainly didn't need light.

"I love that you take care of your sister," she said softly.

Mark chuckled. "You have that backward. She takes care of me. Not to mention that she runs a business."

She shouldn't be shocked. But she was, a little. "What kind of business?"

"She caters birthday parties."

Leah smiled. "That is so cool! And I bet she's great at it."

"Of course she is. She's my sister, isn't she?"

"Well, we all have our burdens to bear."

"Very funny. Would you like some coffee or tea or something?"

"Do you happen to have any wine or sherry?"

"Are you kidding? My sister's a professional cook. What would you like?"

"Sherry, if it's dry."

"Coming up."

He disappeared into the kitchen, and Leah took the opportunity to look around. They had beautiful blown-up nature photographs on their walls that were captivating in their simplicity. The furniture was a little old and worn, and definitely not chosen for aesthetics, but all of the pieces looked either comfortable or functional. She approved. Not that anyone had asked her opinion, but she approved.

Mark returned a moment later and set her sherry and a glass of wine for himself on the coffee table. She followed him to the old couch and sat down.

Her heart was beating a little fast. Funny how just

anticipating talking to a man could get her excited. But if she planned to be honest with herself, she really was excited.

And it wasn't just that he was handsome as sin. It was more that he happened to be about the most intriguing man she'd ever met. He'd had no problem passing himself off as a dimwit, just to do the job he'd been hired to do. This really interested Leah, in a couple of ways. First, she'd had no problem playing dumb, because she'd forced herself to do it to gauge reactions. But she'd have thought it would hit him where it hurt, as a man, to act like a clueless idiot. It hadn't bothered him at all.

He obviously had a pretty good hold on his own masculinity and his mind to allow himself to come off as an idiot.

She hated to admit she admired that about him. She'd *hated* playing a ditz. He'd seemed to enjoy it. Still did, the turkey.

And then, he obviously loved his sister. And truth to tell, she was certain he had layers she knew nothing about. And she wanted to peel them away, one by fascinating one.

But she was such a dork. She didn't even know where to begin peeling.

Taking a sip of her drink, she glanced at him. "What are you smiling about?"

"Are you going to un-Candi yourself anytime soon?"

"Oh! May I? Please?"

"I'd be a lot happier."

"Bathroom?"

"You mean I don't get to watch you deflate your bra?"

"I know it's an exciting proposition," she said dryly.

"You have no idea."

"Maybe next time."

He laughed. "Damn. Well, okay, powder room down the hall. First door on the left."

She had to force herself not to run. She hit the bathroom, tossed off the wig, and shook out her hair. With a sigh of relief she popped out the contacts, and the pièce de résistance was deflating her chest. It didn't matter if Mark was fibbing about liking her au naturel better; *she* liked herself better. So she wasn't very busty. At least she didn't feel like the focal point for everyone she met was a quick trip south of her eyes.

That thought brought her up short. She'd been excited about posing as a sexpot. But now it felt good to shed the entire charade. So she wasn't a beauty. At least if people liked her, they liked her for being Leah. That was good enough.

A thousand pounds felt as if it had just dropped from her shoulders, and she reveled in her new freedom.

She came out of the bathroom sporting a huge smile, her only regret that she wore Candi clothes instead of Leah attire. But there was little she could do about that now. Her good mood must have been contagious, because when she looked at Mark he was grinning, too.

"Feel better?"

"Much."

"You look better, too."

"Not hardly, but at least I'm closer to me."

"There you go."

"Excuse me?"

"Admitting you prefer being you is big."

He was right. Leah took a sip of sherry, then said, "Okay, I came clean. Now you."

"Well, technically, I caught you."

"Don't try to duck the question."

"What do you want to know?"

"Who you are, for starters."

"Well, my real name is Mark—with a k."

She smacked his arm. "Funny you aren't."

He smiled, and every internal organ she owned melted.

"What do you want to know?" he asked her.

"Will you tell me the truth?"

"Am I a handyman?"

"No."

"Correct, I'm not. I'm in security."

"How'd you get into that line of work?"

He hesitated. "I was sort of trained for it."

"Yes? How?"

"Courtesy of the federal government."

"You were in the military?"

"Not exactly."

Leah blew breath out of frustrated lips. "Yes, you're really being forthcoming here."

"I started as a cop."

"Okay."

"Then I worked for the FBI."

Leah went still. "The FBI?"

"Yes."

"As in that Jake jerk FBI?"

"That Jake jerk was my partner."

"So he scared the hell out of me today for your pleasure?"

"Not exactly."

"What was it exactly?"

"It's a guy thing. You probably wouldn't get it."

"Give it a try."

"First of all, remember that you were still on my short list of suspects."

She'd have liked to screech her outrage, but common sense told her she didn't have a lot of solid ground to step on. If the man had figured out she was trying to get a job as two different people, naturally she'd be suspect. "Okay, I accept that, although I'm not sure how that's a guy thing."

"Second, I trust Jake's judgment above almost anyone else's except my sister's."

"So you had him size me up? Is that it?"

"Yes."

"That's a little harder to forgive."

"Third, I was jealous."

"Jealous?"

"Of that dweeb you were making a date with."

"That dweeb was Kate."

"I realized that tonight, but on those monitors I couldn't make out her lovely manicure."

Leah didn't think she'd ever inspired jealousy before. Not that she thought it was a productive emotion, but it certainly felt good that someone believed she was worth it. "I'm beginning to forgive you."

"Hallelujah," he said with a grin.

"Does Jake the jerk still work for the FBI?"

"For now. He's planning on retiring."

"Why did you retire? Or did you?"

He laughed, but it sounded a little pained. "No, I wasn't fired. I retired because . . . Well, I let Jake down."

He looked so sad, Leah wanted to hold him. "How's that?" she asked softly.

"It's a long story."

"Get me some more sherry and I have time."

They walked into the kitchen together and Mark started talking. Pretty reluctantly, Leah thought.

"I inadvertently put Jake and a couple of innocent civilians in danger. I brought a witness Jake and I were protecting to where he was vacationing. The thugs hoping to silence her found out where we were, and followed us. They mistook someone else for the witness, which forced Jake to take that woman away. But the bad guys kept following them."

"Seems to me it was the bad guys' fault."

He stopped in midpour and looked over at her. "That's what LeAnne keeps saying."

"Who's LeAnne?"

"The owner of the spa where Jake was staying. She was the one they mistook for the witness."

"But she's okay now, right?"

Mark smiled. "She's better than okay. She and Jake got married just a couple of months later, and they're expecting their first kid right now."

"Oh, that's wonderful! So what's your problem? It sounds like it was fate. Who knows? If they hadn't had to deal with that, maybe they wouldn't have gotten together."

"They were destined to fall in love from the first time they laid eyes on each other. They didn't need to be threatened with death to figure that out. In fact, the danger and the threat nearly drove them apart. Again, my fault."

"Yeah, Jake seems real mad at you, Mark."

He shook his head. "He's not and he never was."

"Then why are you?"

"Why am I what?"

"Mad at you?"

He blew out a breath. "I told you. I nearly got them killed."

"So you gave up?"

"I did not give up. I changed direction."

She digested that for a moment, then nodded. "Basically, you don't put people in danger any longer; you try to protect them from it."

He riffled a hand through his hair, head down. "You

make it sound noble. It's not. It was just a decision I had to make."

"I think it was the right one."

"Yeah? Why's that?"

"Well, if you hadn't, I'd never have met you, now, would I?"

He snorted. "Like that was a good thing."

"If nothing else, you've been entertaining."

He looked at her, then set his wineglass on the counter and stepped toward her. "I could be a lot more entertaining if you'd let me."

Her pulse took off like a space shuttle. She had to wait a few moments before she trusted her voice. "What kind of entertainment are we talking about?"

He cupped the back of her neck and settled his lips on hers. It was gentle but demanding. She'd never felt anything so wonderful in her life.

He broke the kiss and smiled. "Anything you want, pretty lady."

Chapter Thirteen

"Well, the kind of entertainment I was thinking about we can't engage in here," Leah said, her voice shaky.

"Why not?"

"Shelley's here!"

"I promise she won't barge in on us."

Leah shook her head, cheeks flaming. "What happens to a woman who loses her sight?"

"What do you mean?"

"How does she compensate?"

"Through her other senses."

"Like hearing?"

"For one, yes."

"There you go."

"Leah, I'm not following you at all."

"Hearing!" she said, wondering if there was more to his dimwit act than she'd thought.

Finally, some of his brain cells decided to get in on the act. "Oh! You're afraid she'll hear us."

"Bingo, Einstein."

"We can be quiet."

"Maybe you can."

He stared at her. "Are you saying . . . you're a talker?"

"And a moaner and, if you've got it in you, kind of a screamer."

"Oh, Lord," he muttered, scrubbing his face.

"I'm sorry if that bothers you. I can't seem to help it."

"Bothers me? You're kidding, right?"

"Well, you never know." Leah put her head in her hands. "I wouldn't be telling you all this if you hadn't plied me with liquor tonight, you know."

"Trust me, right now I'm glad I did. It will not bother me." He hesitated. "I could have sworn you were—"

"Pure as the driven snow?"

"Well, something like that."

"I hate to disappoint you."

"Oh, yeah, I'm almost ready to cry."

She smiled. "So the honest truth is, I wouldn't enjoy myself at all if I were really self-conscious about Shelley hearing us."

He seemed to mull that over. "Okay, I hear ya. Or, more appropriately, I *want* to hear ya."

She looked at her watch. "Another truth. It's a school night."

"You could always play hookey tomorrow."

"Sorry, no can do. Leah's pulling double duty tomorrow, seeing that Candi is quitting."

"You're getting rid of Candi?"

"If I never see another blond wig or Pump You Up bra again in my lifetime I will die happy."

"But your experiment!"

"It's over. It wasn't scientific in the least, and I think I've learned more than I wanted to know."

"I'm going to sort of miss Candi."

Her jaw dropped. "Are you serious?"

"Oh, honey, you were good for hours and hours of entertainment."

"I'm glad I amused you," she said, a little miffed—but not much. "I was that bad, wasn't I?"

"You don't know how to be vacuous, Leah. And believe me, I'm thrilled by that. Brains are so much sexier than breasts."

"Don't let other men hear you say that. You might be kicked out of the species."

He shook his head. "There are a bunch of us out there."

"Is it a secret society? Do you have a special handshake?"

He laughed. "The men who were more interested in your chest size aren't worthy of your time."

She was getting goopy all over again. Because she could tell he meant it. It was one thing to hear such sentiments from her brother and Gramps, but it was completely different from a man who was genuinely interested in making love to her. Especially a man like this one, who, she was certain, could have a woman with any chest size he wanted. She sighed. "Speaking of time, I really should get going."

He looked pained. "What are we going to do? You don't want to be with me here, and you've already mentioned that your house is off-limits."

She patted his chest. "You're a smart FBI guy. You'll probably figure something out."

"I pretty much have to. I'm not going to get any sleep until I do."

"Poor baby." She smiled. "Thanks for tonight. I actually had a good time."

"It could have been better," he muttered. But as she turned to go, he pulled her back. "Lady, if I'm not getting any sleep, neither are you." And with that he gave her a kiss that curled her toes and sent her pulse into aerobic levels.

Leah felt a little droopy the next morning, mostly because she'd hardly slept, thanks to a certain security specialist who kissed with a passion that she'd never experienced before. She tried to remember if anyone had kissed her like that in her life, and the honest answer was never. If she thought about it, kissing had always just seemed like a perfunctory prelude to getting naked. Mark kissed like it was his sustenance.

She'd marched into Mr. Thorndike's office this morning and announced that Candi had called her the night before to say she was quitting, and could Leah cover until they found someone else. It had almost been comical to see the relief on Thorndike's face.

On her morning break she trudged her way up to Steve's office. Luckily he wasn't in a meeting, and his secretary sent her right in.

"Howdy, big brother."

Steve's eyebrows rose. "What are you doing here?"

"Candi's dead."

"Excuse me?"

"Candi quit."

He sat back in his chair and tossed his pen on the desk. "And why is that?"

She dropped into a guest chair. "She wasn't really reliable anyway."

"You're finished playing dress-up?"

"I wasn't playing. It was—"

"An experiment. Yes, I know. So you keep telling us." She shrugged. "Whatever, it's done."

"Gramps will be very relieved. He was beginning to worry."

"Like you haven't added a few gray hairs to his head?"

"That'll be over soon, too."

"Thank God. You're not a very attractive girl."

"Speaking of attractive, what was with that date last night?"

"Just someone I know."

"William Shakespeare? What parent in his right mind would name a kid that?"

"I don't think they had a clue."

"Don't you think he's a little . . . um . . . effeminate?"

"I'm not marrying him, Steve. It was just someone to have dinner with." She frowned at him. "Speaking of which, what was with the ambush? Can I expect you to show up every time I have a date?"

He waved. "It was Colson's idea. He wanted to see what you were up to, and with whom."

"Well, the cat's out of the bag with him. Which is why Candi got a fast send-off."

"What do you mean, the cat's out of the bag?"

"I told him my real reason for playing Barbie doll."

"Did you tell him you're my sister?"

"Not yet. But I will eventually."

He gave her a hard, piercing look. "And you feel the need to bare your soul to Colson why?"

"I like him."

"Funny enough, I approve."

"Oh, well, then I can die happy."

He grinned. "I'm still your older brother."

"Speaking of which, why don't you come clean about Stephanie to him?"

"I will, but only right before I announce it to the staff."

"Mark wouldn't spill the news, Steve."

"I'm ninety-nine-point-nine percent certain you're

right. It's more a matter of feeling like I owe it to the employees to be among the first to know."

She nodded. Knowing Steve and his ethics, it made perfect sense. But there was something about Mark that made her want to clear the air completely. Deception didn't sit well with her, she'd recently discovered. And she knew it hadn't sat well with Steve all these years, either. She'd be very happy when his charade was over with.

"Anyway, I just wanted to let you know that I'm filling in for the time being, but I'm going to be handing in my notice, too. It's time for me to start looking for a job in my own field."

He smiled. "Thorndike won't be happy to hear that. He says you're great."

That gave her a warm fuzzy. "I'll kind of miss working with you," she said. "Not a lot, but a teeny, tiny bit."

"Don't break down in tears or anything," he said.

Leah grinned. "You'll miss me, too."

"Do I have to?"

"Yes."

"Well all righty then."

Leah stood up. "Well, back to the salt mines." She turned to go, then swung back. "Just an observation?"

"What's that?"

"The best part of this experiment was seeing how much your employees like and respect you."

He went still. "That's nice of you to say."

"Are you kidding? You're my tyrannical big brother. I would have loved nothing more than to inform you that you're a jerk on the job."

"I'll bet. But you know, there's still at least one traitor among us."

That had her marching right back to his desk. "You really believe that?"

"I do."

"Do you still think Kate knows about it?"

"I don't know."

"I don't believe it for a second."

"How are you so sure?"

"I'm a sociologist with a minor in psych. I'm a better judge of character than you are. And I believe her."

"How do you know so much about Kate all of a sudden?"

"Now don't get mad."

"Of course not. I never get mad at you . . . At least not more than once a day."

"We've become friends, Steve. At least tentatively. I honestly believe she's a good, honest, fun person."

"I hope you're right."

"You do?"

"Yes."

"I thought you hated her."

"So did I."

Leah hid a smile as she turned to go, but once out of his office, she couldn't help it. She nearly skipped to the elevator.

Her brother was toast.

Leah was a little miffed at Mark. It was almost noon and he hadn't bothered to stop by to see her all morning. Not that he was required to, just that she'd sort of expected a "Good morning" at least. And she'd held out a little bit of hope that he'd ask her to lunch, although until she quit the firm altogether, it probably wasn't a good idea.

So she went to plan B. She grabbed her cell phone and headed to the bathroom. She didn't know if or how her office space was bugged, and that annoyed her.

She dialed Kate's number.

Kate answered on the third ring. "Well, hello."

"Hi, William."

Kate laughed. "It was a spur-of-the-moment thing."

"It was hilarious."

"Thanks. Their faces were priceless."

"No kidding. Listen, I know it's short notice, but are you free for lunch?"

"Actually, I was about to have my secretary send out for a sandwich, but getting some fresh air sounds good."

"Do you know where Lacy's Deli is?"

"Yep. Good stuff."

"About a half hour?"

"See you then."

Mark spent the morning taking Jake on tours of clients' facilities and explaining the intricacies of the different systems his company had installed in the last few years.

As Mark knew he would be, Jake was a quick learner. Of course, they'd had to learn a lot about security over the years with the FBI, so it wasn't a stretch.

They stopped for lunch at a diner on Route 7. After ordering burgers, Mark said, "So what do you think?"

"I have to say, I'm pretty excited about the opportunity."

Mark smiled. "Great." Working with Jake again, even if they weren't actually in the same location, was a superb opportunity. "But are you positive you want to leave the Bureau?"

"Were you positive?"

"Not at all. I just knew it was the right thing to do. For *me*."

"Well, I can't say I won't miss some of it. But I won't miss how much time I'm forced to be away from

LeAnne, and I sure as hell don't want to be away from the baby."

Baby. Even the word brought back an ache in Mark's gut. His child would be almost ten years old now, if—

No, he wasn't going there. He cared too much about Jake and LeAnne to resent their having what he'd lost a decade ago. He conjured up a smile. "So it's a boy, huh?"

"Yes. I should have known. Once LeAnne decides something, she usually gets her way."

"Stubborn wench."

"Tell me about it," Jake said, but he had the goofiest grin on his face.

"Picked out a name?"

"No. LeAnne wants him to be Jake Junior and call him J.J. I'm still fighting that. No kid should have to be named after me."

"You can always name him Mark."

"J.J. it is."

Mark laughed. "Tell LeAnne she's welcome."

Their food arrived and they dug in. In between bites they discussed the logistics of setting up an office in Richmond.

"We'll have to rename the company. How about C and D Securities?"

"Why not D and C?"

"Because it sounds like a female medical procedure."

"Good point. We don't have to rename it at all if you don't want. You founded the company."

"No. This is a partnership, pal."

"Speaking of partnerships, what's up on the dating scene? Why aren't you hitched yet?"

Mark stopped chewing. "You know why."

"That was a long time ago."

"Not long enough."

Jake shook his head. "When are you going to figure out that Heather was an aberration?"

"Heather was an abomination."

"She was one woman. Giving her this much power over you still is a loss on your side, and a win on hers. Why are you letting her get away with this for so long? She's not worth it, buddy."

"I know."

"Then let it go already."

"I'm working on it."

"You'd think I'd be the last person to say this, but when you find the right lady, it's the greatest thing that will ever happen to you."

"You stole the last great lady."

"That's because I'm so charming." He put down his burger. "Seriously, aren't you interested in it at all? Are you even looking?"

"Interested in marriage? No. Interested in a relationship of some sort? Possibly."

"Why does the name Leah pop into my head?"

"Since when did you become such a matchmaker?"

"You've got to admit, she's beautiful."

"Yes, she is."

"Except in that getup. Jeez, what was she thinking?"

"Believe it or not, she was experimenting."

"Now that I think about it, in that getup she's just your type."

Mark could hardly dispute that. "I'm not so sure about that anymore."

"Then you finally *are* growing up."

"Anyway, she has this idea that she's so plain that she's almost invisible."

"Oh, so she's blind." Jake stopped. "I'm sorry, that was a really dumb thing to say."

Mark waved. "Not a problem. Shelley sees Leah better than Leah does."

"Doesn't surprise me. Shelley's one smart and intuitive lady."

"Guess what Leah told me last night?"

"What's that?"

Mark looked around to make certain no one could overhear them. He probably shouldn't even be telling his best friend. Leah would not be happy. But he had never professed to be anything but a dumb, hormonal male. And he knew he could trust Jake with his life—had had to on many occasions. "She thinks she's a screamer."

Jake grinned. "What do you mean, 'told you'? You mean you don't know?"

"Not yet."

"You're slowing down, buddy."

"Well, she's also shy about it. I haven't had the opportunity to find out."

"Do you want to?"

"More than take my next breath."

Chapter Fourteen

Kate and Leah sat down at a window booth in the deli. Leah marveled that the beautiful woman before her didn't translate well into a man. Of course, Steve wasn't exactly the most breathtaking female, either.

Kate wore a simple cream suit with a turquoise silk blouse underneath. Her hair was loose and slightly curled at the ends.

She'd be perfect for Steve, just as soon as he stopped viewing her as the enemy.

Leah ordered the tuna salad and Kate went with chicken salad. Then they smiled across the table at each other.

"I had fun last night," Kate said.

"So did I."

"Stephanie can be nice when she's not talking to me."

"I think she's mellowing about that a little bit. She's been listening to Steve, and he's definitely having doubts about your guilt on this one."

Kate's smile turned soft, but then became a little troubled. "Can I ask you something really blunt?"

"Sure."

"Have you ever . . . wondered about being with a woman?"

Leah almost fell out of her chair. "Um, no. Not that there's anything wrong with that!" But there went her plans for Steve and Kate. "Why?"

Kate shook her head. "I don't know. As much as I'd like to punch Stephanie in the nose . . ." Her voice trailed off. Then she added, "Trust me, this is brand-new to me, too. I mean, I *love* men."

Oh, boy.

Kate waited until the waiter deposited their iced teas, then dug into the pail on the table filled with chunks of kosher pickles. "I don't even know why I'm telling you this. Forget I said anything about it."

"No, really, it's all right. But has it ever occurred to you that you might find Steph attractive because she looks a lot like Steve?"

Kate stopped in midcrunch. "I never thought of that." She finished her pickle piece, then shook her head. "No, I don't think that's it. Or not all of it. Steve's really good-looking, no doubt about it. And I think he has the potential to be a really decent guy. But there's something about Stephanie that is kind of . . . I don't know . . . stimulating?"

"Maybe you enjoy the heat of battle?"

"Maybe. Because Lord knows Stephanie isn't cover-model material. No offense."

"None taken."

"I mean, if I wanted a woman, why wouldn't it be someone like you?"

Leah sat back and laughed. "Because I'm not cover-model material either?"

"Oh, please. I'd use you in my ads in a second."

GET TWO FREE* BOOKS!

SIGN UP FOR THE LOVE SPELL ROMANCE BOOK CLUB TODAY.

LOWEST PRICES EVER!

Every month, you will receive two of the newest Love Spell titles for the low price of $8.50,* **a $4.50 savings!**

As a book club member, not only do you save **35% off the retail price**, you will receive the following special benefits:

- **30% off** all orders through our website and telecenter (plus, you still get 1 book FREE for every 5 books you buy!)

- Exclusive access to dollar sales, special discounts, and offers you won't be able to find anywhere else.

- Information about contests, author signings, and more!

- Convenient home delivery of your favorite books every month.

- A 10-day examination period. If you aren't satisfied, just return any books you don't want to keep.

There is no minimum number of books to buy, and you may cancel membership at any time.

* Please include $2.00 for shipping and handling.

NAME: _____

ADDRESS: _____

_____

_____

TELEPHONE: _____

E-MAIL: _____

_____ I want to pay by credit card.

__ Visa   __ MasterCard   __ Discover

Account Number: _____

Expiration date: _____

SIGNATURE: _____

Send this form, along with $2.00 shipping and handling for your FREE books, to:

Love Spell Romance Book Club
20 Academy Street
Norwalk, CT 06850-4032

Or fax (must include credit card information!) to: 610.995.9274.
You can also sign up on the Web at <u>www.dorchesterpub.com</u>.

Offer open to residents of the U.S. and Canada only. Canadian residents, please call 1.800.481.9191 for pricing information.

If under 18, a parent or guardian must sign. Terms, prices and conditions subject to change. Subscription subject to acceptance. Dorchester Publishing reserves the right to reject any order or cancel any subscription.

"That's sweet, really."

"You should know me well enough by now to know I don't do sweet."

Their lunch arrived, and they were silent for a bit. Leah was so taken aback by Kate's confidences regarding her attraction to Stephanie, and her unexpected compliment, that she almost forgot why she'd called the other woman to meet in the first place. Her mind had shut down.

Suddenly Kate said, "Do you think Stephanie's gay?"

That jarred her mind awake. "Definitely not. Not unless she hides it well. And she's too honest to hide something like that."

"Oh. I was thinking maybe I was picking up on vibes or something."

"But you don't get those vibes from Steve?"

Kate mulled that one for a bit. "I hadn't thought about it. But I suppose I do. Except Steve is so *reasonable*."

"Because I kept thinking you two would make a great couple."

"Oh, jeez. Steve might be a nice guy, but he'd never date me as long as Stephanie hates me so much."

Leah wiped her mouth on the paper napkin. "So that's a really good reason to prove to Stephanie that you're not spying on her company."

"Why are you so willing to believe me?"

"Because I'm a great judge of character, and I like you."

"See? Now why couldn't you be gay?"

Leah laughed. "Sorry."

"You know, I've been so busy going on and on about myself, I haven't even asked if there was a reason you wanted to do lunch."

"There was, but it kind of slipped my mind."

"Does it have anything to do with last night?"

"Oh! Right. First of all, Candi has been permanently retired."

"Really? Why? She was kind of fun."

"She's outlived her usefulness. And if I had to wear that bra one more time I couldn't be responsible for the many felonies I'd commit."

Kate laughed. "Good point."

"But here's the funny part. You were caught last night."

"Stephanie knew?"

"No, she's dumb as a brick when it comes to observing people."

"Then who?"

"Mark."

"Is that right? Why didn't he call me on it?"

"I asked him not to."

"Why?"

"Because I was kind of hoping you'd get to know Stephanie from a different perspective."

"Well, in that you succeeded. She was almost human."

"Amazing, isn't it?"

Kate smiled and glanced out the window. Leah followed her gaze when her eyes narrowed. "That looks like Harvey Murphy's nephew. Wonder what he's doing riding his bike on this side of town."

Leah turned back to Kate. "You know Jimmy Slater?"

"Sure. Not well, but I've met him a few times at his uncle's picnics. Harvey loves to throw barbecues."

"Who is Harvey?"

"One of my chemists. Why?"

"Isn't that interesting?"

"Why?"

"Jimmy's one of our interns."

166

* * *

Mark raced back to the Just Peachy offices after receiving a frantic, almost incoherent voice message from Leah.

When he got to her office she was pacing, and her body screamed agitation.

"Who died?"

She practically jumped a mile, then raced to him. "Let's go for a walk."

"Why, honey, I didn't know you'd miss me so much."

"Shut up, dummy, and walk."

They headed to the park across the street, and if Mark weren't so concerned over what had Leah so riled up, he'd have taken more time to appreciate the way she filled out the navy suit she was wearing.

When they were nearly half a block away, she looked over her shoulder at the building, then turned back to him. "I might have a lead on our mole."

"Excuse me?"

She quickly told him about the relationship between Jimmy Slater and an Apple Blossom employee.

"It might not be anything, but then again it might," she finished up, and sucked in her first breath since she started blurting out the news.

"It sure is worth looking into."

"You think so?"

"Of course."

"One other thing. Kate wants to know if she can hire you, too, if anything comes of this. She's as appalled at the possibility of corporate espionage as we are."

He shook his head. "I'd have to clear it with Stephanie and Steve. It could be a conflict of interest."

"Or it could benefit both companies."

"I'd still need to clear it."

"Okay."

He smiled. "Ya done good, sweetheart."

She beamed with pride. "Yeah I did, didn't I?"

It was a gray day overhead, but that smile felt like the sun had just come out shining in all its warmth and glory. Something strange twisted in his chest that he hadn't felt in a long, long time. "Will you go out with me Friday?"

Her smile instantly turned shy. "What are we going to do?"

He had no idea at the moment. All he knew was that it had to be something completely private and farther out of town. "Someplace where none of your employers can drop in to check up on their little spy."

Leah gulped. "Little spy? I'm not a spy."

"Jake's still assessing the situation."

"Why haven't you said anything?"

"I was waiting for you to tell him off."

"I couldn't tell him off playing an airhead, now, could I?"

"You gave it the good old college try."

"Well, he's investigating you. I didn't like that."

"No, he's investigating you, sweetheart."

"This is a disaster," she said. "I just wanted to be wild. I never wanted to cause an international disaster."

"I don't think the world will self-destruct."

"So where will we go?"

"It's a surprise."

Her eyes lit up. "I love surprises."

"Me too."

That afternoon Steve and Mark and Leah met in Steve's office.

Mark immediately asked, "Where's Stephanie? She should be here."

168

"She had to fly down to Charlotte this morning," Steve said smoothly.

"She didn't mention anything about a trip last night."

"It just came up this morning. We had a problem at one of our factories."

"Can we conference call her?"

"Doubtful. I'm fairly sure she's touring and in strategy meetings, and she won't want to be disturbed."

Mark frowned. "I thought she considered this a top-priority issue."

"It is, but she certainly trusts me to make a decision on how to proceed."

Right then Steve's phone buzzed. "Yes, Mrs. Leeds?"

"Kate Bloom is here to see you."

Leah suddenly found great interest in a paperweight. She was the one who'd phoned Kate and told her to come and help.

Steve scowled and covered the receiver. "What's she doing here?" he asked Mark.

"I have no idea."

"I asked her to come," Leah finally confessed. "I thought we should all talk this through."

"You realize you're consorting with the enemy."

"I don't believe she's the enemy," Leah countered. "Having her on our side is in our best interests."

"No offense, little sister, but you're a secretary here."

"Little sister?" Mark said.

Leah and Steve looked at each other. Finally, Steve said, "Did I forget to mention that?"

Mark didn't appear happy. In fact, he appeared downright ticked. "Yes, apparently you left that out."

"Oops," Steve said.

"You know, this is really getting irritating," Mark said. "How am I supposed to do my job when the three of you are lying to me about little facts that just *happen* to be important?"

"We didn't think it mattered in this situation."

"Don't you realize I was focusing a lot of time and attention on her," Mark said, hiking a thumb in Leah's direction, "because you thought it was cute that I didn't know she was your sister?"

There went their alone date this weekend, Leah thought glumly. But she rallied, because right now they had more pressing issues to address. "It's my fault," she said to Mark. "I didn't want anyone to know because it would color the way people reacted to me."

"I was ready to bust your butt, babe," Mark growled.

"Can we talk about this later?" she asked.

"Oh, we most definitely will."

Leah nodded, even though she felt a sudden need to run to the bathroom and throw up. "Steve, Kate wants answers as much as we do. Working together gives us strength."

Mark's thundercloud expression faded slowly, but it did finally fade. He nodded and stepped forward. "If it weren't for Leah and Kate, we wouldn't have this lead. I think we should hear Kate out."

Steve rolled his eyes, but finally he spoke into the phone. "Send her in."

He relaxed back in his chair and put on his conciliatory face. But the moment Kate walked through the door, something fired up in his eyes that Leah—though not an expert—considered a huge sign of appreciation and interest.

Steve stood and straightened his tie. He rarely wore a suit, but he never came to the office without a tie. "Hello, Kate. Have a seat."

"Thank you," she said, sitting down beside Leah and

crossing her mile-long legs gracefully. "And thank you for letting me talk this through with you."

Steve nodded. "We might as well pool information."

Mark and Leah exchanged glances. Apparently Steve had made up his mind to at least listen. Leah saw approval in Mark's eyes, right below his promise of future retribution.

"I want you to know I'm as eager to get to the truth as you and Just Peachy are, Steve. If we have traitors among us, let's both get them."

Steve looked hard at Kate for a moment, then offered a curt nod. "I just want to warn you of one thing, Kate."

"Yes?"

"If we find who and what we're looking for, and that person or those people claim that you had knowledge of their activities, we will sue."

"As well you should."

"And ask that criminal charges be brought."

"As well you should." She leaned forward. "But let me just tell you something, *Mr. Smith*. I might be ambitious and I might be trying to grab some of your market share, but there is no way in hell I'd do anything illegal or unethical to achieve those goals. I can beat you people the good old-fashioned way. So stick that where the sun don't shine."

Leah had to hold her hands tightly to keep from clapping.

Steve sat back as if he'd been sucker punched.

Mark made something of a strangling noise.

And then all was quiet for a moment.

Finally Steve sat forward. "Okay, let's do it."

Kate leaned forward in response, and Leah could practically see the sparks flying between Kate and her brother. And they weren't sparks of anger; that was for sure. It seemed to be a mixture of two people bonding together to right a wrong, two people ready to join forces marching into battle, and two people who'd just gained a modicum of respect for each other.

Leah didn't care in what proportion. What mattered to her was that the sparks weren't only heating up their warring instincts.

If she'd ever witnessed two people who suddenly discovered basic attraction, this was it. Well, except the first time Mark had gazed at her with that smoky, passionate look in his eyes, and she'd just about done a snow-cone-in-the-desert routine.

She had the feeling Mark had seen and been affected by it, too, because he surreptitiously ran a finger up her spine. And she had a hard time keeping from shivering. Or jumping up and throwing herself at him. Except she didn't know if his touch was of a sexual nature, or revengelike.

It took her a moment to realize she'd zoned out on the discussion. She tuned back in.

"Steve, let me hire Mark to work with us as well."

"Why would I do that?"

Kate threw up her hands. "Why wouldn't you? We're working for a common goal, and Mark knows more about the case than any security firm I might hire on my own."

"She has a point," Leah said.

"How do I know you won't try to get Mark to come over to the dark side?"

Leah gasped and jumped up. "Does he look like Darth Vader to you?" she practically screamed.

"It's okay, Leah," Mark said, grabbing her arm. "It's a legitimate question."

She shrugged off his hand and leaned over the desk,

glaring at her brother. "This guy has worked his tail off for you. He's ex-FBI. You honestly think he'd betray us that way?"

Steve grinned. "No. But I was sort of expecting the indignation to come from him."

"Oh." Leah slumped back down in her chair.

Kate chuckled. "Don't worry, Leah, I know where Mark's first allegiance lies. All I'm asking is that he helps me catch a thief. And proves that I knew nothing about it."

"Oh." Leah felt her cheeks flush in embarrassment. "I'm an idiot."

"You're not an idiot," Mark said.

Steve looked at Kate and Mark. "Just Peachy doesn't consider Apple Blossom's hiring Colson Securities in this investigation a conflict of interest."

"What about Stephanie?" Kate asked, her nose wrinkled.

"Leave Stephanie to me," Steve said.

Mark looked at Kate. "When's a good time for us to talk strategy?"

She checked her watch. "How about four this afternoon at my office?"

"Works for me."

Leah had to fight the tiniest inkling of jealousy. After all, Kate was about the most glamorous and beautiful woman she knew. But she tamped it down with a little bit of effort. Steve looked at Leah pensively. "You know, Jimmy has a huge crush on you."

She snorted. "He has a huge crush on Candi's boobs."

"So get him to talk to Candi's boobs."

"Right. He's going to tell my boobs that he's a thief."

"I don't want him talking to Candi's boobs," Mark said.

"Okay, bad idea," Steve agreed. "Let's catch him the old-fashioned way."

"Candi's boobs *would* be the old-fashioned way," Kate said. "But right now I don't like it, either."

Mark nodded. "We'll get him the new-fangled way—with modern technology." He paused. "We hope."

And with that, they concluded the meeting, although Kate said, "I have one more thing to talk to you about," to Steve.

Leah and Mark took the cue and left the office.

"Well, that went well," Leah said, trying to forget her stupid and irrational outburst. She should have known Steve had been teasing.

"Yes, it did, Tiger."

Apparently Mark wasn't going to let her forget so easily.

Chapter Fifteen

"Are we still on for Friday?" he asked as they walked to the elevator from Steve's office.

"After what you just learned, I didn't think you'd want to," she said, trying to keep the glumness out of her voice.

"Oh, I still want to."

Hope bubbled. "So you aren't mad?"

"Of course I'm mad."

"Then why would you want to?"

"Because the Leah I want to see Friday is the private Leah. This was business." They stopped at the elevator doors and he punched the button. "Unless there are secrets the private Leah is keeping from me."

Leah swallowed hard as her conscience kicked in. Was the Stephanie thing private? Not really, her mind argued. Stephanie was all about Just Peachy. That constituted business. And besides, it was not her secret to tell.

She shook her head. "The private Leah is in the clear, I think," she said.

"Good," he said, then waved her into the open elevator. "I'm really looking forward to it."

Oh, me too! her heart screamed. But she just smiled. "Friday."

With Leah and Mark out of the office, Steve looked at Kate, trying not to notice how beautiful she was. That would be dangerous. Not to mention stupid. If she was lying about all of this, he'd feel like a total idiot for allowing her to snow him. But he couldn't help really, really hoping she was telling the truth.

But he didn't think he wanted to know why.

"So, what else?" he asked, hoping it would be a lengthy discussion so she'd stick around longer.

"I'm suggesting full disclosure with each other."

"What do you mean?"

"We can't tie Mark in knots by making him feel he has to constantly be concerned with client confidentiality. I promise I will give him free rein to discuss with you what's happening at Apple Blossom if you promise he can do the same with me."

Steve shook his head. "What are we doing here, Kate? We're competitors."

She sighed. "Do you follow sports?"

"Yes, why?"

"You know how the Cowboys and the Redskins hate each other during the regular season?"

"I do, although what this has to do with face cream and perfume is beyond me."

"And do you know that during the All-Star game, Cowboys and Redskins band together as a team to win?"

Damn, she was good at analogies. "I get your point."

"Good. Full disclosure. Both ways. We're playing the All-Star game right now, buddy. And just as soon as we learn the enemy's game plan, and beat him, we can go back to trying to kick each other's butt."

His admiration for her was climbing at an alarming rate. He had to watch that. "Okay, coach, full disclosure."

She smiled, and his heart did a double take. He rarely was blessed with a smile from Kate.

"One more observation," she said.

"That you think I'm cute?" He wanted to bite his tongue as soon as the words slipped by him.

She laughed, a smoky sound that was causing belly fires. "Granted. But you're still a Cowboy."

"No, I'm a Redskin."

"Cute, but ornery," she said dryly.

He grinned. "Okay, what's your *real* observation?"

"I have this funny feeling that Leah has it bad," she said, her head jerking toward the office door.

"I have the funny feeling Mark isn't far behind."

"I think you're right."

And they smiled at each other and Steve felt lost. It took him a moment to say, "Anything else?"

She stood up and he jumped up right after her. "Nope, that about does it," she said. When he shook her hand he didn't want to let go. He had to force himself to loosen his grip so she could escape.

"Thanks again, Steve," she said, then turned toward the door.

Right before she got there, he stopped her. "Kate?"

She looked over her shoulder. "Yes?"

"It's a pleasure to be working *with* you for once."

She laughed. "Don't be so sure. I still plan on kicking your butt in the market."

"Don't you wish?" he said, but he grinned too. When she began to leave again he said, "Kate?"

"Yes?"

"For what it's worth, I believe you."

She stopped and took a short, loud breath. "Whether you believe *this* or not, that means a lot to me. I believe in your integrity. I can't wait to prove mine."

And then she left, and Steve stared at the door for a long time, a sick feeling in his gut. His integrity was going to be called into question very soon. Because he'd been living and acting a lie for years now.

And soon, very soon, Kate was going to realize that.

Chapter Sixteen

"Where are you two going tonight?" Steve demanded Friday morning, as Leah drank her juice.

"I don't have any idea."

"Well, get an idea."

"Why? It's a surprise. I like surprises."

"Well, I don't. I want to have some clue here."

She smiled and patted his cheek, then handed him his orange juice. "I think the entire point is that you *don't* know. We'd just as soon you don't show up with another entourage to keep an eye on me."

"I don't—"

"Oh, but you do. Your track record in keeping your nose out of my business isn't stellar."

"You're my little sister."

"Who is all grown-up now."

"What's this all about?" Gramps said in the doorway. It was obvious he'd come back from his morning walk. The man woke up way too early.

"Leah has a date tonight."

"My, we're getting popular these days. I hope you're not going on this one in the blond getup."

179

She poured Gramps his juice, then took it to him and kissed his cheek. "Nope, I'm all me tonight."

"Good." He gulped down about half the glass at once, then said, "So why the yelling in here?"

"We weren't yelling."

"Yes, you were."

Leah pointed at Steve. "He's driving me nuts."

"And life goes on," Gramps said.

Steve pointed at Leah. "She's going out tonight and she won't say where."

"So? What business is it of yours?" He turned to Leah. "Where are you going tonight?"

"You just said it was none of your business!"

"I said it wasn't *his* business. But I'm your grandfather."

If she didn't go crazy in this household, it would be a miracle. Or maybe she'd already gone crazy in this household, and she was too crazy to realize it.

"I don't know where we're going, and even if I did, I wouldn't tell either of you. I'll have my cell phone, and if there's an emergency, something like Steve finally getting a life—"

"Hey!"

"—just give me a call and I'll crack open the champagne." With that she slammed down her juice glass in the sink and sailed out of the kitchen, nose raised high.

She stomped to her bedroom and looked through the closet. The problem was, she had no idea what they were doing, so figuring out how to dress was a dilemma. She liked surprises with the best of them, but she sure didn't want to show up in an evening gown to go to a honky-tonk, and she didn't want to wear jeans to a five-star restaurant.

She was beginning to resent surprises.

Gramps came to her bedroom and knocked on the partially open door. "Come on in."

He'd refreshed his juice and just stood silent for a while. Finally he said, "I'm not trying to interfere. But we like this guy, right?"

"We do. We think. This is just new, Gramps."

"But you're going to some undisclosed location."

"I told you, I'll have my cell phone."

"Can you maybe call just to tell us where you are when you get there?"

She sighed. "Gramps, I love you dearly, but I'm twenty-eight years old. I can take care of myself."

He held up a hand. "Of course you can. And you deserve your privacy. You're just my baby, Leah."

She instantly teared up, and quickly waved her hand in front of her eyes. "I know."

"I love you, little girl."

"I love you too, Gramps."

"Well, that's about it." He turned to go and then turned back. "You know, there's one thing I heard on the Sandra show."

She resisted the urge to roll her eyes. "What's that?"

"Always stick a clean toothbrush in your purse. Just in case."

She gaped at him for a moment. "Well, thanks, I'll keep that in mind."

"Leah?"

"Yes?"

"If you intentionally don't plan to come home tonight, please call. Just so I know to turn off the porch light."

She smiled and choked up all at once. "I promise."

Mark called her midafternoon. "Are you ready for tonight?"

She wanted him to define "tonight," but figured asking was probably not very tactful. "I'm game if you're game," she said, holding her hand to her chest to keep it from bursting.

"Should I pick you up, or are you still scared to let me know where you live? After all, I've pretty much guessed why you didn't want me to know before now."

"Do you want to go through the grilling from my family?"

"Umm, I can if you want me to."

"How about if I come to your house and we can leave from there?"

"That sounds good," he said, his tone obviously relieved. "Seven?"

"I can be there, but Mark, I have no idea what to wear."

"Come completely casual. Shorts or jeans, whatever's comfortable."

"That sounds wonderful. I'll see you then."

"I can't wait."

She smiled as she hung up the phone.

Leah made the mistake of arriving ten minutes early at Mark's house.

"He had a meeting that ran late. He's in the shower. He'll be out in a sec," Shelley said. "Can I get you anything?"

"No, thanks, although something smells really good."

"I hope so," Shelley said, which was sort of a strange response. "Come on in and sit down."

"Do you have a birthday gig coming up?" Leah asked.

"Six in five days," Shelley said with a sigh. "Tomorrow's a clown theme. Between you and me, I hate those. Perfectly good pies being thrown in people's faces for a few laughs."

"I never liked pie-in-the-face gags."

"I never liked clowns."

Leah had about a zillion questions she'd love to ask Shelley, both about herself and Mark, but she was too afraid of being rude.

"So are you going to use and abuse my brother tonight?" Shelley asked, apparently not nearly so worried.

"Umm, do you want me to?"

"Hell, yes!"

"Then I'll do my best."

"I want him crawling home whimpering."

Leah laughed. "I'm not certain I'm capable of that, but you know, I'd hate to disappoint you."

"Just work on it."

Before she could respond Mark came sprinting out of his bedroom, combing his wet hair with his hands. "I'm so sorry."

"Not a problem. Shelley was just giving me some very sage advice."

Mark glared at his sister.

"Stop glaring at me," his sister said.

"Your advice sucks," Mark said.

"And your technique needs work."

Leah felt like she was watching a tennis match.

"What's Leah wearing?"

Mark looked at her and smiled. "A black denim miniskirt and a paisley kind of short-sleeved button-down thing."

Shelley nodded while Leah's skin went hot. "Sounds pretty."

"It is."

"Okay, I approve. Go away."

"I'll call you, okay?" Mark said.

"Only if you're not going to be home. I don't want to have to leave the porch light on for no reason."

Leah couldn't help it; she burst out laughing.

"What?" Mark said.

"We have *got* to introduce Shelley to my grandfather. They'd become best friends in minutes."

Leah had been worried all week that Mark would try to wine and dine her in some ridiculously expensive, romantic restaurant. So when he'd told her to dress casually, she'd actually felt a huge sense of relief. He'd be taking her to some off-the-beaten-path diner or something. She'd never in a million years expected this.

"You want to time the windmill just right," he advised. "Otherwise the golf ball is going to fly right back at you."

They were Putt-Putt golfing at a place outside of Leesburg.

She nodded at him, trying to keep a straight face. "Thanks for the advice." She teed up the ball, took a couple of looks, then swung. It sailed smoothly through the device and dropped like a stone into the hole.

He stared at the green, at her, and then at the green again. "You've done this before."

"Every Friday night with my gramps."

"You tricked me."

"You never asked."

"Okay, this is war."

She laughed, and the feeling of happiness and contentment was almost like a drug. She'd have never believed a man like Mark would choose Putt-Putt as a prelude to a romantic night. But what a perfect choice.

She flung her putter over her shoulder. "Care to make a few friendly wagers?"

"I might," he said. He set up and looked. And

looked. And looked. Then shot. The ball flew back at him and almost took him out in a place she most definitely didn't want injured.

"About those wagers," she said.

"Not one chance in hell."

Their next destination thrilled her so much she almost clapped with delight. A county fair! She hadn't been to one of these in ages. They parked the car and strolled down the midway, inhaling the scents, goggling at the sights. At some point Mark casually took her hand in his, and she reveled in the warmth and strength of him.

Mark pointed out a shooting gallery. "You might be fairly good at Putt-Putt, sport, but how's your shot?"

"Fairly good? I beat you by fifteen strokes, buddy."

He steered her toward the booth. "It's rude to rub it in."

"And it's rude to try to bolster your male pride by challenging me to a shooting contest, especially since you've been wearing a gun most of your life."

"Those guns were just sissy little Glocks. These are rifles. Big difference."

"I've never held a gun in my life, and I'm not about to begin now," she said.

"Chicken."

"That's right. But don't get me alone in the dark with a putter in my hands."

He almost choked. She didn't understand what was so funny about that until it occurred to her that what she'd said could be taken a couple of ways. She smacked his arm. "Men!"

"Come on," he said, dragging her to another booth, bypassing the shooting gallery, she realized thankfully. "How do you feel about water pistols?"

"I think I can handle one of those."

Ten minutes later Leah walked away with a teddy bear. Unfortunately, Mark had won it.

"You know, if you ever get into a mortal water-pistol shoot-out, you'd be a goner," he said.

"Gloating is so rude."

He grinned. "I know. Your humility after the Putt-Putt win was an inspiration."

Leah looked down and smiled.

"How do you feel about Ferris wheels?" he asked, draping an arm across her shoulders.

"Love them."

"Then let's go."

They climbed in and within seconds were underway. After a few breathtaking turns, they found themselves stopped at the top of the wheel. "Nice view," Leah said.

"Beautiful," Mark responded, but he wasn't looking at the fair beneath them.

She caught her breath as their eyes met. And before God and everyone else, Mark lowered his mouth to hers.

Their lips were a little chilled from the wind, but they warmed up fast. And Leah felt almost high on something as her senses all came to life. His mouth moved over hers, coaxing and demanding, soft and hard. She didn't know how to explain it. She just knew it could go on forever and she'd be happy.

She was so lost in the sensation of him, she didn't even feel them begin to move. Not until they came to a slightly jerky stop. And she heard someone loudly clearing his throat.

Reluctantly she broke the kiss, then almost squealed with mortification when she realized they were down on the platform and the ride attendant was waiting for them to unload.

"Oh!" she said, trying to untangle their limbs, which had somehow become intertwined during the kiss.

"Sorry about that," Mark said to the man, but there wasn't a speck of regret in his tone. Instead he was laughing.

Leah tried to make the best of it and gave the man a wobbly smile. But she wanted to disappear in a puff of smoke when the people waiting in line to board the ride began applauding.

Mark hadn't had this much fun in he couldn't remember how long. Even getting his butt kicked at Putt-Putt had been a blast. He'd suspected after their date at the drive-in that Leah would prefer simple pleasures to opulent wooing.

And her delight was like an aphrodisiac that just kept on giving. He had hoped she'd be willing to play instead of go the snob route, and he hadn't been disappointed at all.

After watching a magic act that had her oohing and ahhing with wonder, he said, "Hungry?"

"Oh, yes."

"Well, good, because the next show's about to begin. But first I need to get something from the car."

They hurried back out to the parking lot, and Mark retrieved the picnic basket Shelley had prepared for them.

Leah's eyes lit up, and right there and then Mark decided he'd like to spend the rest of his life surprising her. Which was a scary thought, but he didn't want to spoil the night by analyzing the notion too closely. He steered her down a cobblestone path to the left of the main festivities. It led them into a small patch of maples and oaks and weeping cherry trees.

When they emerged into a clearing, Leah gasped. Smack-dab in the center of a large grassy area was a picturesque lake.

Other people had settled on the lawn, but they had

no trouble finding a fairly secluded spot under a huge maple. Mark opened the basket and pulled out a plaid blanket he'd laid on top. He draped it over the ground and they settled down.

"Ready for some sustenance?"

"That depends. Did Shelley prepare this, or did you?"

"You're a real card. And I'll have you know, I can cook. I've been a bachelor for a long, long time."

She went still. "I thought you said you'd never been married."

He shook his head. "Not even once."

She gnawed on her lower lip, then asked, "Ever come close to tying the knot?"

Mark busied himself sorting through the basket. Finally, when he felt her eyes on his and realized she expected an answer, he said, "Sort of close, yeah. Many years ago."

"What happened?"

He touched his fingers to her cheek. "You know, I'm having a great time tonight."

She nodded. "I understand. You don't want me to spoil it by asking about things that are none of my business."

"I didn't say or mean that. I meant I don't want to spoil it for either of us by bringing up a subject that tends to sour a mood."

"Gotcha. I'm sorry I asked."

"Don't be. Really. I'm not hiding anything. In fact, you make me want to tell you all about the past. But just not tonight."

She smiled and nodded again. "So did Shelley make the picnic?"

"Yes. But I could have if I'd had time!"

Leah patted his leg. "Of course you could."

He growled at her, but then turned his attention back to unpacking their dinner.

"It smells delicious," she said, leaning over the basket to get a peek. That brought their lips in dangerously close proximity. Mark was nothing if not an opportunist, and he leaned an inch closer and kissed her, marveling at the softness he found there.

She pulled back far too soon, but he assumed she felt shy about too much PDA, especially after being embarrassed by the crowd at the Ferris wheel. He was no exhibitionist, but it didn't bother him in the least to be seen kissing her. Who wouldn't envy him? "I'd rather be kissing you than eating."

"Tough. I'm hungry, and this smells delicious."

He noticed a folded note and grunted. "Shelley says I'm supposed to ask you if you're allergic to any foods."

"Nope."

"Do you like artichokes, caviar, cheese, fruit?"

"Yes, yes, yes, and yes."

Leah savored all the offerings, licking her fingers clean and moaning in pleasure with each new taste. Her unconsciously erotic actions drove Mark crazy with desire, and he longed to make her moan like that with another type of pleasure. By the time she patted her tummy and said, "I couldn't eat another bite," Mark was aroused almost to the point of pain. He opened his mouth to suggest they leave instantly when the scheduled fireworks display began across the lake. Leah sat up in delight, softly clapping her hands together in excitement.

He groaned inwardly and gritted his teeth, hoping the show was a really, really short one.

Strangely enough, Mark was content to hold Leah during the fireworks, letting her use his shoulder to pillow her head. The most kissing that went on under the tree was when he nuzzled her temple occasionally, just to feel her skin and inhale her shampoo.

The fireworks were spectacular, and the company was spectacular, and he hadn't felt this good in a long time. They strolled to the car in silence. He did not want the night to end, but he cared about her feelings too much to insult her by making any assumptions. "Do you want me to take you home?"

"Do you want to take me home? I'm sure I look like hell."

"You're beautiful. And I have an alternative. But you have every right to say no."

"What is it?"

"I arranged to borrow a small hunting lodge about ten miles from here from a friend of mine." He pulled her head close just in case she looked at him in disgust or outrage. "Only if you'd like to," he said. "I will not be upset if you'd just like to end the date now. My intent wasn't to get you in bed, Leah. It would be my wish, but it wasn't my intent. My only aim for the night was to finally spend some time alone with you."

"Were you disappointed?"

"Would I be asking you to spend the night with me if I were disappointed? This was the nicest date of my life. That's the truth, I promise you."

"Nice sounds boring."

"Nice isn't boring. Nice means no awkward moments. Nice means laughing and playing and eating and holding you. Nice means spending time with you has no hidden agenda. I could take you home right now and still smile about this night for years."

She looked up at him with tears in her eyes, but she didn't appear distressed. And he noticed that she was a pretty crier. Some women just didn't cry well. Right now he could stare into those watery green eyes for weeks. Or months. Or years.

"I've always wanted to stay at a hunting lodge," she whispered.

"I was hoping you'd say that. It still isn't a demand for anything but a good night's sleep."

"Are you kidding? Gramps didn't make me carry a new toothbrush in my purse for nothing."

Mark laughed and leaned down to the abandoned picnic basket at their feet. He pulled out the final un-used item inside—a toothbrush.

Her laughter was soggy. "Shelley?"

"Shelley." He sighed. "Speaking of which, I have to call her to let her know I won't be coming home."

Leah chuckled softly. "And I need to call Gramps."

Their eyes met and in perfect unison they said, "Porch lights."

Chapter Seventeen

Steve didn't know why he followed through on an impulse to call Kate. After all, it was a Friday night. There was no way that a beautiful woman like her would be sitting home, twiddling her thumbs. She probably had a dozen men jockeying for any scrap of time she'd honor them with.

So when he found her number and picked up the phone, he was already prepared to find her out, or to have her in, maybe, with plans. But if he didn't try, he'd sit here all night wondering—

"Hello?" she said in that soft, husky voice that could turn positively wintry when she was angry.

"Kate? It's Steve Smith."

"Hello, Steve," she said, and although her voice dropped a couple of degrees in temperature, it also wasn't cold as ice, either.

"Have I interrupted anything?"

"A Bogie movie and a glass of wine. Why?"

"With company?"

"Yes, my parrot, Gabby."

He was nervous as a schoolkid asking out his first

crush, which was weird, because even as a schoolkid asking out his first crush he hadn't been all that nervous. "I was wondering if you'd be able to meet me somewhere for a drink."

"Is something wrong?"

Yes, lately I haven't been able to stop thinking about you. "No, not wrong, exactly. It's just that you and I couldn't seem to coordinate schedules this week, and I really wanted to get together and talk about what you and Colson have planned from your end of this investigation."

There was a long pause, and Steve ran a hand around his collar.

Finally she said, "I'll share our plan of attack if you'll share yours."

He didn't realize he'd been holding his breath until he blew it out in a gust. "Great. So can we meet?"

"Why on a Friday?"

"Because I'd like the weekend to digest the plan of action so that when I see Mark Monday morning I'll have a better grasp on the situation." That was such a load of bull he almost felt guilty. But not quite. Having common ground and possibly a common problem and enemy was as good a place to start as any. "But if you're busy . . ."

"I've seen this movie at least a dozen times, and I've been craving a margarita all night, but all I have in my place is wine."

He was pretty sure that was a yes. "So, tonight?"

"I'm in my nightgown, so you'll need to give me an hour or so. Where would you like to meet?"

Now there was an image he wouldn't be able to wipe out of his mind anytime soon. "Well, we have two choices. We could go to some noisy bar, or I could run to the store and pick up the fixings for margaritas and come to your place. That is, if you don't mind giving me your address."

Again she hesitated. "I'd actually prefer not to go to a noisy bar."

"Well, if you don't mind, I'll just stop over there."

"Still give me an hour, okay?"

He wanted to say, *Don't get dressed on my account,* but he had the feeling she wouldn't appreciate it much. In fact, she might flip the dead bolt and refuse to open up for him. "An hour it is."

"Great. Have a pencil? I'll give you my address."

The hunting lodge was much larger than Leah had expected. For some reason she'd had the impression that many of them were no more than tiny shacks big enough to roll out a sleeping bag.

This one was first-class rustic. And no dead animal heads on the wall, either. The front door opened into a great room that functioned both as a lounging area and a dining room, with a scratched wooden table long enough to seat at least twenty people on matching wooden benches.

A huge maroon leather couch divided the room in two, sectioning off the living room area. It faced a big brick fireplace, and was flanked by two black leather chairs with ottomans. Instead of a bearskin rug lying in front of the fireplace, there was a slightly threadbare Persian rug in maroon and black and heather green.

The place smelled of pine oil, and Leah couldn't find a speck of dust anywhere.

"This is really nice," Leah said. "Who owns it?"

"My installation manager," Mark said.

"Does he actually hunt?"

"No, he uses it mainly for poker-party weekends."

Mark nodded at wooden stairs at the far side of the

room. "Those lead to a loft that has about eight or ten bunk beds." He pointed to a dark hallway. "That leads to the bathroom and the master bedroom. And the door behind the table leads to a pretty large kitchen."

"One bathroom for twenty inebriated poker players?"

He laughed. "Leave it to a woman to be practical. No, there's one bathroom in the master bedroom and another one upstairs.

"Before anything," he added, taking her purse from her shoulder and hanging it on a coatrack by the door, "this." He took her in his arms and kissed her mindless. Wrapping his arms around her, he laid one hand on the small of her back, and the other brushed up and down between her shoulder blades. Leah pulled her arms out from under his and raised them up and around his neck. His body heat beckoned her, and she pressed herself against him.

Mark groaned into her mouth, and the sound traveled straight down to her belly. His tongue touched her lower lip, then slipped inside.

In a fog she marveled once again at the sensuality he brought to the mere act of kissing. Without his caressing a single intimate part of her, she felt that he was making love to her.

Finally he pulled away, and they stared at each other, their harsh breaths mingling.

Then he bent again and nuzzled her neck. "You smell so good," he said, then nipped her earlobe, and a shiver raced straight down her spine.

"Oh," she moaned. "I never knew kissing could be like this." Her hands slid down to his shoulders, then his arms. "And I love your body. It feels so hard and hot and big, and I can't wait to see you naked."

He chuckled into her neck, but it sounded a little painful. "Leah, I never meant to bring you in here and drag you straight to bed. I was going to build a fire and open some wine and just talk for a while. I didn't want to rush you."

"Drag me. Rush me."

He straightened and looked down at her. "You're sure?"

"Or I can drag you and rush you," Leah whispered, her green eyes dazed and filled with need.

That was all he needed to hear. "Let's take turns," he said, and bent, cradled the back of her knees, and lifted her up into his arms. "Me first."

He carried her down the hallway and kicked open the door. Turning on the light, he walked her over to the bed and laid her down.

Opening the bedside table he took out a pack of matches, then walked around the room lighting the dozen or so candles Harry kept there. Then he flicked off the overhead light. The room softened to a soft yellow glow.

"I love the way you walk," Leah said. "Sort of like a panther or something."

That was a new one to him, and he smiled as he dropped the matches back into the drawer. There were a dozen or so condoms sitting in there, too, but he'd get to them when he needed them. He was in no hurry.

When he began to lie down beside her, Leah said, "Wait."

"What?" he asked, thinking he was going to keel over dead from need if she changed her mind now.

"Undress for me."

"Excuse me?"

"Undress."

"I thought I'd let you help me with that."

"Not this time. I want to watch you undress."

"You want me to do a striptease for you?"

"No. I just want you to take off your clothes the way you do when you're getting ready for a shower."

"Uh . . ."

"You're not shy, are you?" she asked, her voice teasing. She stacked some pillows and reclined back in a half-sitting position.

"No, but—"

"Please?"

Mark was at a loss. A woman had never asked him to do something like this before. Especially a woman who seemed so shy at times.

But he shrugged. "Okay, but I can't say that I undress sexy."

"Just seeing you baring a little skin is sexy."

He took off his loafers.

"No socks. That's so sexy," she said softly. "And you have gorgeous feet."

He unbuckled and unzipped his jeans, then let them drop, kicking them away.

"Oh, boxers. I love boxers. You have such powerful legs, I bet you played football or something in school."

"Soccer," he answered her, but she didn't seem to be listening. She was almost in a lust zone of her own.

He grabbed his polo shirt and pulled it off.

"Oh, my God, you're a 'from the back' guy. I *love* when guys take their shirts off that way."

Mark was beginning to believe her assertion that she was a talker. He hoped she was right about being a moaner and a screamer, too. His initial embarrassment was beginning to give way to intense arousal, and even in boxers he had the feeling it was fairly apparent.

"Your chest is breathtaking. Just a slight sprinkling of hair. It's perfect."

And now he was down to his skivvies, and so turned

on that he probably tore them off a lot faster than he did when he was undressing for a shower.

"Oh, my God," she whispered. "You are so beautiful. I've never been with a man as gorgeous as you are."

Okay, her running commentary practically had him on the brink, so he had to kiss that mouth quiet for a while so he didn't do anything stupid, like tear off her clothes and thrust himself into her.

"Now undress me, Mark," she demanded, tossing one of the pillows aside and lying down, stretching like a cat.

"My pleasure," he murmured as he fell on top of her. He cupped her face and slanted his lips over hers. Unfortunately, being body-to-body, lips-to-lips, didn't have the "slow down" effect he'd been going for. The feel of her soft clothes abrading his skin was erotic in a way he'd have never thought possible. And her hands gliding over his arms and shoulders and back felt like a huge slice of heaven.

Her hands slipped down his waist and hips and skimmed over his buttocks, which instantly tightened with pleasure.

And she moaned softly into his mouth.

He wanted to devour her. His lips brushed over her cheeks, her forehead, then down to her neck, where he found her pulse point, beating feverishly.

And she'd forgotten to mention she was a whimperer, too. Her hands became more frantic on his flesh, and her nails dragged over him. He had the feeling he'd be a marked man by morning, in the best possible way.

Mark slid to her side and began fumbling with her blouse. As he worked the buttons free one by one, his lips followed the path of her exposed flesh. Pulling the shirt from her skirt, he finished with the buttons and spread the halves aside.

Her skin glowed in the candlelight, soft and irresistible. He touched her ribs, and then his fingertips traced the lace of her pale green bra.

Air whooshed out of her lips. She sat up and shucked her shirt completely, tossing it somewhere; he didn't know where. The woman had the sexiest collarbones he'd ever seen.

"Damn," he said, kissing them.

"Oh, Mark, that feels good."

Her bra had a front clasp, and he snapped it open, then brushed both sides away to expose her breasts. And he just about came right then and there. "Good God."

"Touch them, kiss them," she commanded.

And he did, suckling one nipple with his lips while kneading her entire other breast with his hand.

She arched up with a long, low moan. "Oh, Mark, that's good." And her hand came up to touch his nipples as well. Bolts of excitement traveled straight from his chest to his groin.

He went from one breast to the other, wetting them, blowing on them, then nipping them, and her cries became shorter and sharper. "I need more."

He sat up and worked on her skirt, feeling around until he found the side zipper; then he pulled it down her legs.

"Your panties match your bra," he said.

Before pulling the skirt all the way off he slipped her sandals from her feet, taking a moment to finger her ankle bracelet. "That's about the sexiest damn thing I've ever seen," he said, then shed the denim.

Pushing her legs apart slightly, he knelt between them and bent to kiss her flat belly, then moved lower and kissed her sweet spot over her silk panties.

Leah cried out and latched onto his head. "Oh, oh, please."

"Patience, baby," he murmured, rubbing his finger along the wet spot of the silk.

"No. I . . . don't have any left. It's been so long, and it's never felt like this. Please, Mark, help me."

There was no way he could ignore this woman's cry for help. He maneuvered her panties down her legs. "I just want to taste you."

"Yes, taste me," she rasped. "Then I want to taste you."

He wouldn't survive it. His body was throbbing, a primal need to plant himself inside her that was almost too intense to ignore. But he bit his lip and touched her, finding her wet and so ready. Thrusting a finger inside her, he leaned down and licked her. She writhed and gasped and spoke words he couldn't understand, and the moment he felt her pulse around his finger, she screamed.

Mark didn't stop until he felt her walls stop squeezing his finger. Then he moved up her body to her mouth and kissed her parted lips.

She answered him with a fervor that stunned him, but then pushed at his chest. "I want you now. I want you to feel that. I want to make you explode like you made me. But first let me taste you."

"Leah, I am so close, I'm afraid I won't survive."

She laughed, but her eyes were drowsy in a way that said her body was happy. Which made him so ecstatic and full of emotion for this woman who loved how he cherished her.

"Lie down," she whispered. "I'll be gentle."

He couldn't deny her anything at this moment, so he gritted his teeth and rolled to his back.

Her hands stroked over him as she talked and kissed her entire way from his chin to his manhood, and when her hand wrapped around him and her lips covered him, he jerked and groaned his pleasure. It took every ounce of self-control he possessed to hold off, so when he exploded, it would be inside her.

Finally he grabbed her arms and pulled her up his body. "I have to, Leah. Now."

"Oh, yes, please do."

He pushed her to her back, then twisted to the drawer and grabbed a condom, ripping ferociously at the wrapping.

Rolling it on, he turned back and spread her legs wide, fingering her wetness for some moments until she began whimpering again.

Then he positioned himself between her thighs and looked at her. "I want this so much. I've wanted you from the moment I saw you, Leah."

"Yes."

And he entered her, trying to be gentle until she got used to him. But she grabbed his buttocks and started chanting, "Harder. Harder. Harder."

Nothing, nothing on earth could feel this good. The pressure built in his groin until there was no way to stop the explosion. "I'm coming," he whispered. "Come with me, baby."

And she grabbed his back and arched up into him, pushing him deep inside her.

Mark felt fireworks going off all over his body, and nearly passed out from the pleasure. As he groaned and rasped, "Oh, Leah," she screamed again.

Steve arrived at Kate's gated community in McLean five minutes late, thanks to the ineptitude of a store clerk who hadn't yet mastered the codes for produce. The guard checked his name against the guest list, then opened the iron gate and directed him to visitor parking.

He reached her seventh-floor condo and rang the bell. Kate opened up with a smile.

Unfortunately, she was not in a nightgown, but instead in low-riding jeans and a red cotton top that barely reached her belt. Her hair was held back in a casual ponytail, and she'd obviously not bothered to reapply makeup. She looked exquisite.

He'd never seen her in casual clothes before, and, not surprisingly, she more than did them justice. He'd also never seen her without lipstick, and her bare lips were just as beautiful as when she had them painted.

She never wore much makeup, and he now knew it was because she didn't really need it.

But he still would have loved to see that nightgown.

She glanced at the paper bag in his hands and said, "Whoa! What have you got in there? I was expecting tequila and mix."

"My grandfather considers himself something of a gourmet. He'd whip my butt if I ever considered making drinks with a mix. I hope you have a blender."

"Sure. Come on in."

Her small foyer was long and narrow, and led to a living room that was tastefully decorated in blues and creams, with dark mahogany furniture. She turned to him and said, "Home sweet home."

"It's great," he said. And he wasn't just talking about the decor; he was also commenting on how she filled out a pair of jeans. He didn't think he'd ever been jealous of a piece of clothing before.

"Anyway, the kitchen is back down the hall to the right."

He stepped aside and followed her into her kitchen. It was fairly large, and he set the bag on a small, round oak table. "Thanks for meeting on such short notice." He felt a need to keep using words that didn't give her the impression he considered it an actual date, because he didn't want her calling security and having him tossed out.

"No problem. Like I said, I had nothing better to do." She leaned down to a bottom cabinet, showing off her own bottom half to great advantage and pulled out a blender. After setting it on the counter she turned to gaze at him. "Anything else you need?"

He'd have liked to say, *Yes, everything you keep on the bottom shelves.* Instead he said "Not a thing."

"Can I help?"

"Yes, keep me company."

"Okay. This should be fun to watch." She sat down at her kitchen table and crossed her legs.

Mark turned away and began unpacking the sack, so she didn't see reflected in his eyes the flare of lust that burned through his veins. "Frozen or over ice?" he asked.

"Over ice."

"Regular or strawberry?" He held up a carton of the fresh fruit.

"Regular. We can eat the strawberries with cream."

Okay, visions of sugarplums were dancing through his head. He was surprised by his strong physical attraction to her. He'd always considered her beautiful, but their rivalry and his suspicions of her company's actions had made it impossible for him to feel anything but appreciation for the package and contempt for the inner workings. Somehow the contempt had dissipated with her passionate defense of her innocence. He hoped he wasn't letting his judgment go south, so to speak.

"Salt, no salt?" he asked.

"I'd love salt. But I probably shouldn't."

He began dumping the ingredients in the blender.

He'd had Gramps go on the Internet to find a good recipe and print it out. And while he'd dressed after his rushed shower and shave, he'd made Gramps recite the ingredients and directions over and over again so he wouldn't look dumb reading instructions to fix the drink for Kate.

"So, want to hear the game plan Mark came up with?" Kate asked.

"Yes."

"He decided on a three-pronged attack. He's putting one man in our lab where Harvey works. He's putting one man in as a new maintenance guy so that the man can look around at night when the lab is empty, and he has a man who's going to be following Harvey to see if he has any meetings with his nephew, Jimmy."

"Sounds like a plan. But shouldn't he also be trying to get hold of Harvey's financial records to see if he's been making payments for information, or receiving money from some source for obtaining the information for Apple Blossom?"

"He mentioned that. And he said he has sources in law enforcement who could obtain that information, but until we discover anything suspicious that would give his friends cause, it would be walking a fine line. If Harvey—or any of my employees—turns out to be guilty, I want the charges to stick, and not get tossed out because of technicalities."

"Well, Mark should know the best way to build an airtight case."

"Okay, how about your strategy?"

"We've already spent a ton of money on internal surveillance, and Jimmy is now what Mark is calling 'a person of interest' so the guards have been briefed about keeping a close eye on him in the lab. But he's also added a man to tag the boy. Because as much as he and his uncle have plenty of contact at family functions and things, they could very well be smart enough never to exchange information at events like that. So he's got a guy who's going to be following him and keeping a log and picture gallery of everyone the boy has contact with."

He added the tequila, and the conversation came to a short halt while the blender did its thing. When he was finished, he turned. "Glasses and ice and we're good to go."

"Yea!" she said, with a smile that made his mouth go dry. She jumped up and went to an upper cabinet to retrieve a couple of stem goblets.

Steve revised his estimation. Upper cabinets were good, too, because reaching made her shirt ride up and reveal skin, and the cotton stretched over her full breasts. This was most definitely a man-friendly kitchen.

She filled the glasses with ice, then set them down on the counter. He poured, then handed her a margarita.

"Want to go sit out in the living room?" she asked.

"Whatever you want."

"Okay, living room. Just be forewarned: My parrot's called Gabby for a reason. And she's learned some interesting phrases."

They headed to the living room, and this time he noticed a big bird cage hanging from the ceiling by a chain. Gabby was beautiful—bigger than Mark realized parrots were. As soon as Mark walked toward him, the bird said, "You lookin' at me?"

Mark turned on his heel and said, "Nope."

"Stool pigeon!"

"Gabby, behave," Kate said.

"No."

Mark had to laugh. "Cheeky thing, isn't she?"

"Unbelievable. I leave the TV on during the day so she can listen and not get bored. One night when I came from work, the first thing she said to me was, "'*Yo quiero* Taco Bell.'"

"No way."

"Scout's honor. She hasn't said it in a long time, though." Kate sat down on a chair and folded one leg under the other. She gestured to the couch. "Get comfortable."

They sipped their drinks, and Kate closed her eyes and murmured, "Mmmm. That's wonderful."

He felt inordinately proud. "I'm glad."

"So," she said, "let me ask you this bluntly."

"Hit me."

She grinned. "There are times I've wanted to."

"I probably deserved it."

"And wanted to slug Stephanie."

"She's really not that bad. She's just very protective of the company."

"If we find a culprit, will Stephanie pursue a lawsuit against Apple Blossom, even if it's proven he or she acted alone and without my company's knowledge or approval?"

"We talked to our lawyer about it. She says we could easily sue for some damages, and for a percentage of the profits you've made from the products your employee stole."

"Oh. Our lawyer said basically the same thing. I was hoping your lawyer was dumber than ours."

He laughed, but sobered quickly. "We're not pursuing it, Kate.

If it was an individual acting alone, we're not coming after Apple Blossom. In fact, we discussed our two corporations working together to make certain it never happens again."

She chewed her lower lip, so he added, "There's enough of a market for both of us to succeed. And may the companies give each other a run for their money. Honestly. We have no desire to put you out of business with a lawsuit."

"I can't believe Stephanie agreed to this."

"Like I said, she's not as bad as you think. She'll give you a fair shot if you deserve a fair shot. She's not afraid of honest competition."

Kate was silent for a long time, sipping her drink occasionally. "I'm sorry for all of the nasty things I've ever said about her."

"She's not all that proud of the things she's said about you, either. That is, once she's completely convinced that the corporation didn't sanction the actions."

"I swear we did not. I swear it, Steve."

"I believe you."

She smiled. "You're a better man than me, Charlie Brown."

"Actually, I'm very glad you aren't a man at all."

She stared at him so long that he held up a hand. "I'm sorry. Please don't take that the wrong way."

"I'm not. Actually, I'm kind of flattered."

"Want to be in on my meeting with Mark on Monday?"

She shook her head. "I can't. My schedule is full." After a second she said, "But if you like enchiladas, you can come over for supper Monday night and fill me in."

Steve couldn't believe it. She was inviting him over for supper? "Yes!" he said, a little too quickly. "I mean, I'd like that."

"And now would you like to share a little *Casablanca* and finish off these margaritas?"

"I couldn't think of anything better." Well, he could, but he didn't feel like getting slapped.

"Play it again, play it again!" Gabby squawked.

Chapter Eighteen

For the first time in his life, Mark had to cry "uncle." It was almost three in the morning before he and Leah emerged from the bedroom at the lodge, she wearing only his shirt and her panties—and that sexy-as-sin ankle bracelet—and he had on only boxers and jeans.

He loved seeing her in his shirt, which swam on her and reached nearly to her knees. She just looked so darn cute.

Her hair was a mess in the best possible way. Her lips and cheeks and chin worried him a little, though. They were definitely the worse for wear.

He built a fire while she sat on one of the chairs, her legs folded under her. For some reason he kept looking back at her, half-afraid she was a dream that would disappear if he even blinked.

When he got the fire going, he asked, "Some wine?"

"Mmm, I'd love a glass. Although right now I feel almost drunk already."

Once again not wanting her far away, he took her hand and led her to the kitchen, where Harry kept a wine rack. "Preference?"

"Red, please. Dry."

He chose a cabernet and opened it with a corkscrew he grabbed from a utensil drawer.

Leah laughed softly and he turned to her with eyebrows raised. "What?"

"You know where everything is. My guess is you've attended a poker party or ten in your time."

"I've been here once or twice."

"Right."

"Okay, maybe a few more times than that," he conceded. "I felt it was my duty. I want to support my employees."

"I'm sure."

When he'd poured the wine they padded back out to the living room and sat down on the couch. He draped his arm around her shoulder and she laid her head on his, practically purring. They were silent for a long time, enjoying the warmth of the fire in the chilly morning air.

"Leah?" he said finally.

"Hmm?"

"I don't know about you, but what we just shared most definitely wasn't meaningless to me."

"No, it wasn't meaningless to me, either. I'm just not sure exactly what it meant."

"Meaning what?"

"I don't know."

"I don't either."

"Do we have to define it right now?"

"I guess not." But that didn't quite sit well with him, and he didn't know why. It wasn't that he was ready to express undying love to this woman, but the thought of their being nothing more than a short, pleasurable fling sat like a sour lemon in his stomach.

Something incredible had happened in that bedroom. He might be too tired right now to experience it again tonight, but never? That was almost unthinkable.

"You're remarkable," he said quietly.

"You too," she said, then yawned.

The goblet wobbled in her hand, and he took it from her and set it down. "Come here, pretty lady." He folded her in his arms and guided her head to his chest.

She threw her arm around his waist, and they just sat there for he didn't know how long. He felt like there were important things to say, but he didn't know what they were. He probably should think about it before something came out of his mouth, leaving room for his foot.

With luck, they had plenty of days and nights ahead to straighten it all out. And to have more mind-blowing sex.

But somehow calling it merely great sex cheapened it in a way Leah didn't deserve. She'd given all of herself tonight, had trusted him with her body. It was more profound than great sex.

"Mark?"

"Hmm?"

"Who was your first?"

He stared down at the top of her head. Her chestnut hair shimmered with gold highlights in the firelight. "My first what?"

She chuckled into his chest. "You don't play a good dimwit, either."

That's what he was afraid of. "The first girl I made love to?"

"Yes."

"Why would you want to know that?" he asked, a little uncomfortable with the honest answer.

"I'm just curious. Who was she?"

"Her name was Jenny. Jenny Palmer."

"How old were you?"

"Sixteen."

"Was she your first girlfriend?"

"No."

"High school sweetheart?"

"Not exactly."

"What was she, exactly?"

"Umm, well, she was a teacher."

She shot up straight. "You're kidding me! You made love to one of your teachers?"

"Well, sort of."

"You mean she wasn't your teacher?"

"Yes, sort of."

She shot him an exasperated look. "Spit it out."

"She was my driver's ed teacher."

Her mouth dropped open, but after a moment she burst out laughing. "Let me guess. You did it in the car."

Mark pressed his lips together.

"You did!"

"Yes, but it's not what you're thinking."

"You have no idea what I'm thinking."

"First, she was only twenty-three. It wasn't like an older woman situation."

"Well that's good," she said dryly. "We wouldn't want you to be seduced by a really old person. So what happened?"

"We were on a drive and she told me to take a left at this fork in the road, and we ended up at . . . Before I go on, I had no idea this place existed."

"Oh, please, tell me more."

"Well, it was this bluff above a small lake."

"Very secluded, right?"

"During the day, yes. I'd been told it gets a lot more activity at night."

214

"And this place was called what?"

"You don't want to know."

"Oh, you betcha I do."

He felt a tick in his jaw and he looked away from her prying eyes. "Makeout Mountain."

There was a moment of stunned silence, followed by peals of laughter. When he finally forced himself to look at her, she was doubled over. "Oh, God, that's . . . that's unbelievable."

"I told you you wouldn't want to hear it."

"Oh, no, that's priceless, really." She sat up straight. "So your driver's ed instructor took you for a ride, did she?"

He was totally embarrassed, yet he couldn't help but chuckle. "You could say that."

"She seduced you."

"You could say that."

"Were you surprised, or did you pretty much know she wanted to hop your bones?"

Mark stared at pretty, demure little Leah, not realizing she even had bawdiness in her. But then he just shook his head. He'd gone this far. "I had no idea until . . . well, until . . ."

"Until what?"

"You sure are a nosy little thing."

"I know. Until what?"

"Until . . ."—he searched for a delicate way to put it—"she invited me to check out the upholstery in the backseat."

"I take it you didn't object too strenuously."

"To tell you the truth, it wasn't that I was naive; I wasn't. But I certainly wasn't expecting it."

"Was it fun?"

"It was awkward and uncomfortable."

"And fun."

He rolled his eyes. "Yes, it was fun. It was my first time. I was thrilled at the chance. But trust me, it wasn't exactly magical."

Leah shook her head. "These days she could be thrown in jail for that."

"I didn't tell anybody!"

"Please. Boys brag. It's in their genes."

"I swear to God, Leah, you are the first person I've ever told about that."

Her eyes went wide. "No way."

"It's the truth."

After another moment of shocked silence, she laid her head back on his chest, and he felt her smile against his skin. "That's so sweet."

He had no idea what was sweet about it. To him it was embarrassing. "I've improved since then."

"Oh, yes, you certainly have."

"Your turn."

"What?"

"Your turn. What was your first time?"

She didn't hesitate. "Nothing even close to as exciting."

"Everything about you is exciting. When was it? High school?"

She found that uproariously funny. "With Steve as a brother? I never even had a date in high school."

"Not even for the prom?"

"Steve offered to take me."

"Ouch."

"I declined."

"I can't believe the boys weren't running after you."

"Oh, please. I bet there isn't a boy from my high school who'd remember who I am."

216

He found that hard to believe. "So who was he?"

"A guy I met in college."

"Did you love him?"

"Love him? I didn't even date him."

"Excuse me?"

She looked up at him. "This is going to sound so bad."

"No it won't. Tell me."

"He was my study buddy."

"For what class? Biology?"

"Close. Sex ed."

"No way."

"Yes. We met every Thursday night to study, because we always had quizzes on Fridays. The night before finals we were laughing about some position, because we couldn't believe it was possible."

"So you . . . what? Decided to do some hands-on research?"

"Umm, yes."

"Did you . . . find out what you wanted to know?"

"Well, I learned a lot that night, to say the least. So did he. It was his first time, too."

"But you didn't fall in love with him?"

"No. And he didn't fall in love with me. We were *experimenting*, Mark. We were curious, and we were studying this stuff together."

"I can't believe he didn't fall head over heels."

"Trust me, he didn't. But I'll always think of him very fondly. We weren't any good at what we were doing, but he was really sweet. And that's when I learned that I really like sex."

"You sure do."

She punched his shoulder. "I am so grateful to him for being my first. It meant the world to me."

"But you didn't love him!"

217

"No, I didn't. That's why I was glad. I really liked him, but there was no scary pressure to try to live up to a guy I was ga-ga over. You know?"

"I'm working on it."

Leah sighed. "I don't know how to explain it, other than I respected him and he respected me. That meant a lot to me. I knew he wouldn't hurt me. We were young, curious kids."

"I wish I'd been him."

She stared up at him. "Why?"

"I just would have loved to be young and curious with you."

"You'd have thought I was a total dork and idiot."

No, he'd have thought he got the chance to touch Leah for the first time. It was a weird feeling. He shied away from virgins at every opportunity.

Although come to think of it, he'd been attracted to her even before she'd admitted she was no virgin. "I would have felt honored. He should have felt honored."

"He didn't use me and go away, Mark. We've been great friends ever since. I was at his wedding. He's happily married to the nicest woman in the world. And I couldn't be happier for him. I love him for what happened. I couldn't have picked a more caring, wonderful guy. But I would never have loved him the way I'd need to love a man to marry him or anything."

"What do you need to love a man . . . that way?" he asked, because even speaking the word "marry" gave him hives now.

"If I knew, I'd either be married or be depressed I couldn't find him."

Mark was a little irritated that she hadn't pointed right at him and said, "You." Why, he didn't know. Ego, maybe. "Are you depressed you haven't found him?"

"Not yet. It's not number one on my priority list."

"What is?"

She grinned. "Maybe becoming a driver's ed instructor?"

"I need lessons," he said, as fast as he could.

"I've seen you drive. Yes, you do."

He wanted to grab her and drag her back to bed, but his body said no way. "I'll sign up for lessons the moment I can raise my arms again."

She smiled and patted his chest in a "you poor thing" kind of way.

"What was this guy's name?" he asked, realizing there was a little jealousy involved here.

"Gary."

"The guy was a fool if he didn't hold on to you. He should have been head over heels."

She laughed. "You've been with me. You're not head over heels."

Mark wasn't so sure. But he wasn't so sure about anything anymore. Which really made him uncomfortable. "Well, I guess there's something to be said for education after all," he said, because he didn't know what else to say. "Thanks for telling me."

"And thank you. I'll never look at a driver's ed car the same way again."

They sat that way for a long time, with only the crackling of the fire sounding in the night.

After a while he heard her breathing deepen, and knew she'd fallen asleep. He'd feel guilty for exhausting her so much tonight if it hadn't been Leah who'd kept coming back for more. He shifted forward slowly so as not to jar her, set down his wine beside hers, and then picked her up and carried her back to the bed and tucked her in.

She immediately turned on her side and then went still.

Mark returned to the living room to bank the fire, then headed back and slipped into bed beside her. Wrapping his arm around her waist, he felt a contentment he hadn't remembered in a long time.

His last thought before succumbing to sleep was that even in slumber, he liked her beside him.

Leah awoke the next day filled with a powerful feeling of abandonment. She turned over, and sure enough she was the only one in the bed.

Had she only dreamed those strong, protective arms holding her all through the night? Had Mark decided to sleep on the couch?

But then the delicious aroma of coffee reached her, and she heard noises coming from another part of the lodge. She stretched, then winced as she began taking stock of every muscle she possessed, because every one of them was screaming that she'd sorely abused them.

She didn't mind the ache, because it was a delicious reminder that what had happened last night hadn't been a hallucination.

Shivering as she left the body-warmed sheets of the bed and felt the chill of the floor and the air, she headed down the hall. Spying her purse, she sighed with relief and silently blessed Gramps for the sage advice of bringing along a toothbrush. She hoped there was toothpaste in the bathroom.

She was digging around in her bag when she heard, "Good morning."

She whirled around, mortified she hadn't combed her hair or washed her face before Mark got his first glimpse of her. She wasn't exactly a raving beauty anytime, but mornings she was definitely at her worst.

Clutching her toothbrush, she ducked her head. "Hi."

"Coffee's brewing," he said.

"It smells wonderful. But let me go freshen up first, please."

"Sure."

She practically sprinted to the bathroom and looked in the mirror. It was worse than she thought, and she groaned. "Whoa, Nellie."

Brushing her hair, teeth, and splashing water on her face didn't improve her much, but she felt slightly more human.

When she returned to the bedroom, the first things she spotted were the number of opened condom packages on the bedside table, and she repeated, "Whoa, Nellie." She was surprised they both weren't dead.

It wouldn't do to leave the sheets on the bed before making it, so she began stripping it. When she pulled off the pillowcase that Mark had used, she brought it to her nose and inhaled the faint scent of sandalwood and man that she savored every time she got close to him. She'd never forget his scent as long as she lived.

"What are you doing?"

She froze, then turned to the door slowly, lowering the pillowcase. "Stripping the bed."

He was still bare chested, seeing that she was still wearing his shirt. "You don't need to do that. Harvey has a service that comes in every Monday to clean."

"I feel guilty leaving a mess."

"Honey, compared to Mondays after poker weekends, the service will probably think no one was here all weekend."

She dropped the pillowcase and scooped up the pile of condom wrappers on the table. "Not if they see these."

He chuckled. "Want some coffee?"

"Oh, yes." She looked down at herself. "Just let me get dressed and you can have your shirt back."

"Do you want to shower before we go?"

"Oh, I'd love that."

"Me, too. Let's have a cup of coffee first, then grab a shower."

"Okay," she squeaked. He turned and left the room, Leah staring at him. Was it her imagination, or had he implied that they were going to conserve water? She sure hoped so.

Leah wasn't sure how much water they'd conserved, since they were in the shower for a very long time. Mark was sweet and gentle as he soaped her all over, which was a good thing, because her body felt like it had been through a train wreck.

The ride home was quiet, but not in an uncomfortable way. Mark looked over at her often and smiled, and every once in a while he took her hand or rubbed strands of her hair before returning his attention to the road. It was close to a half an hour before they spoke.

"Thank you for last night," he said. Then he added, "All of it."

"I had a wonderful time," she answered him.

"Will you go out with me again, Leah?"

"On one condition," she said.

"What's that?"

"That you aren't asking because you feel . . . I don't know . . . chivalrous."

He chuckled. "I don't have a chivalrous bone in my body."

"Yes, you do. And if I ever discovered you were asking me out because you felt obligated after last night, I'd be mortified."

He was quiet for a moment. "Leah, yeah, I'm asking

you out again because of last night. Because I had a fantastic time, and I'd like to have more just like it. I'll even allow you to beat me at Putt-Putt again."

"Oh, please, I could take you blindfolded."

"I was being chivalrous."

"Right."

He smiled as he made a quick check of the rearview mirror. "I want another date because I want another date. It's as simple as that. And if you're worried it's all about the mind-blowing lovemaking, I'll be happy to prove to you it's not, by being pure as the driven snow for as long as you'd like."

"Why would I want that?" She could hear the horror in her own voice at the thought.

"I don't know. I don't really profess to have a complete grasp of the female mind."

"Well, that's not it at all. In fact, if you wanted to go out just for the sex, I could understand that. I just don't want to be a pity date."

"You are so far from a pity date, you're in two different universes."

Her heart smiled. "In that case, I'd love to."

"How about tonight?"

"Well, Gramps is planning a special supper, but . . . wait, I've got an idea!"

"What's that?"

"Why don't you and Shelley come over for supper tonight?"

"I'd hate to impose on such short notice."

"Oh, Gramps won't mind. And I'd love for him and Shelley to meet. If nothing else they can fight over cooking techniques and recipes."

"I'll ask Shelley. If she doesn't have any other plans or obligations, I'm sure she'll be thrilled to come."

"Great. I know they'll love talking."

He grinned. "Speaking of talking . . ."

Leah ducked her head. "I warned you."

"That you did. And you came through like a champ."

"Was it irritating?"

"Hell, no! Talk to me, moan to me, scream to me anytime you want, lady. It's sexy as all hell."

Leah opened her mouth, but just then Mark's cell phone buzzed.

He reached into his chest pocket and flipped his phone open, an irritated look on his face. "Leave it to someone to break in on a very fun conversation."

After punching a button he said, "Yeah?"

He listened, then glanced over at her. "Yeah, Steve, what is it?" He listened some more, and his expression grew grim. "We're about ten minutes from the Beltway. We can be there in about fifteen, depending on traffic." Then he looked at her again and said, "Hold on. Leah, do you want me to drop you at my house first so you can pick up your car?"

"What's going on?"

"Emergency meeting in your brother's office."

"About the thief?"

"Yes."

"Heck no, I want to be there."

He put the phone back to his lips. "About fifteen." Then he flicked the phone shut.

"Do you know what it's all about?"

"Looks like one of my men has already turned up some incriminating information."

It actually took them closer to twenty minutes to reach Steve's office due to an unusually high amount of traffic for a Saturday. When they arrived, Steve was sitting at his desk, looking tense. Also standing or sitting around the room were Kate, Jake, and two men Leah didn't recognize.

Steve glanced up and nodded, then did a double take, raking his gaze over Leah's face, finding she didn't know what. Then his narrowed eyes moved directly to Mark.

Kate must have followed the play of expressions on his face, because she glanced over her shoulder at them. But instead of the dark look Steve had given them, she broke out in a wide grin.

Mark nodded at Kate, but then peered closer at her, and it was his turn to look at Steve, eyebrows raised. Leah didn't understand what everyone was seeing that she wasn't, but whatever it was, Steve had the grace to turn a little red in the face and drop his gaze.

Leah glanced at Kate again, and noticed that Kate's lips were a little swollen, and her cheeks a little red. Understanding dawned. If Leah looked in a mirror right now, she'd be mortified, she was sure.

Mark introduced Leah to the two men. She smiled at them, but didn't actually catch their names because she was too busy trying to hide her face and ignore all the looks that were passing between everyone. An unspoken language was taking place, even between Mark and a smirking Jake, but she didn't want to interpret.

She had the feeling the next time she and Steve were alone, the words would be less than silent.

"So what's the deal?" Mark asked.

The taller of the two strangers stepped forward. "I installed the new digital copier in Lab B the first night. No unusual activity that night or Thursday. But last night the suspect stayed late, long after everyone else had cleared out."

"That's not unusual," Leah piped up. "Jimmy often stays late to clean up."

"Right. Well, last night he stayed late to clean out."

"I'm sorry?"

"He stayed until six forty-two. Between six o'clock and six twenty-four he copied an entire file."

Leah shook her head. "I don't get it. That's part of Jimmy's job. He's an intern."

"But," Mark chimed in, "he's only supposed to make copies of memos and other correspondence, like invoices, for filing. He's never supposed to copy formula notes. Those are classified to only certain individuals."

"Okay."

Mark turned to Leah. "The new copier archives all the work it does, so we can document what's being reproduced."

"Oh. So you can make duplicates of the documents he's been copying?"

"Exactly."

"Ain't technology grand?" Jake said.

"This is the file he copied," Steve said. The label was marked JP 1023-4.

"What's it for?"

"A miracle antiaging face cream Just Peachy chemists have been working on," Steve said with a grin.

"What's so funny?"

"I deliberately drew attention to it. I sent out a memo telling the staff that it was imperative we speed up the development of the cream. I implied in cryptic terms that it could be the biggest breakthrough Just Peachy has had since we opened up for business, and the sooner we get it on the market, the better."

"He also made two copies of the memo," the tall man said.

The shorter man chimed in, looking at some notes. "He placed three calls during that time. The first number was traced to a Daniels residence. Apparently his girlfriend. The second turned out to be a pizza joint at Tyson's Corner. The Slater boy works there part-time, as well. The third was made to his own home."

Jake picked up the story. "The camera recorded him going into the men's room, where of course there is no surveillance. He brought the file folder back out with him and refiled it."

"So?"

"The old bait and switch," Mark said. "He takes the copies in with him, hides the contents on him somewhere, then brings the file folder back out, empty. The next day, or whatever, under the pretext of cleaning out file cabinets, he pulls the empty folder out and sticks it with the other unused office supplies."

"Oh." This spy business wasn't for sissies, she decided.

The shorter man picked up again. "We tailed Jimmy to the pizza place, where he began work. This girl"—he tossed down a black-and-white photo—"came in about a half hour later. She and he disappeared in the back for a few minutes. She left about ten minutes later. My guess is they didn't just head back there to neck, but who knows?"

"Is this enough to constitute probable cause?" Steve asked Mark.

"On the kid, yes, but not on his uncle. We need to know that his uncle receives the information, then does something with it." He turned to Kate. "Do you have regular development meetings?"

"Every Tuesday morning."

"Until and unless we catch Harvey receiving the papers, and/or he pitches a formula that closely assimilates the notes in that file, we don't have enough to charge him with fraud."

They talked about tweaking strategy in terms Leah

didn't understand, but she was impressed. Mark knew his stuff. She felt a huge burst of pride just watching him in his element.

The meeting broke up about fifteen minutes later. After Jake and Mark's two security men left Steve, Mark, Leah, and Kate chatted casually. Leah watched with intense interest as Steve and Kate interacted. Their gazes toward each other were softer, their smiles much more frequent, and there was a decided lack of the biting undertones that usually accompanied their civil conversations.

She didn't know what, but something had happened. And it had to have happened recently—like last night.

"Ready to go?" Mark asked her.

She held up one finger. "Kate, what are you doing tonight? Do you have plans?"

"Um, no."

"Well, listen, my grandfather is making a special gourmet meal. Mark and his sister are coming. Why don't you join us?"

"Oh, I couldn't intrude."

"You wouldn't be intruding," Steve said quickly. "Gramps loves to show off his cooking to anyone who will eat it."

"Yes, but I wouldn't want to cause any tension. With Stephanie, you know."

"She won't be there," Steve and Leah said at once.

"She . . . has a standing Saturday-night date with her boyfriend," Leah elaborated. But guilt seeped in, because she was teetering dangerously close to lying about personal stuff, something she'd sworn she wouldn't do. And she was going to murder Steve later for it.

"Stephanie has a boyfriend?" Mark and Kate said in unison.

"Yes," Leah said, still silently cursing her brother, "Really nice guy. Professional wrestler."

Mark and Kate said, "Ohhhh," and nodded, as if that explained a lot.

"Come," Steve said.

Kate hesitated. "If you're sure your grandfather won't mind."

"He won't."

"Great," Leah said. "Around six for cocktails?"

"Sounds good."

Leah and Mark waved and left. As they turned the corner, Leah danced a little jig and punched a fist in the air. "Yes!"

"Don't congratulate your matchmaking skills too much, darlin'. My guess is they kind of did that all on their own."

"Who cares?" she said.

And as they headed down in the elevator, Mark took her in his arms and kissed her silly.

"Aren't these elevators being monitored?" she asked when they came up for air.

"Who cares?"

Chapter Nineteen

The Smith family home was teeming with controlled chaos. Delicious scents wafted from the kitchen, where Gramps and Shelley had disappeared minutes ago, arguing the relative merits of parsley versus cilantro.

Two additional table place settings were added when Mark called to say that Jake's wife, LeAnne, had driven up from Richmond, and could they join the crowd? Gramps was thrilled. He loved cooking for a captive audience, and he loved being in the company of young people, because Oprah had had a guest on once who spouted the theory that to stay young, you should surround yourself with the young.

Steve was playing bartender, and everyone was sitting or milling around in the informal parlor. LeAnne, Kate, and Leah had all converged in one corner to chat.

"Congratulations on the baby, LeAnne," Leah said, smiling.

Jake's wife was an auburn beauty, with a serene, ethereal air about her that seemed in stark contrast to Jake's barely leashed tension and energy. But whenever Jake looked around to check on his wife, which was often, his expression softened and his blue eyes sparked. "Thank you," LeAnne said.

"You're pregnant?" Kate asked, staring at LeAnne's still-flat tummy.

"Yes, our first."

"That's wonderful!"

LeAnne grinned. "We'd been trying for a while, but when it finally happened, Jake almost fainted. 'A baby?' he said, as if I'd just announced I was giving birth to a Martian."

"Men are such wimps when it comes right down to it," Kate said.

LeAnne nodded sagely. "Mark and Jake could face down armed thugs without blinking an eye. Tell them they're about to learn to change diapers and they cower in fear."

Just then Jake looked over at LeAnne and beckoned for her to join him. LeAnne said, "Excuse me," and strolled toward her husband.

"They make a pretty striking couple," Kate said.

"They sure do."

Kate swirled her margarita around, took a sip, then leaned closer to Leah. "Guess what?"

"What?"

"I've had a revelation."

"What's that?"

Kate practically giggled. "I like boys."

Leah had a hard time keeping a straight face. "You've figured that out, have you?"

"Yes."

"Now would this be 'boys,' plural, or 'boy,' singular?"

"Oh, I'm pretty sure I like boys, plural. Maybe just some more than others."

Leah held up her wineglass. "This calls for a toast." They clinked glasses.

"And how about you?" Kate asked. "I couldn't help but notice that your lips looked like they went seven rounds with a boxer today."

"I . . . don't have a clue what you're talking about."

"Right. And it can't be our handsome Mr. Colson, because I think he might be a little light in his loafers, if you get my drift."

Leah, unfortunately, had been sipping wine to cover the blush creeping up her cheeks. She practically sprayed a mouthful across the room.

Somehow she managed to choke it down, but then coughed while Kate patted her back sympathetically.

"Excuse me?' Leah said.

"You heard me."

"Um, what makes you say that?"

"Don't tell me you didn't notice?"

"Notice what?"

"When Mark leaned over the desk to look at the surveillance photos, there was the distinct scent of Passion's Promise wafting from his shirt. Speaking of which, isn't that the perfume you wear?"

"Uh—"

"Maybe he's sneaking yours while you're not looking? Or maybe he's snitching bottles from Just Peachy?"

"Very funny."

"So, did we have fun?"

Leah pressed her lips together to keep a goofy grin off her face. She nodded rapidly. "How about you?"

"Not as much as you two, apparently, but I'm not complaining."

"I'm so glad for you! And for Steve. It's about damn time."

"Steve said the same about you."

"Really? Could have fooled me, the way he was glaring at Mark and me today."

"I think he was just issuing a silent warning to Mark that he'd better treat his little sister right."

"I could do the same for you with my big brother."

"Oh, don't worry. I've never met anyone like him. He's so open and honest and sweet."

Uh-oh. "And don't forget loyal. He'd do anything for the people he loves, even if he doesn't much like it."

Leah and Kate made their way over to the makeshift bar, where Steve was wearing an apron over his clothes that read, *Kiss the guy with the bottle in his hand.*

Leah said, "I'm not volunteering. How about you, Kate?"

"I think he'll have to settle for a tip."

Steve laughed as he refreshed their glasses. "What can I say? Wishful thinking."

Jake, LeAnne, and Mark came and joined them. Jake said, "Leah, is it rude to ask for a tour of the house? It's beautiful."

"Of course!"

The four of them started to walk toward the doorway, but Jake put a hand on Mark's chest, halting him. "This is a private tour. You're not invited."

Oh, boy. Leah smelled a setup. So did Mark, judging by his irritated scowl. Leah glanced at LeAnne, but the woman met her gaze with an expression of total innocence. Leah didn't believe it for a second.

Mark said, "All right, pal, but remember you have the right to remain silent. Use it." He pointed at LeAnne's nose. "You too."

"Me?" LeAnne put a hand to her chest. "I'm the soul of discretion."

"Uh-huh," Mark grunted.

Leah sent one final pleading look at Mark, but he just

shrugged. "He's the guy with the badge and the gun. I'm just a lowly citizen."

So, with slightly dragging feet, Leah led them first to the formal living room. "Oh, it's beautiful," LeAnne said. "Did you decorate it?"

She shook her head. "I don't know chintz from china. It was my grandmother."

They headed to Gramps's library. Jake pretended intense interest in the thousands of books. "Has your grandfather actually read all of these?" he asked.

"Many more than once. These are just his keepers. He's given five times this many to the local library."

"He seems like a really nice man."

"With the patience of a saint. He raised us himself since we were still little kids when my parents died."

"Raising three small children," Jake said. "I'm scared out of my mind by one."

Leah had to think for a moment how he came up with the number three. Then she remembered he was Mark's friend, and Mark still thought Stephanie existed. "A big, bad guy like you? Piece of cake."

"When I met him," LeAnne chimed in, "he didn't even know how to raise a dog."

And Mark's story came back to her. "That's right! I forgot what you all went through. I'm so sorry."

Jake came back to them and put his arm around his wife protectively. "It was pretty bad at the time. But I met LeAnne, so I can't exactly regret it."

"Too bad Mark still does."

Both Jake and LeAnne stared at her. Finally LeAnne blew what was probably a gasket for someone who was so soft-spoken. "That idiot. He can't still be carrying that load of garbage around with him."

"I'm afraid so."

"Don't believe him, Leah," Jake said. "It's just not true."

"He was a hero," LeAnne said.

"He still is," Jake said.

Leah's heart sung and stung at the same time. She wondered if Mark would ever get over the guilt.

"So, not meaning to be nosy, Leah," Jake said, "but Mark's my best friend, so I'm going to ask anyway."

"Okay."

"Where do you see your relationship going?"

"Well, that was blunt." She looked to LeAnne for help in telling Jake to mind his own business, but LeAnne seemed just as interested in the answer. "The truth is, I don't know."

"You seem really nice, Leah," LeAnne confided. "And it's about time Mark got serious about someone, as far as I'm concerned. But we're worried because, just like with the guilt over the Wilson case, he has a hard time letting go of what he perceives to be past failures."

"Why do you think he hasn't dated anyone for longer than a few weeks since—"

LeAnne elbowed Jake in the ribs, and he let out an "Oomph."

"He's told me about that."

"He has?" LeAnne and Jake said at the same time, shock on their faces.

"Well, not the whole story. He alluded to a past serious relationship, but when I asked what happened, he didn't want to talk about it."

"That's Mark," LeAnne said with disgust.

"In his defense," Leah said, "we haven't known each other that long." She sipped her wine. "I don't suppose you'd like to fill me in."

"Well—" Jake started, which earned him another elbow to the ribs. "Ow!"

"Let Mark tell you in his own good time. That's the way it should be done."

"You're right, of course. However, I have no idea where my involvement with Mark is going, so I probably won't ever know." That was a depressing thought.

Jake snorted. "Mark has been my best friend since Quantico. Trust me on this one. He's hooked."

LeAnne nodded. "I haven't known him nearly as long. But I've watched how he's treated the parade of women in his life. He's never looked at them like he looks at you."

"Don't get my hopes up," Leah said with sigh.

"Conversely, Leah, please don't get his up if you don't mean it. I'm not sure he'd survive another heartbreak."

Leah wanted to laugh hysterically. "Little chance of that. I've never gotten a man's hopes up in my life, and a heartbreaker I am not."

Gramps had added an extra leaf to the formal dining table, so everyone would have plenty of room. The table already seated eight without a leaf, but Gramps had taken one look at the cumulative size of Mark, Jake, and Steve and decided adding the leaf would be prudent.

He and Shelley sat at either end, as he deemed her honorary hostess of the dinner party, even if she sometimes used dried basil in her béarnaise sauce.

Shelley retorted that Gramps wouldn't know a good tomato sauce if it bit him in the butt.

All through supper they traded barbs, and by the end of the meal they were practically best friends. It was a friendship built on a love of cooking and a strong desire to best the other in that department. They declared Wednesday evenings cook-off nights, and both were practically rubbing their hands with glee at the prospect. Mark and Leah smiled at each other across the table. They'd known the two would probably get along, but they hadn't dreamed it would be this fast and this stimulating for them.

After dessert and snifters of brandy, Jake and LeAnne said their good-byes first, Jake stating that LeAnne needed her mommy sleep. When LeAnne hugged Leah good-bye, she whispered softly, "Take care of him." Leah almost cried, because she was well aware that Mark didn't need anyone taking care of him.

Kate left next, and Steve walked her out to her car. Leah and Mark and Gramps took positions at the front windows. "We really shouldn't be spying on them," Leah said.

"Sure, we should," Gramps said.

"You people are spying on them?" Shelley said indignantly.

"Yes," Gramps said.

"That's disgusting."

"Probably."

"So give me a blow-by-blow," Shelley said.

They were all disappointed when Steve was a perfect gentleman, just handing Kate into her car. But before she drove off, she rolled down the window and he leaned in and laughed at something she said. Then he stepped away and waved, and trotted back up the sidewalk to the front door. They all barely had time to find something to make them look busy and uninterested.

"Cut the innocent act," Steve said. "Your noses were fogging up the windows."

"You're a real disappointment, son," Gramps said, then turned away and began clearing the table, something he never let guests help him do.

Then it was down to Mark and Shelley. "We need to get going, too," Mark said.

"Gramps?" Shelley said.

Gramps put down his armload of dishes and walked over to her. "Night, Shelley. It was wonderful to meet you."

She held her cheek up to him and he gave her a buss.

Shelley grinned and said, "The chicken and artichoke hearts weren't bad."

"Weren't bad?" he said, indignant. What Shelley couldn't see was that he was grinning from ear to ear. "I dare you to top that recipe."

"You're on. See you Wednesday."

Then Gramps took his load and headed into the kitchen.

Leah smiled at Mark and waggled her fingers at him. *Night,* she mouthed.

"Like hell," he said, and grabbed her and kissed her.

"Oooh, cooties!" Shelley said.

"I won't be at Just Peachy tomorrow," Mark told Leah.

"Oh?" she said, trying not to sound disappointed. Not that she saw him that much even when he was there, but for some reason it just felt good to know he was in the same building.

"I have a job beginning in Reston, and all of my men and women are in place at Just Peachy, so there's no reason for me to be there."

"Oh. Well, my last day is Wednesday, anyway. Thorndike already found a full-time replacement."

"Oh." Now he looked disappointed, even though he'd just said he would barely be around himself. "Well, I'll call you."

"Okay."

But after Shelley and Mark said their thank-yous and good-byes, after they'd gotten into his Toyota and driven away, Leah stood at the door, feeling somewhat bereft. She wasn't quite sure why.

* * *

Mark called Leah Sunday, but didn't ask to see her again. They talked in generalities, and he seemed distracted, so she didn't keep him on the phone for long. To take her mind off of troubling thoughts, she worked on updating her résumé.

Monday, he was at another job site, so he didn't call her all day at work. She kept herself busy training the woman who'd be taking over her job.

He *did* call Monday evening, but just to tell her that he had to fly to Richmond in the morning to meet with Jake and a corporate attorney to map out a plan for setting up the Richmond office.

That evening, while she watched Steve walk around the house whistling while getting ready for a date with Kate, Leah made a decision: No pinning hopes on Mark Colson. It was a recipe for disaster.

Steve showed up at Kate's, a bottle of wine in one hand, flowers in the other. When she opened up the door, he just about swallowed his tongue. She wore a sleeveless peasant dress and open-toed sandals, and her hair was long and loose.

Once again, no makeup. Once again, she didn't need it.

"Hi."

"Hi."

Soft music played in the background, and the place smelled like heaven. They decided to save the wine for supper, so Kate poured iced tea instead. She placed the flowers in a vase and set them on the coffee table; then they settled on the couch.

"Thank you so much for the roses. They're beautiful."

"I'm glad you like them," he said, loving the soft look

in her eyes as she fussed to arrange the bouquet just so. "How was your day?" he asked her.

"A little tense. Tomorrow's going to be worse, facing Harvey across the conference table, waiting to see if he proposes a breakthrough antiaging cream."

"Mark doesn't think he'll do it this soon. Harvey will want to test it first, and then he's going to want to change the composition enough so that he thinks Just Peachy can't accuse him of theft. He'll claim something called simultaneous invention, when two people just happen to come up with the same idea at the same time."

"This is really stringing out my nerves, Steve. I just want it to be over."

He pulled her closer and draped his arm around her shoulders. "I know. I know very well." And he wasn't just talking about the corporate theft. "Let's forget about work tonight, okay?"

"Wonderful idea."

"So, you've met my family," he said. "Tell me about yours."

She smiled. "Typical middle-class."

"Are your parents still alive?"

"Oh, yes. They live in Saint Louis. My father's a phys ed teacher and the high school football coach. My mother teaches kindergarten."

"So, do you like football?"

"I love every sport known to peoplekind. In my family, it would be blasphemy not to."

"How about those Skins?" he asked, grinning.

"Sorry, Rams fan."

"Brothers and sisters?"

"Two older sisters, one younger brother. Sarah is married with four kids and counting. She runs a day-care center from their house. Liz is an accountant and aspiring author. Jeff is just finishing law school. Maybe. He still sponges off my folks while he tries to find himself."

She sounded totally disgusted, which would make sense of a driven woman like Kate.

"Wow, you're a diverse group."

"Our parents' house is a zoo during holidays," she said, laughing.

He set his iced tea on a coaster. "Any boyfriends?"

"Not a one. I was a nerd in high school and college, and I've been too busy ever since. You?"

"Not a boyfriend in the bunch."

She laughed. "That's good to hear. How about the young ladies?"

"A few in college. None that took my breath away. After that . . . work."

"We're a sorry pair, aren't we?"

"Until now, I haven't really minded it."

She looked at him with those blue bedroom eyes. "And now?"

"And now I can't believe what I've been missing. Then again, I don't think I've let any great opportunities pass me by—yet." Steve paused, letting his gaze linger on her lips. "I've always thought you can't be who you are without having been where you've been."

She laughed. "Psych 101?"

"Gramps 101."

Kate brought her feet up onto the couch, smoothing her dress over her legs. "So tell me, what's the craziest, most outlandish thing you've ever done?"

Yikes. He didn't want to answer that one. *Just a few more weeks, Kate, and I promise it will all be out. And we'll laugh about it. I hope.* "Hmm, about the craziest thing I did was go skydiving." *Sorry, Gramps, for lying.*

"You rebel."

"Naked."

"Yeowch! Any lasting side effects?" she asked, a wicked gleam in her eye.

Mark grinned. "A complete aversion to skydiving."

"How about being naked?"

"As long as it's not at twenty thousand feet, I'm okay with it. How about you? Craziest moment?"

"Don't get mad, okay?"

He frowned. "Why would I get mad?"

"Because you're so protective of your sister."

"Leah's sheltered. Someone needs to look after her."

"Not *that* sister."

"Oh."

"Anyway, it wasn't really a practical joke on her directly."

"Go on."

"Well, did Stephanie ever tell you she saw Leah at supper—as Candi that night—and a date of Leah's?"

"I vaguely recall that. Seems to me she said the guy was a total dork."

"Hey, I'm not *that* bad!"

He stared at her. "*You're* William Shakespeare?"

She nodded, a proud expression on her face. "That would have been me."

His first thought was to be irritated. Especially since Leah had never told him. His second thought was that he had no right to be angry. So he just said, "Well, you sure fooled Steph. She thought Leah had lost her mind."

"We tried to stick to darkened corners of the restaurant."

"It must have worked. Steph didn't see through it. Which really shocks me. I'd never mistake you for a man." *Except I did. What an idiot. And Leah's hearing about this.*

"It was the most fun I've ever had."

"Now no offense, but Steph thought Leah was up to something. She just didn't know what."

"You weren't there! How would you know?"

"Steph described you."

"I'd make as good a man as you'd make a woman," she said, then leaned over and kissed him.

You have no idea, Steve thought.

Chapter Twenty

By Wednesday morning, Leah had decided her new motto was "Live and learn." It didn't make Mark's rejection hurt any less, but being philosophical made her feel as though she had some measure of control.

At least Steve was in heaven, and that meant the world to her. Her big brother deserved all the happiness he could get, after basically giving up his personal life to build a business that he'd hoped would secure his and his family's future. It was his turn to have some fun now.

Obviously it wasn't hers. Although when she'd talked to Steve last night, he'd gotten a little exasperated with her. "Mark's *busy* with a lot of things, Leah. You can't expect him to just drop everything for you."

And Steve had been right. Four days wasn't a long time not to see Mark, although it felt that way. But it was forever in terms of him not finding time to give her more than a two-minute phone call. And a distracted phone call at that.

Then again, he'd asked if she'd like to go out again. He hadn't asked for a relationship.

Leah was confused, and she'd have loved nothing better than to talk things over with Kate, but Kate was busy trying to catch a spy and juggle a new relationship with Steve. It was only Leah who seemed aimless.

Well, that was going to change. She'd had a number of inquiries regarding jobs from both government agencies and the private sector alike. So far the two positions that held the most interest to her were with the Georgia Bureau of Investigation and the Perch Group, a political and market-research firm. The Perch Group was located in Los Angeles, and she'd miss her family horribly if she had to move that far away. On the other hand, Leah thought maybe it was time she started making her own way, and stopped depending on her brother and grandfather so much.

She was mulling all of this over sitting at the park across from the office. Although technically this was her last day, the woman taking over her position, a nononsense grandmother of five, would have been ready to take the reins by yesterday afternoon. Leah just felt an obligation to be nearby if some last minute questions cropped up.

She sighed and stood up. She ought to at least be pretending to be working in the office. As she went to step in the street, however, her cell phone rang. She stepped back and pulled it out of her purse.

"Hello, pretty lady," she heard Mark's deep, rumbly voice say.

She tried to go for cool and aloof, but didn't quite have it in her. "Hello."

"I'm home."

"Welcome back."

"You sound thrilled."

"I'm happy you're home, of course."

"Don't be doing any cartwheels."

246

She had to smile. "I would, but I'm in a skirt, and I don't want to scare anyone."

"You can scare me like that anytime."

She didn't know what to say. Although her heart was racing, it was also scared.

"Hmm, are you mad at me for some reason?" he asked.

"Not at all."

There was a long pause. "Well, okay. I guess I'd better let you go."

She wanted to scream, *No!* but all she said was, "I'm sure you have a lot to do."

"That's true. Well, I guess I'll talk to you later."

"That would be nice."

" 'Bye."

"Good-bye, Mark."

"Wait, wait, wait!"

"Yes?"

"That sounded like a kiss-off good-bye if I've ever heard one."

"It wasn't."

"I was hoping I'd get to see you tonight."

She almost sobbed. "I'd like that," she said, because she wanted nothing more in the world.

He took a noisy breath. "Good. Remember what tonight is?"

"No."

"Cook-off at the OK Corral."

"Oh, yeah! You want to come over and watch and be a judge?"

"Hell, no. I want you to come to my place because we'll have it all to ourselves."

"Would you like me to make us some supper?"

"How does delivery pizza sound?"

"Wonderful."

"I'm dropping Shelley off at six o'clock. Is that too early?"

"No."

"See you then?"

"Yes."

Mark stared at the phone after he'd disconnected. He had no idea with whom he'd just spoken. Leah's natural shyness couldn't account for her standoffish tone. After a moment he dialed Steve's private line.

"Steve Smith."

"Colson."

"Hello. Back in town?"

"Yes." Mark considered asking for an update on news at work, but he could get that at the office, and besides, at the moment he didn't care. "What's wrong with Leah?"

"What do you mean, what's wrong with Leah?"

"The woman I just talked to is an alien. I almost didn't recognize her voice."

"Why don't you ask her?"

"Because she said nothing's wrong."

"There you go."

"Bull. I haven't known her long, but long enough. Something's wrong. Did something happen to her while I was gone?"

"Not that I know of."

"Did she meet another man?"

"Mark, it's been four days."

"Is she sick?"

"No."

"You're being very helpful."

"Again, you are asking the wrong person."

"But you know, don't you? You're just not telling me."

"I have my suspicions."

"Just a hint. I'm begging here. I'm seeing her tonight, and I don't want to screw it up."

"She's a woman."

"I had noticed that detail," Mark said dryly.

"If that isn't a clear enough reason, you've been going out with the wrong women."

"Well, thanks. You were a big help."

"Glad to be of assistance." And Steve hung up on him without saying good-bye.

All Mark wanted to do was kiss Leah senseless when she opened the door to Shelley and him. But Gramps was there, so it probably wasn't prudent.

Then all he wanted to do was kiss Leah senseless once he got in the car with her. But Gramps was probably at the window, running commentary for Shelley, so he held himself in check.

And on the drive to his place all he wanted to do was shake her and force her to tell him what was eating her. But that could cause a car accident. So he settled for chitchat.

"Happy to be free from that job?" he asked.

"It wasn't so bad, if you don't mind not having to use your brain."

Strikeout number one.

"Anything exciting happen while I was gone?"

"The grass grew."

Strikeout number two.

"Any progress on the Steve and Kate front?"

For the first time, he saw a genuine smile. "He's not saying. He doesn't kiss and tell. But if I were a betting woman, I'd put my money on a whole lot of kissing going on."

"Excellent. Good for them."

And then she lapsed back into silence. Now he was

249

getting irritated. But before he could say anything irrevocably dumb, they arrived at his house.

They entered and he immediately pointed to the couch. "You're not getting any sustenance until we get to the bottom of this. Sit."

A stubborn frown creased her brow, but then she moved to the couch like she was marching to Pretoria.

He tossed his keys on the desk by the door and came and planted himself firmly in front of her.

"What's going on? And don't tell me nothing, because I'm not that stupid. I left you Saturday night and I thought everything was great. I come back today and I don't know who you are."

"Maybe that's it; you don't know me at all."

"I think I do."

"One night of sex doesn't instantly gain you access to my mind."

He almost reeled back from that one. "We've had a lot more than just one night of sex."

"Have we?"

He growled. "How is it that you talk so much when we're making love, and now I can't drag the time of day out of you? And don't give me that old 'If you don't know, I'm not telling you' routine. I *don't* know. I can't read your mind. Just tell me what I did wrong."

She wrapped her arms around her waist. "It's just . . . just . . . I'm scared."

"Of what?"

"I don't know! I know it's not fair to tell you one day that I don't mind if you just want to date me or have my body when you want it, then get mad when you take me at my word."

"How do you figure I took you at your word?"

"Well, you barely called, and when you did it was like a duty call. You weren't even there."

And finally, the stupidity drained from his confused brain. Of course. For someone who placed so little value in her worth as a woman, any sign could be taken as rejection. She had to get over this. He'd love to make it his mission to show her how much he valued her. But damned if he knew how.

He was used to two kinds of women: those who thought so highly of themselves that they made a man feel like he should be honored to be in their illustrious company—Heather fell into that one—and those who placed so little value on their self-worth that they just didn't care. Just about every other woman he'd ever been with fell into that category.

He'd never been with one who wanted desperately to be seen and heard, but felt like she'd been invisible all of her life—and insecure about her worth to those around her.

Right now he was sitting beside this kind. And he didn't know what to do with her.

"You're mad because I didn't call more?"

"I'm not mad. Seriously, I'm not." She took a breath. "And I'm not saying another word until you offer me a beverage."

She was trying his patience, but he figured a small break might be a good opportunity for both of them to sit back and take a few deep breaths. "What can I get you?"

"Are we still having pizza? Or am I close to being kicked out?"

"We're still having pizza."

"A beer, please."

He chuckled on his way to the kitchen. He wondered if she'd ever cease to surprise him. She was so refined and elegant, he'd never have expected she'd order a cold one. He pulled two out, poured them into chilled mugs, and brought them back out. By the time he got there, he felt ready for round two.

"Okay, let's have it."

She took such a slug of beer that she had to lick foam off her upper lip, and no matter how frustrated he was right now, the action managed to fire up hormones all over his body.

"The thing is, Mark, I don't have much experience in this whole dating thing."

"Okay."

"I had so much fun on Friday and Saturday, and then Jake and LeAnne sort of mentioned they thought you were having fun too. I don't know. I guess I expected more than I should have. And when you called me those couple of times at the beginning of the week, it was like you didn't really want to talk to me, but felt obligated. So I decided to give you an out."

"Okay, I can deal with this," he said, and he finally sat down beside her. "First of all, I don't spend my personal time with anyone out of a sense of obligation. If I'd rather have been doing laundry tonight, I wouldn't have asked you over. I'd be pouring fabric softener. Got it?"

"Yes," she said, but there was still a concerned frown on her face.

He took a deep breath and decided to attack this from another angle. "Let me explain a few things, okay?"

"Okay."

"I was an agent with the FBI for years. One of the things they drill into you is that when you're working an assignment, that assignment and your goals in that assignment are your major focus. Not only because they're paying you to do it, but because taking your mind off the task could cost you or someone else or the government. It sounds melodramatic to say it's life and death, but the truth is, sometimes it is."

She nodded, her eyes wide.

"I didn't automatically lose that mind-set when I quit. First my focus was on making this business work, and once it worked and I had clients, the focus was on making sure I secured my clients' goals, not just because I wanted to be a success or rich or anything like that, but sometimes those clients need me. And it matters to me that I don't fail them."

"I understand that."

"It wasn't that I didn't think about you while I was gone; it was that I was focused on the mission of the trip. And it never, ever occurred to me that you would interpret it any other way."

"I'm sorry, Mark. Even with a minor in psychology, I can be really lousy at reading other people."

"No, I'm a lousy communicator."

"No, you're not. I'm a dunce when it comes to dating."

"No, you're not. I'm a dunce when it comes to women."

They stared at each other for a moment, then burst out laughing.

"My God," Leah said. "We deserve each other."

"Let me add one more thing, just to put this into perspective. For a long time, the only women I dated were Candi types. They were easy—easy to find, and easy to walk away from. And I have never, ever called another woman while on assignment. That's the God's honest truth. I'm not saying you should feel like I bestowed some great honor on you. I'm saying that I missed you enough that even in the middle of poring over documents, I just wanted to hear your voice, even for a minute."

To his horror, tears popped into her eyes, and she flung herself at him. "I'm so sorry, Mark!"

"Don't be sorry, sweetheart. I'm not promising I'll be calling you five times a day when I'm away, but I will promise to find a way to make you realize I'm thinking about you."

She shook her head. "No, no, you don't have to. You really don't. Now that I understand, everything's good. I promise. And besides, you don't owe me anything. You didn't even owe me that explanation."

"Maybe not, but I *wanted* you to have it. And trust me, you're the first woman in forever I've felt a desire to explain something to."

"Can we start over?" she asked, looking up at him.

God, he'd missed her. "Absolutely."

"Welcome home, Mark."

"It's good to be home." And then he kissed her, and truer words had never been spoken. Her lips felt like home. Her scent smelled like home. The silky feel of her hair and skin felt like home. He was home.

When he lifted his head, she was smiling. Her eyes opened slowly. Stormy green. He knew that look. And his body quickened. He'd made a promise to himself on the flight home that he wouldn't just pick her up and ravish her tonight, no matter how much he wanted to do exactly that. He was going to show her that getting her naked was not the only thing on his mind. But he wasn't about to deny her if she wanted—

"Let's make love," she whispered.

"No pizza first?"

"I'd rather work up an appetite."

"Whatever the lady wants," he said, and led her back to his room.

"Not a chance," Leah said stubbornly, looking around Steve's office at three expectant and hopeful faces.

Mark came and stood in front of her chair and leaned over, his hands on the chair's arms. "Please, Leah, we need your help."

"Why me?"

"Because Jimmy Slater had a crush on you a mile wide when you were working here. He'd be so thrilled to see you, he'd let down his guard."

"He had a crush on Candi."

"Exactly."

"I gave up Candi for good."

"Resurrect her for just a little while."

"Name me one good reason I should do this."

"I'll name you five," Mark said. He held up his fingers and began ticking them off. "For Stephanie. For Steve. For Kate. For Just Peachy. For Apple Blossom."

By her count he left off a very important one. *For Mark.* "We have no way of knowing that bringing Candi back is going to help at all. And I'm not a spy."

"Doing nothing certainly isn't going to help," Mark said. "And you don't have to be a spy. I'll coach you through what you should do."

"Is there any danger in this?" Steve asked. "Because if there is, we'll find another way."

"No danger whatsoever. We're going to have her waiting to follow Jimmy after work to the pizza place. She'll just go in and dazzle him. That's it."

"Are you sure?" Kate asked.

Leah was at least gratified that Steve and Kate were worried about her welfare. Apparently Mark wasn't so concerned.

Then again, Mark was the pro. She had to believe that he was certain this wasn't dangerous. She had to believe that he cared at least that much.

"But that Pump You Up," she moaned. "It's torture."

255

"I'll make it up to you, sis," said Steve.

Okay, if she was going to be tortured, she was milking it. "How?"

"Well, we'll pay you, for one," Kate said.

"There isn't enough money to make me willingly put on that contraption again."

The three others looked at each other, apparently at a loss. She almost felt sorry for them. Everything she held dear she pretty much already had, or was well on her way to working toward.

"Free Apple Blossom products for life?" Kate said.

"Ditto for Just Peachy," Steve said, which was a joke, because he already gave her those. In fact, she was often his guinea pig when his company was about to introduce a new product.

She shook her head. "On one condition, and only one condition."

"Name it," they all said in unison.

"You!" She pointed at Steve. "And you!" She pointed at Kate, "agree that you will talk up Mark's security company to every corporate bigwig you know."

"Done," said Steve.

"Done," said Kate.

Mark just stood there staring at her.

She ignored him. "I mean it, you two. I want to see results. Between the two of you, you know every head honcho in town and in the industry. I want it to be known that if they don't have a Colson security system, they're idiots. I want it to be known that your companies banded together to wipe out a corporate espionage scheme, and Mark got it done for you. Got it?"

Kate smiled at her. "I'll do you one better. At our next national convention, I promise to hold a workshop on how banding together makes companies—and the industry—stronger. And just how Stephanie"—she got a bit of a distasteful look on her face—"and Steve and I benefited from using a company like Mark's."

"I want his company name-dropped at least five times during the workshop."

"Easily."

"I'll do the workshop with you," Steve said.

"As long as it's you and not Stephanie," Kate retorted.

"Done."

Leah stared hard between the two of them. "You'd better deliver."

"We will."

Suddenly they all remembered Mark was still in the room.

Leah looked up and saw the expression on his face, and wasn't sure if he was angry or in a coma.

"Good God," Steve said, "you've rendered the man speechless."

Leah was feeling saucy, but also a little worried that she'd really ticked him off. So she decided a dramatic but quick exit was her best bet. "Excuse me while I go bra shopping," she said, jumping up and heading toward the door, feeling it prudent to get the heck out of there.

"What happened to the bras you already have?" Kate asked, as Leah turned the knob.

"I burned them."

The meeting was far from over, but Mark finally found his tongue. "Excuse me," he said to Kate and Steve. "I'll be right back."

"Take your time," Kate called as he strode after Leah.

He caught her at the elevator doors, jabbing the buttons and looking over her shoulder as if she feared the devil was after her.

When she spied him approaching, she offered him a weak don't-hurt-me smile.

Right as he took her arm, the door opened, and a messenger stood gazing at them a little warily.

"You looking for this floor?" Mark said.

"Yes." He glanced down at the package in his hands. "Steve Smith's office?"

"Then go ahead. Down the hall and to the left."

The kid scrambled, and Mark dragged Leah into the elevator. She looked around, apparently to see if she could locate the monitor so she could cry for help if she needed it.

He grabbed both her arms and turned her to face him. "Why did you do that?" he asked.

"I . . . couldn't think of anything else?" she squeaked out.

"Leah, you could have asked for anything."

She pulled away, crossed her arms, and shot him a belligerent look. "That's what I wanted. I'm sorry if you don't like it, but—"

He shut her up with a hard kiss. He didn't stop until he felt her body soften and melt into his. Then he broke the lip-lock, albeit reluctantly. "That was the nicest thing anyone's ever done for me," he said, and it wasn't a lie. He'd had partners in law enforcement who watched his back, and on too many occasions saved his life. But that was their job. His family had always been good to him, but that was their job, too. This was so different as to almost be alien.

"I wasn't being nice."

"No? What were you being?"

"I was thinking that if you start getting millions of clients, you can afford to make someone else put on that damn bra."

"Okay, the receiver is on the right side; the microphone is on the left."

Leah couldn't believe Mark was fastening things inside her bra. She couldn't believe she was doing this at all. "Are you sure this is going to work?"

"Not at all. But it's worth a shot."

"I don't know if I can pull this off, Mark. You yourself said I stink at the bimbo business."

"Trust me, Jimmy believed because he wanted to believe."

"But I don't know how to do what you do."

"I gave you a loose script. You don't have to follow it verbatim. Just improvise and have fun."

"Have fun? Are you out of your mind?"

"Yep. Over you. Now listen, we're going to be right outside, or be following wherever you go. You are not in any danger whatsoever. Just say the word, and we'll be there."

"What's the word?"

"Whatever you want it to be. Name it."

Leah thought about that. "How about *Titanic?*"

He laughed. "Okay. Why *Titanic?*"

"Because I have the feeling I'm going to sink."

Leah had to don the Candi getup for three days before security signaled that Jimmy had taken the bait they'd planted. Mark kissed her and said, "Go get 'em, slugger."

She waited until Jimmy had pedaled down the road out of sight before hopping into her car and zooming past him to get to the pizza place before he showed up. She kept running the lines she was supposed to say through her mind, certain she was going to screw this up.

In her ear she heard Mark say, "Can you hear me?"

"So far so good," she said. "But I forget which boob is which."

"You'll be transmitting from the left, hearing us from the right."

"Right, hear; left, laugh," she said, just to try to find something to keep them straight.

She reached the pizza place and sat down. The waiter came over and stared at her breasts. Great. She was hating this already.

"Can I get you something?"

"No, thanks, I'm waiting for my . . . girlfriend."

About ten minutes later Jimmy walked through the door. He had a knapsack slung over his shoulder. He also didn't see her.

She jumped up. "Jimmy, is that you?" she squealed. "Long time, no see!"

He turned, and the look on his face would have been priceless if it didn't kind of give her the willies. The kid couldn't be older than twenty.

"Miss Devereaux!" he said, heading straight for her. "It's so good to see you again."

Left, laugh. She grabbed his arm so her left breast was closest to him. "How are you, sugar?"

"Just fine. But we sure do miss you at the office."

"Isn't that sweet of you to say, you silly thing," she simpered, and had to keep herself from gritting her teeth when she heard a deep chuckle in her ear. "I sure miss y'all, too. Especially you, you cute thing."

The boy blushed right down to his throat, which almost made her feel bad for him. "Do you work here, too?" she asked.

"Yes. For extra money. I deliver," he said, and then winked at her. Suddenly she didn't feel so bad for the kid.

"I have *always* wanted to know how that works," she heard in her ear.

"That is so cool, because I've always wanted to know how that works. I'm thinking of applying."

Jimmy glanced around, then turned back to her. "If you want, I'll take you around tonight. It's not supposed to be allowed—you know, insurance—but I'd be happy to show you the ropes."

"That would be super!"

"Let me clock in and I'll be back and let you know what to do."

"You are just the cutest!"

Still more laughter in her ear.

Jimmy disappeared and she leaned down toward her left breast. "I'm going to kill you."

"I'm sorry. Okay, go on his rounds with him. See if he drops anything more than pizza anywhere."

"Will you be following us?"

"I told you we would."

"Well, you'd better," she said. "I've already got the creeps."

"We'll be right behind you."

"You'd better be," she whispered. "Otherwise I'm suing for inflammation of character."

Mark's laughter filled her ear, and she was torn between irritation and pleasure at the sound of his deep chuckle. No one's laugh should be that sexy. Especially when he was laughing at her.

"You owe me," she said.

"What?" Jimmy said beside her, looking at her strangely. Probably because she was talking directly into her left breast.

"I said my favorite pizza is pepperoni."

The laughter in her ear could possibly cause damage. Oh, Mark was in trouble.

"Well, I have my first five deliveries," Jimmy said. "I

bet I could filch us a couple of slices of pepperoni for the ride."

She wanted pizza right now about as much as she wanted to get in the car with the thieving little twerp. "That would be great!"

"So here's what you do," Jimmy said, bending lower.

Leah tried to surreptitiously thrust out her left breast in his direction so he came in loud and clear.

"The car is in back," Jimmy continued. "Go on out to the side and I'll pick you up. No windows on that side for anyone here to see you."

Leah smiled and wiggled out of her booth and headed out the door. "Lecherous little demon," she said.

"Sounds like he's done this before," Mark remarked.

"You'd better not lose me, because I've got the creeps."

"We're with you, honey. I'm not letting anything happen to you."

"Why me? Doesn't the police department have undercover females who are good at these things?"

"He knows you. Instant familiarity."

"You owe me," she said again.

"I know, pepperoni. I'll buy you lots of it."

"Buy it in those long casings so I can thwap you with one."

"You're doing great. Just remem—"

"He's coming; don't distract me."

Leah slid her bottom into the cheap, smelly car and pretended to be fascinated. "Where are we going?"

"All of these are deliveries to Falls Church. They try to give us sections of town. I always take Falls Church. Less traffic."

"Oh, how smart of them."

Jimmy made four deliveries that seemed routine enough to her. But what the hell did she know? He talked about each tip and tipper, griping sometimes, elated once.

"Does this make you much extra cash?" Leah asked after the fourth delivery.

"Yes. I make really good money," he boasted.

"How?"

"I know the right deliveries to make," he said.

"Special pizzas?"

"That, and other things." He looked over at her, smiled, then laid a hand on her leg that would have her washing it off for a week. "I make good money in lots of ways."

"Do you make that much money at Just Peachy? Because I sure didn't make enough to keep me in lipstick."

"I make a lot there," he said.

He was either boasting to impress her, or referring to something else, because she knew for a fact that all interns made minimum wage.

"You're that good?" she asked, going for wide-eyed and impressed.

"I know how to turn a profit. I could take you out on the town."

Over my dead body.

"Over my dead body," she heard Mark mutter in her ear.

She smiled.

"You'd like that?" Jimmy asked.

"That would be so cool!" She was running out of expletives.

"We have one more to go; then I want to show you something before we head back for more delivery orders."

"Excellent!"

They drove into the heart of Falls Church, and Jimmy pulled up to a very upscale town-house complex. "I'll be right back, Candi," he said, obviously feeling they'd moved into first-name familiarity.

Leah was so rattled, she forgot which boob she should be talking to. So she split it down the middle. "He took his backpack with him this time."

"Where are you?"

"On a pretty side street. I'm sorry I didn't get the name. But we're right across the street from tennis courts, and what looks like a government building. Police station or something."

"Can you get a street number, at least?"

"It looks like two-eleven." She took a breath.

"Bingo. Two-eleven Park is Harvey's address."

"Are you nearby? Because he's planning on showing me something I'm not sure I want to see."

"We're about a half mile away. Don't worry, honey; we have your back."

"Just make certain you have my front and all points in between. I'm creeped out, Mark."

"Nothing will happen to you. I promise."

"This is the first time he went inside," she reported. "The last few stops, he never made it past the porch."

"Gotcha. We're almost home."

Leah tried to get her breathing under control while she watched Jimmy approach a few minutes later. He was grinning.

When he got into the car she said, "You look happy."

The idiot waved a twenty at her, obviously to impress her. Cheating paid well, apparently. Even for morons.

"Wow!" she said, all breathy. "That was some big tip!"

"This a relative of mine. I make sure he gets extra cheese, if you get my drift."

She got his drift, all right. The boy was cheating her brother. She wanted to strangle him.

"I think I'd like doing this job," she said, "if it pays this well."

"You probably can't expect this much money," he warned her. "Unless you think you could get your job back at Just Peachy. Then we could do some serious business."

Murder was too good for him.

The last destination scared the spit out of Leah. The boy was steering them out to some solitary place in Great Falls. He drove them down a dead-end street and parked.

"What are we doing here?" she asked, having a hard time keeping up her high-pitched bimbo voice.

"I thought you'd like to give me a thank-you kiss for all of the advice."

"You know," Leah said, talking to her right boob, "you remind me of that guy in the *Titanic*. It's like you're the king of the world."

He tried to grab for her, but she shoved open her door and flew out. Talking to her left boob, just in case the right one was the wrong one, she said, "This even reminds me of the *Titanic!*"

"Come here, sweetheart," said the little creep. "One kiss."

He caught her before she could get ten feet away. "You know you want this too."

"Want this?"

He tried to grab at her breast, which was bad for many reasons. She pulled away and said, "I don't know what you mean. And I'm not that kind of girl."

"Of course you are."

She was going into a new career, and it wasn't as an undercover bimbo. "I'm not."

"I'll teach you."

"As much as I'd love that lesson, you're a little young to know much. Call me in a decade or so."

"Just show me a little skin. And I'll show you what I can do with it."

Leah was boggled that this young kid was such a disgusting lech. She tried to wiggle around as much as she could to keep his hands from connecting with what weren't her breasts. And to possibly mess with her lifeline. "You know, you even remind me of Leonardo DiCaprio from the *Titanic*, dammit!" she almost screamed at her chest. "So suave and herolike."

If blaring sirens and lights hadn't blasted them right then, Leah feared she'd have had a serious panic attack. The boy was sick.

But just in time a police car pulled up, and a big, burly guy she didn't recognize lumbered out with a flashlight that could light up Manhattan in a pinch.

"Ma'am?"

"Yes?" she breathed, wanting to rush into the guy's arms.

"Are you Candi Devereaux?"

"Who's asking?" she said, because she thought sounding tough might be a good idea.

"I'm the Maytag Repair Man," the guy said. "I hear your washer's broken. Are you Ms. Devereaux or not?"

Time to get out of here. "Have you ever seen *the Titanic*?"

"He's a cop," Jimmy said, rather irrelevantly.

"The captain and I are on a first name basis," her rescuer said.

"Yes, I am Candi Devereaux."

"Well, then, ma'am, you'll have to come with me."

"Why is that?" Jimmy asked.

"She's wanted."

"Wanted?" she and Jimmy said at the same time.

"Yes, for solicitation."

"Solicitation?" Jimmy said.

"Yes, sir. I'm afraid she's a lady of the evening."

"Excuse me?" Leah said.

"She's a prostitute."

"I might never speak to any of you again," Leah said.

"You got us what we needed," Steve reminded her.

"I'm out of the spy business for good."

"Yes, you are," Mark said, looking grim. "I didn't think the kid would go that far."

Leah studied Mark's face, and realization hit her. He was going to blame himself for this forever. It didn't matter if he liked or hated her; he was going to feel like he'd failed her. And the guilt would eat him alive.

That wasn't going to happen on her watch.

She looked at Kate and Steve and said, "Get out."

Steve said, "Excuse me?"

"You heard me. Get the hell out of here, now."

"Leah, this is my off—"

"Get out. Now."

Steve looked at Kate. "Feel like a doughnut from the lunchroom?"

"Sounds good to me," Kate said, as she nearly jumped out of her chair.

"Close the door behind you," Leah demanded.

The door closed with undue haste.

Leah waited a few seconds, looking at the agony on Mark's face, and her heart broke. "I complained too much," she said softly.

He shook his head, still staring at something on Steve's desk. "I can't believe I asked you to do that."

"You promised you'd be at my back, and you were."

"You could have been—"

She didn't like thinking about could-have-beens either. "I wasn't, Mark. I'm here; I'm whole; I'm fine."

"Leah, I—"

". . . don't want to talk about it. I know. You'll just eat yourself alive with guilt. Well, I'm sick of it. You weren't responsible for what happened to Jake and LeAnne. You aren't responsible for what that little pervert did. No one could have foreseen that the pimply little bashful kid was a lech."

"I should have."

Leah took a deep breath. "Let me ask you this."

He finally looked up, and the agony in his eyes just about laid her low. "What?"

"Do you think Steve would have let me go out there tonight if he'd have foreseen this?"

"Of course not."

"Guess what, brainiac? Steve was all for this plan."

"He didn't know any better."

"None of us did. And guess what again? Steve and Kate, who signed off on this, are not out there eating themselves up over it. They're just grateful you and your men were there. And so am I.

"And I'll tell you one other thing, and then you let this go or I'll kick your butt. If you asked me to do it again right now, I would. As long as I knew you were sitting on the other end of my lifeline."

He finally showed a ghost of a smile. "I don't deserve you."

"That's true. I'm a pretty damn good spy."

He laughed, then pulled her to her feet. "I'll concede the Putt-Putt issue, but honey, you suck at being a bimbo and you suck at being a spy."

"You flatterer, you."

* * *

It took over a month for the police to get all of their ducks in a row. Although everything caught on tape from Leah's foray into spying was inadmissible as evidence, they had gathered valuable information by keeping surveillance on the house where Leah had seen Jimmy receive the envelope of money—information that the police hoped would eventually help to make an airtight case against Jimmy and Harvey. And then the wait began for Harvey Murphy to make his move. Finally, it happened. One Tuesday morning in a development meeting, Harvey proposed a new antiaging cream, claiming he'd just invented the next best thing to face-lifts.

The waiting had taken its toll on Kate, who desperately wanted this to be the answer to the mystery, and for her to be able to clear her name and the company's reputation.

She knew Steve believed her, and she adored him for it. Still, it was human nature, in her opinion, for someone falsely accused to want to be able to throw proof in the accuser's face that she was utterly innocent.

Fortunately or unfortunately, Stephanie Smith had been almost nonexistent the last six weeks or so. Kate had to wonder what the woman was up to. Both Steve and Leah had been strangely reticent about the whole thing.

Kate called Steve after the meeting was over, and when he answered she said, "We've got him."

"Are you serious?"

"I have his proposal and his notes in my hot little hands."

"Okay, I'll call Colson, and he'll pull in the cops. Let's meet this afternoon."

"On one condition," she said. "I want Stephanie there this time."

"We can't do that, Kate."

"Why not?"

"She's not in town."

"Where the hell is she, Steve?"

"I can't tell you that."

"Is she in detox somewhere or something?"

"I can't tell you."

"No Stephanie, no proof."

"Kate, be reasonable. We need to move on this now."

"No. She's been accusing me from day one. I want to see her face when I hand her this file."

He paused. "I'll see what I can do. But it won't be until tomorrow."

"Fine."

"This is a mistake, Kate."

"Why?"

"Because Stephanie is a figurehead. I'm the one who runs this company."

"Find her and get her in there." And she hung up.

She locked the file in her floor safe, then sat back. She was missing something here. What was it?

Were Steve and Stephanie at odds of sorts? Was he trying to take the company away from his sister? Lord knew they didn't spend much twin buddy time together. In fact, she'd never once seen them in the same room. It was either one or the other, like a tag team. Or was it—

"Oh, my God," she whispered, as a ton of bricks slammed into her head.

She sat back a minute, just to make certain she wasn't losing her mind. Had she *ever* seen the two together? She racked her brain, praying to remember at least one instance when she had been in the same room with the two of them.

She couldn't recall a single one. Steve and Leah, yes. Stephanie and Leah, yes. Steve and Stephanie, no.

Her face heated up as she thought about the times she'd been around Stephanie, and no matter how aggravating the woman had been, she'd come away oddly stimulated.

She almost gagged, remembering her conversation with Leah, confiding that she was a little concerned about her strange attraction to Leah's sister.

And Leah's reaction? She'd asked if maybe Kate was attracted to Stephanie because she looked so much like Steve.

She thought back to all the times that either Steve or Leah or both had made excuses for why Stephanie was absent.

And worst of all, she thought of all of the nights she and Steve had spent together, watching movies, making love, talking. And all of that time, he'd kept up the lie.

Their entire relationship was a farce. Had he sweet-talked her into bed for a different purpose altogether? It hurt like hell to believe it, but she'd be a fool not to. She hadn't gotten as far as she had by turning a blind eye to lousy news. And this was as lousy as it got.

She felt used. She'd fallen for Steve so fast and hard that she hadn't stepped back to assess the situation. She'd blindly believed his words and his gentle touch.

Oh, God, if she was right, she'd never feel that gentle touch again.

Kate breathed in deeply. She couldn't think about the losses. She had to keep the anger flowing.

He'd used her. He'd used her. He'd used her.

Worse, she'd allowed herself to be used.

There, that thought worked. She was furious at herself for being so stupid. Now to confront the man who'd duped her.

With a vengeance she unlocked the safe and snatched out the files, slamming them into her briefcase. She stalked out of her office, toward her secretary, who looked startled.

"I'm going out," she said.

"But your three-o'clock—"

"Cancel it."

"You bastard," Kate said as she stormed into Steve's office, nearly knocking over his secretary along the way.

"Mr. Smith, I tried, but—"

"It's okay," he said, standing. "Close the door behind you, please."

He waved Kate into a chair, but she stood stubbornly still. "What's wrong, Kate?"

"You're Stephanie."

"What?"

"You heard me, you creep. Go ahead; try to deny it."

A flush crept up his face. "Kate, listen."

"You are, aren't you?"

"There are reasons I had to do it."

"Oh, my God, you are."

She began pacing. "All this time. How stupid could I be?"

"You weren't stupid, Kate. No one knows it, not even anyone in this office."

"Have you been sleeping with anyone in this office?" she asked sarcastically.

"Of course not."

"You lied to me. You made a fool of me."

"No! I never meant to do anything like that. The Stephanie thing had nothing to do with you."

"It had everything to do with me when you used her as your excuse to accuse me of stealing from you."

"It wasn't like that."

"It was exactly like that. Here you sat pretending to be the conciliatory underling, apologizing for her every step of the way, then turning around and making my life hell under her disguise."

"Look, let me come over later and I'll explain everything."

"That'll be the day. Don't you come within a mile of me ever again."

"Don't do this, Kate. Hear me out."

"I hope I never hear your voice again as long as I live."

"Kate, I love you."

Her laughter was embarrassingly hysterical. "Right. Funny way of showing it, you jerk."

If she didn't leave, she was going to burst into tears, and there was no way she'd give him that satisfaction. She dug through her briefcase and pulled out the file. "There's your proof, you idiot. Do what you will with it. But from now on, I talk only to Mark Colson about this case."

He started to walk around the desk.

"No! You come near me and I'll scream my bloody head off." An involuntary sob slipped through. She nodded at the file. "You've got what you wanted from me. Now leave me alone."

"Kate—"

She headed toward the door. Right before she flung it open she said, "You know, Steve, you make an ugly woman. And right now you make an even uglier man. It turns out you're a pretty ugly human being."

"Kate, it's Leah. Please call me. I know you're hurt, but you have to understand all this before you judge Steve so harshly. He had reasons, good reasons why he couldn't tell *anyone* about this."

Kate sat on the couch in her darkened living room, clutching a pillow to her chest, listening to about the tenth message from Steve and Leah. She didn't want to hear it. Nothing could justify his deception. Nothing. And she wanted to lick her wounds in private.

"I'm sorry, I'm sorry," Gabby squawked.

"Thank you, Gabby," she whispered. "Me too."

God, what a fool. She'd fallen for all of Steve's bull, hook, line, and sinker.

"Kate, I'm your friend," Leah said. "I hope you know that. I've hated that we haven't been able to tell you."

Her friend? That was the last straw. She snatched up the phone. "Leah, listen to me and listen good. You aren't my friend. You're as much of a fraud as he is. Do you people get your jollies making everyone look like fools? Don't ever, ever call here again."

"Kate, Steve loves you. And I . . . I truly value our friendship."

"You know, it takes a lot of nerve to say that. Last I looked it up, part of the definition of friendship included honesty."

"Okay, don't forgive me. But please give Steve a chance."

"You know, it just occurred to me: He's such a coward that he lets his fake sister and his real sister do his talking for him."

"He has no idea I've been calling you."

"Right."

"Kate, he called me at home and told me what happened. I almost didn't recognize his voice. He's out of his mind over this."

"You know, Leah, right now I don't give a damn. Good-bye."

"Wait!" was the last thing she heard before she hung up.

"I have to tell Mark, Steve. Kate's going to tell him eventually, and I don't want him hearing it from her."

Her heart broke for her brother as he sat on their couch, bent over, head in his hands.

"Go ahead," he said. "It doesn't matter any longer."

"It does to the company."

"I'm calling a meeting tomorrow and announcing it."

"You can't do that! It's too soon! What if your backer calls in the final note?"

"It'll be a blow, but not a final blow. Today was a final blow."

"Oh, honey, I'm so sorry."

"I know. Go find Mark, Leah. I don't want him hearing it from Kate either."

"Give her time. She'll come to understand."

"No, she won't. I broke a trust."

"You did what you had to do."

"As soon as things started getting personal with us, I should have told her. At least then she could have made an informed choice. As it was, our relationship happened so fast, and I was too afraid of losing her. I deserve this. I deserve how she feels about me."

"You listen to me. You have the biggest heart of any man I've ever known. You pulled off this Stephanie gig far longer than anyone should have to because you were looking out for Gramps and me and Just Peachy and its employees. You would never intentionally hurt anyone. Kate will realize it eventually. Just give her time to simmer down, and time to remember how she feels about you deep inside."

He shook his head. "Go to Mark, Leah. Salvage that, at least."

"What's wrong, Leah?" Mark asked. "You call me in the middle of a meeting, tell me it's an emergency and to meet you at my house, and now you're pacing my carpet bare. Talk already!"

"I want you to understand something."

"Well, if you want me to memorize your walk, I've got that one down. Otherwise, say something."

She stopped and faced him. "Several years ago my brother tried to get financing for a new business."

"Okay."

"He was turned down."

"Okay."

"Because he was a young man."

"It's a hard sell in his business."

"But someone called a . . . a . . . venture something, approached him and said he'd be willing to put up the money if Steve could get a woman to front for him as head of the company."

"Why would that matter?"

"Who knows? I know nothing about business."

Mark sat there for a second. "Okay, I'm starting to get it. So he enlisted Stephanie's help. She's merely a figurehead. No wonder Steve does all the work."

"Not exactly."

"What then?"

"Steve isn't a twin, Mark."

"Then who's . . . Ohhhhhhhhhhh. You're kidding, right?"

She shook her head. "He made her up. He didn't want some other woman acting as the head of the company and then somehow coming back and trying to actually take it over." She waved. "Steve didn't want to take any chances with the business."

"Are you saying . . . Steve has been playing Stephanie all of these years?"

She nodded, mute. Her eyes were so distressed, Mark wanted to pull her into his arms. But there was more to this. "Okay, so he fooled us all. Good for him. It worked."

She stared at him. "You're not mad?"

"I'm mad at myself for not catching on."

"I have a theory that people see what they are told to expect."

"I saw through you. I saw through Kate."

"What can I say? We're bad at this."

It was like he didn't hear her. "I'm irritated that he didn't confide in me. I should have known the complete story so I could give him the best advice possible. But mad that he did what he had to do to achieve his goals? No, I'm not mad at him."

Unfortunately, that was something of a lie. He felt a slight bite of betrayal. Nothing nearly as hard-hitting as when he and Jake learned their boss had set them up, then tried to kill them. That was a little more extreme, and it had knotted his gut. Not like Heather's betrayal, because even after what she'd done, he was devastated more for their child. This kind hurt in a different way. It had settled in his chest.

"Are you mad at *me?*"

"A little."

She ran around the coffee table and sat down, grabbing his hand. "I wasn't trying to deceive you, Mark. I swear. It was just . . . He's my brother. And the company means so much to him."

"From what he told me, Just Peachy has been turning a profit for a while now. Much sooner than expected, and that's even with reinvesting in expansion. Why'd he keep it up?"

"He wanted it to stay that way until he had the loan paid down. Then he was going to announce that Stephanie was retiring and he'd be the new CEO. It would be a smooth transition. No one would panic because he's been running the company so long anyway." She grabbed a shaky breath. "And he was so close. And

277

then all of this stuff happened with Apple Blossom, and that set him back a little be-cause he was determined to figure out how his competitor was getting hold of his company's innovations."

Mark sat there for a while, chewing on it. He finally looked into her worried eyes and laughed, more at himself than the situation. "Looking back on it, it all makes sense. You know, he's a really unappealing woman."

Leah tried to smile, but it wasn't ready to work its way into full-blown humor, by the looks of her.

"And I could never get the two of them together. It was one or the other. How stupid was I?"

"He wasn't playing you for a fool. I swear."

"No, that's not Steve's style."

But truth didn't seem to be in Steve's style either. Or Leah's, right now. And here was the woman he would have sworn would tell him anything he asked her. But for weeks now she'd been keeping up this ruse with him. Perpetuating it, even. She'd also lied about her relationship to Steve. He'd found out by a slip of the tongue that they were brother and sister.

Then there was Steve allowing him to pursue Leah as a suspect, when he knew damn well it was a dead end. And there was Leah, who'd wasted his time by putting on that show with Kate dressed as a man, and making him wonder if she wasn't the one infiltrating Just Peachy.

Mark shook his head, trying to equate the Leah he knew so intimately, who talked openly about herself, to the one who made excuses for Stephanie's absences at any given moment.

"He truly respects you and your work," she said, slicing into his darkening thoughts.

278

"He'd have canceled my services long ago if he weren't happy. I'm not sure that equates to respecting me."

She collapsed back on the couch. "So you are angry."

He looked for a word that worked better. He couldn't find one, because he wasn't certain what he was feeling right now.

"Don't give him grief."

Mark barked a laugh. "Trust me, I'm not letting him off easy. He did leave out some key things that might have helped us a long time ago."

"Mark?"

"Yes?"

"Please, he's going through a lot."

"Such as?"

"Kate found out."

He whistled. "Steve finally told her?"

"No, she figured it out."

"Ah, damn. I bet she didn't take it well." *How am I taking it?* He didn't have an answer. He needed to think.

"World-record understatement." She looked down. "She hates me, too."

"Nobody could hate you."

"Pencil her in as number one."

"I wish I could help."

"It's going to get worse. Steve's making the announcement tomorrow to his employees."

"Tell him to stick to the 'Stephanie's retiring' story."

"Are you kidding? How fast do you think Kate would unveil him, so to speak?"

"She doesn't seem like the vindictive type."

"I hope not. But Steve wants to bare his soul, I guess."

"So, Miss Leah, bare your soul to me."

"What do you mean?"

279

"How many more family and personal secrets are you hiding?" He'd been teasing, but he knew instantly what a huge mistake he'd just made.

Her face turned beet red and she jumped from the couch. "How dare you say that?"

He held up his hands. "I was just kidding." But he realized with sudden clarity that that wasn't entirely true. This news wasn't digesting well.

She stared at him, then shook her head. "No, you weren't."

"Maybe not. I don't know. What are you expecting me to say? 'No problem, Leah. Let's go make love and forget the whole thing.'"

"No, I realize you have to sort it out. I'm just hoping that once you do, you realize it was utterly innocent."

"It's personal fraud."

She sucked in a hard breath. "That's low."

"So's lying."

"Oh, and you, Mr. Spy Guy, have always told the lily-white truth."

"That's different. It wasn't personal; it was professional."

"What Steve did was for professional reasons, too."

"Steve, right. That I semiunderstand."

"But not me, right? And now you believe that you can't believe a thing I say."

As reasonable as you seemed to be about the situation, you just extrapolated."

"Is that a big sociology term?" Well, that came out sounding sarcastic.

"Look it up." That came out even more sarcastic.

Then he decided to become defensively dumb. He resented her dishonesty more than he'd first realized. And it was building out of control. "You have to admit, there's a pattern here."

"For totally different purposes!"

He needed time to think. And he wasn't thinking right now. "I was teasing. Forget I said it."

"I don't think so. And right now would not be a good time to keep this conversation going. I did what I thought was right, which was making certain you learned it all from me first."

"I appreciate that. Leah, your nerves are raw and my nerves are raw and you just clunked me over the head with a hammer. Let's just forget it and watch cartoons or something."

"Good night, Mark."

How did this turn so bad so quickly? He thought he'd been acting fairly reasonably, considering she'd been keeping secrets from him for a long time. "Running away, Leah?"

"Getting fresh air. It's becoming stale in here."

He stood up. The haze finally blew. "How dare you throw this in my face as if it's my fault? Or Kate's, for being angry? As far as I can tell, out of all of us, Kate and I are the only two who have been completely honest."

"Then you and Kate are perfect for each other."

Panic seized him. "Leah, wait. I didn't mean that."

"Yes, you did," she said, her voice quavering as she almost sprinted to his front door. Right before she turned the knob, she said, "Just don't forget that you have secrets you haven't shared either. I figured you would talk to me when you could."

"It's not the same thing."

"Isn't it? I wouldn't know."

The next month was a whirlwind. Mark was running frazzled between Just Peachy and Apple Blossom. He was flying back and forth between DC and Richmond finalizing plans for Jake's incorporation into the company, and the opening of his new branch office. And then there was coordinating with law enforcement to build an airtight case against Harvey Murphy and his nephew, Jimmy Slater.

Mark considered it a blessing. He was busy—too busy to think about Leah. Except he couldn't stop thinking about her.

He wondered constantly how she was doing, how she was feeling, and then in tiny fits of trying put things into perspective, who she was playing this week.

He entered Kate's office, noting right away that she looked like hell. Well, as bad as a beautiful woman could look. He had to wonder if Leah was also suffering. He was pretty sure he wouldn't take home any beauty prizes at the moment, either. And he'd swear Steve Smith had dropped at least twenty pounds in the last weeks.

"Hello, Mark," Kate said. "Have a seat."

He sat. "Kate, the police are picking Harvey and his nephew up this afternoon."

"And then?"

"And then they interview them, and with any luck, get solid confessions about who, what, where, and how."

"Are we allowed to listen in?"

"Not down at the station. But after we pick them up, the first stop is Steve's office. He wants to face them first."

"Well, I want to face them, too. Bring them here afterward."

"Do I look like an errand boy? If you want to sit in on it, come to Steve's office."

"I can't," she whispered.

He sighed. "I understand that. We both were tricked, lied to. But the more I mull this over, the more I absolutely know that Leah and Steve don't have intentionally hurtful bones in their bodies."

"Could have fooled me."

"I know. I feel betrayed, too. And trust me, I have big issues with betrayal. But is it better to be miserable or try to clear the air?"

"I can't look at him."

"Did you hear he made the announcement to his employees?"

"What lie did he come up with?"

"He didn't. He laid it all out on the line."

Her eyebrows shot up. "He did? How'd his employees take it?"

"They listened better than you or I did. And in the end, they gave him a standing ovation."

"They did?"

"Yes, ma'am. Apparently they weren't all that crazy about Stephanie, either."

Amazingly, Kate chuckled, and for the first time in a month he saw a twinkle come into her eyes. "I thought they'd throw tomatoes at him."

"No, that's just what you and I wanted to do."

"Did he get any major resignations?"

"Not a one. He was pretty amazed himself." Mark gave Kate a hard look. "I think it's time you faced him again, Kate. You can't avoid him forever."

"I can try."

"Look, you don't have to forgive him. But have the guts to tell him to his face that whatever you had is over for good."

"I think he pretty much knows that," she said softly. "I know I do. And it hurts."

Mark was a little taken aback by that admission. He countered it with one of his own: "I miss Leah."

"Well, then, why aren't you taking your own advice?"

"I've been busy."

"Coward."

"Look who's calling the bonfire hot."

He stood and, as usual, he felt bone-weary. "Well, I'm heading over there now."

She chewed on her lower lip. "I'm coming with you."

On the drive over to Just Peachy, one thought kept running through Mark's mind: What was Leah doing?

Did she miss him at all? Did she think about him? She'd seemed to really care about him, but she certainly hadn't tried to contact him. He hated to think about it, but a plausible conclusion was that he'd just been a sexual pastime to her. He'd been doing that for years with women. He couldn't make much of a case for it to be a sin for her to feel the same way.

But it hurt. The first woman he'd cared about since Heather, and it had ended badly, too. What was wrong with him?

For some reason, he was disappointed Leah wasn't in Steve's office when they arrived. He didn't know why he'd expected to see her there. He knew that if Steve had even asked her to attend she'd say no, because Mark would be there. Which made it even more painful.

Steve was poring over some notes, so without looking up, he waved a hand at a guest chair. "One second."

Kate said, "I don't have all day."

Steve froze, then looked up slowly, his jaw almost slack. Then he pushed to his feet, and his eyes shuttered. "Kate."

"I asked her to be here," Mark said. "I don't have all day, either."

"I guess that's reasonable," Steve said. "Something to drink for either of you?"

They both shook their heads.

Steve dropped back down into his chair. "The two culprits should be here in about five minutes."

Five minutes was a little too long for Mark to hang out in a very tense atmosphere. He stood up. "Men's room. Back shortly."

Still without meeting her gaze, Steve said, "So how have you been, Kate?"

"Better than you, apparently."

He ran a hand through his hair. "I know. Leah tells me every day I look pretty bad."

"That's not what I was talking about."

"What, then?"

"I heard about your announcement to your company. That must have been hard."

"Not the most fun speech I've had to deliver, but I'm just glad it's over."

"So no more heels for you, hmm?"

"No, thank God."

"Well, congratulations."

"Thanks."

Just seeing him had her heart pounding. The overwhelming desire to smooth the worry lines from his face and kiss his grim lips nearly had her crying. "Steve, look at me."

He finally dragged his gaze up to meet hers. "I can't take any more recriminations right now, Kate. I just can't."

"No more recriminations. Although I can't say I'm thrilled by all of this, I've come to understand why you did it." And she realized that she did. And that if she didn't get past this, she'd lose him for good. How stupid would that be, when she was utterly miserable right now?

He took a noisy breath. "I never meant to hurt you. Never. How was I supposed to know I'd fall in love with you?"

Those words sang straight through her. "And you believed me about the espionage thing. That meant a lot."

"And now you can never believe me again."

"Try me."

He stared at her. "Believe this. I've missed the hell out of you."

"Were you telling the truth when you said you really liked my enchiladas?" she asked.

"Scout's honor."

"How about tonight?"

"Oh, God, Kate. I don't know if I deserve this second chance, but I swear I won't blow it this time."

"I'm counting on it."

Chapter Twenty-one

"Why'd you do it, Harvey?" Kate asked quietly.

The little man held his hat in his hands, staring down at his lap. "I never meant to hurt anyone."

"Then why?"

"I needed the money."

"For what?"

He waved at his nephew, who didn't appear ashamed at all. Just belligerent. "The boy here needed tuition for school."

"Ever heard of student loans?"

"I didn't want him to start out life deep in debt."

"So as an example," Mark said, "you taught him how to be a felon instead."

"It was dumb, I know." He raised pleading eyes to Kate. "I was afraid of losing my job if I didn't come up with some good product. But with the bonuses you give when one of our new items goes into production, I just needed some help."

"By stealing from us," Steve said grimly.

"You have some good developers here."

"Thanks for the ringing endorsement."

"It'll never happen again."

"You bet it won't, Harvey," Kate said. "Because you're going to jail."

"Please don't press charges against the boy. He's just starting out."

"Not in a good direction," Steve said. "He nearly tried to assault my sister."

"Your sister?" Jimmy said. "Candi's your sister?"

"Um, yes."

"You know she's a hoo . . . umm, a, you know."

"No, she's not."

"But, I saw her get arrested."

"You saw her being rescued, you twerp. You're lucky I didn't have you arrested for that."

Harvey goggled at his nephew. "Is this true?"

"She tried to come on to me."

Steve jumped up, Mark took a menacing step toward the little pervert, but Kate stopped them both. "Don't worry. Leave him to the professionals."

Steve sat down slowly and stared hard at Harvey. "You are going to swear out your statement, and you are going to state emphatically that within Apple Blossom, you acted alone. You did, didn't you?"

"Yes. It was just me and the boy."

"You will swear that you had no encouragement from anyone else in the company."

"Yes."

"Especially the president of your company."

"Ms. Bloom had nothing to do with it." He blushed. "She wouldn't do that."

"I know," Steve said, and Kate shot him a smile that whizzed through his body. She was giving him another chance.

And then he looked at the kid. "Well, Jimmy, your

employment here is obviously terminated. Which is a shame, because you were a smart kid with a lot of promise." He stopped. "And I fully believe in second chances because I was recently given one. I might have forgiven the formula stealing part, and asked the police to let you off with probation. But what you did that night with . . . Candi can't be left unpunished. But it's for the courts to decide what to do with you."

Steve looked at Mark. "Will you take it from here?"

"Gladly." Mark filed out with the two culprits, leaving Steve and Kate alone.

Kate looked at him with a smile that could launch a thousand ships. "You know, I think I love you."

Amazingly, Steve Smith's announcement to his company employees met with roaring approval. Apparently they hadn't liked Stephanie much, either. Even the press, who'd picked up on the news, thought it was a great success story. And since Steve had done it all through private funding, and it was a privately owned company, he hadn't broken any laws.

Mark dragged himself home and dropped his briefcase on the floor, then headed straight to the kitchen for a beer. Forgoing a mug, he twisted the top and headed straight for the couch.

He was bone-tired and heartsore, and he didn't know how to fix either one. Sleeping didn't help. Dreams of Leah haunted him. Willing himself not to think about her didn't help; it just made him think about not thinking about her. He was working harder at that than he was at work.

The front door opened, startling him. He stood and whirled, reaching instinctively for his Glock, which was no longer attached to his rib.

When he saw Shelley enter, laden down with Tupperware, he moved toward her. "Hey! I assumed you were in your room. Where have you been?"

"Wednesday, dummy. Just like every other Wednesday."

That pinched, too. Shelley was a welcome guest in the Smith household, while he was persona non grata.

He took the packages from her and headed to the kitchen. "Smells good. What is it?"

"My superb chicken marsala, and Gramps's less-than-stellar sampling. Want to give them a taste test?"

"No, thanks. Too tired to eat."

"You look like hell."

He had grown used to her knowing this without sight. "Thanks a bunch."

"Hard couple of days?"

"You could say that."

After he dumped the bounty on the counter, he turned and hugged her. "Did you miss me?"

"Not particularly. You need to eat, Mark. You're too skinny."

"I can still wrestle you to the ground, brat."

She ran her fingers over his face. "And you look old."

"I feel old. So, did you have fun?"

"Tonight was a little stressful."

"As opposed to most of the nights with the Smiths the last month?"

"Well, it was different."

"How?"

"All emotional. They've been keeping it together, but this is different."

Alarm bells clanged in his head. "Why?"

"Leah's leaving tomorrow."

The alarms lowered to his chest. "What?"

"No biggie. I'm dead on my feet. Heading to bed."

"The hell you are."

He grabbed her around the waist, ignored her indignant shriek, lifted her up, and carted her to the couch. "Sit. Get off your feet."

"What a gracious host you are."

"What do you mean, she's leaving?"

"She got a job."

"What?"

"She's been offered a job in Georgia. She's flying down tomorrow to finalize and sign the contract. So it was kind of teary all around. We had a farewell supper tonight. And my marsala won."

"I could happily strangle you. Why haven't you told me she's been interviewing?"

She shrugged. "You told me you didn't want to talk about her."

"Where?" he asked, the word strangling his throat.

"The Georgia Bureau of Investigation."

He sat down heavily beside her. "She's leaving." And all of the abandonment from Heather came crashing down on him.

"Of course she's leaving, idiot. She was offered a job. Actually six, but she liked this one best."

He couldn't breathe.

Shelley's hand felt for his arm, then latched on. "What did you expect, Mark? That she'd sit around here pining for you until you grew some brains?"

That was exactly what he'd expected, he realized. No matter what had been happening, no matter where he traveled, coming back to DC he knew that if nothing else, Leah would be here. It had been the most comforting thought he'd allowed himself.

"Breathe in, breathe out," Shelley said. "It makes the heart happy. Of course, your brain has been dead for a while now, but we should still keep the blood flowing just in case a miracle occurs in your stupid skull."

"Did they put you up to this?" he asked.

She was silent for a really long time. "You are my brother. So I'm supposed to love you at all costs. But right now, I don't even like you."

She stood up. "I'm going to bed."

"No, wait!"

"No, thanks. There's food in the fridge if you get hungry."

"Shelley, please."

She didn't sit back down, but she didn't move to go. "I have been having supper with this family for a long time now. It's the highlight of my week. They love each other fiercely. They've been going through hell together. And yet they find the time to stick by each other for support. They find time to put all this crap aside to laugh and try to keep their sanity in an insane world. To try to build something good. You go ahead and judge them all you want, big brother. You judge them your way, and I'll judge them mine. And mine is better. And right now, you are despicable."

Coming from his sister, it was like a marksman going for the bull's-eye. "I'm sorry," he said softly.

"Don't apologize to me. I'm not the one who needs it."

"She's leaving."

"Yes."

"Why would she leave her family? They're all she has."

She sat back down. "You're such a fool. She has her education. She has the desire to make a difference. She has the need to make her own way."

"None of that includes me."

"Why should it? Where have you been?"

"Has she talked to you about me at all?" he asked.

"Never."

"Then how do you know all of this?" He laughed. "Dumb question."

Once again, Shelley stood. "I'm going to bed. This is giving me a headache. And I already just barely avoided one after all of the tears at the dinner table tonight. I don't want to succumb now."

"I can't stop her if she wants to go," he said, more to himself than Shelley.

"You also can't stop her if you don't talk to her. But you go right ahead and be a lonely dork. I'll still love you."

"When is she leaving?"

"The car picks her up at six."

"The *car*? They're sending her a car?"

"Well, they asked her to hitchhike to the airport, but she held out."

"She's leaving," he repeated. "I can't stop her."

"That's true. She might be sweet, but she knows what she wants."

"And she doesn't want me."

Shelley shook a finger at the sky. "This is the burden you wanted me to bear, isn't it, Lord?"

"I'm thinking I should do something."

"Did Mom and Dad drop you at birth, perchance?"

He ignored that. "Okay, I'm doing something."

"Like what?"

"I just don't know. I said some things"—he heaved a breath—"that might make asking her anything impossible."

"What do you want to ask her?"

"Not to leave."

"That might be tough. She seemed excited."

293

"Oh."

"Because her family is cheering for her, and she has nothing else holding her here."

"She has me."

"No, she doesn't." Shelley felt her watch. "You have about six hours to convince her she does. Now I'm going off to bed. With luck, you won't be here in the morning."

"Shell?"

"What, already?"

"I love you."

"You should. I'm the only sane person in this household."

Leah came awake, realizing she should have listened to her headache and taken some aspirin, because the pounding in her head wasn't going away.

But then the doorbell rang five times at least, before the pounding began again. She dragged herself from her bed and opened her door, only to see Steve whoosh past her in a robe, so she started shuffling back to the safety of her room to let him take care of it.

A pang, sharp and hard, hit her. It was her last night in her bed, her last night of knowing this was her haven forever.

It had changed over the years. She'd donated the collection of Pound Puppies long ago, as well as her china dolls. It had gone through at least four paint jobs, and several furniture changes, but it had always been her room.

She would miss it. She'd miss Steve and Gramps and—

"She's sleeping," she heard Steve say, his voice angry. "And even if she weren't I wouldn't let you near her."

"Five minutes with her," she heard, and her heart completely splintered. *Mark.*

"Just five minutes."

"No."

Leah ran back to the door of her room and listened shamelessly.

"Let him talk to her," Gramps said. "Apparently the boy has something to say."

"No," Steve said.

"Son, I haven't taken you over my knee in a long time. Don't make me try to do it now. My resulting broken hip will haunt you for decades."

"He hurt her. She's over him."

Leah bit her lip. Over him? Not in this lifetime, at this rate. But she was working on it. And if he came back only to crush her again, she'd have to start over. The last few weeks had been like walking on broken glass. Every step she took drew blood. Her sanity depended on believing she'd be okay in time.

"This is my house, and I'm letting her see him," Gramps said.

"If you do anything to hurt my sister again, I will destroy you," Steve said.

Leah winced. She was a little old for the big-brother routine. And he was up against an ex-FBI guy who knew how to use a gun.

"Leah!" Gramps called. "Company!"

She didn't answer because she was paralyzed by fear. Not seeing Mark had been torture. Seeing him might be worse.

She stood there until Gramps materialized at her door. "Leah, honey, you have company. I think you should talk to him. But it's your choice."

"What should I do, Gramps?"

"Whatever your heart says."

"My heart says, 'No way.'"

"Then I'll just go say so."

"Gramps?"

He turned back. "Yes?"

"What if it says yes, too?"

"The only times you don't say yes is if the yes is pulling into an inside straight and you know you have a bunch of nos left."

"That makes absolutely no sense."

"You want better wisdom, let me have coffee before I find a guy banging on our doors."

"Okay, I'll go. Right?"

"Whatever you want. But if you don't want him running and screaming, comb your hair and wear something sexier than that granny gown."

"I love you, Gramps."

"You should. I'm the only sane person in this household."

Leah wasn't about to show up in something sexy. She came down in jeans and a T-shirt. She did manage to brush her hair and teeth, however.

She looked like hell and she knew it. And strangely, she didn't care. She was even too sleepy to figure out what he was doing here. In any case, he got what he got. She was finished trying to impress him.

Steve was still standing bulldog guard duty.

"Down, boy," she said. "Go away. I can handle this."

"Leah," Steve said. "He's no longer friendly territory."

Mark said, "Can we go somewhere else?"

"Over my dead body," Steve said.

"It will be if you don't go away," Leah said. "Go away, Steve. Now."

"I won't hurt her. I promise," Mark said. "I just want to talk."

"Okay, but you aren't taking her out of this house."

Leah stared at her brother. "Excuse me?"

"Amuse me," Steve said, "by hanging out at home. Don't get in a car."

Mark looked pretty grim. "Are you thinking I'm going to drive her away and ravish her?"

"You've done it before. And look where we are."

Mark stood there for a second. And then he took one step toward Steve that had Leah holding her breath and wondering if she needed to get the baseball bat out of the closet.

But he stopped and didn't lift a fist, so she waited. "I respect your sister more than you do, apparently."

Leah had never thought about it, but a career as a referee might be in her future. "Time-out!"

"No one respects my sister more than I do."

Apparently she needed a bell or whistle or something. "Wait!"

"I respect her for sticking up for your lamebrain scheme. And for lying for you all this time when she's the most honest person I know."

The ref was beginning to feel faint. "To your corners," she thought she whispered.

"We love her," Steve countered. That must have been his right punch.

"Of course you do." Lame left jab from Mark.

"You obviously don't." Sucker punch. Point, Steve.

"I love her more than any woman I've ever met, you jerk."

Technical Knock-Out.

That was pretty much when the ref passed out.

* * *

Leah was either in heaven or hell, and three angels or devils were hovering over her.

Or maybe she was in a shopping mall. Two of the angels looked suspiciously like Steve and Gramps, the other like the key to heaven. She squinted and pointed. "I'll take that one." Then she smiled. "I just made a bad choice, right? I picked the devil. Gramps taught me better than that."

"Where can I take her?" she heard her first choice ask. "And may I please have water and a cold compress?"

"She needs a doctor."

"She needs me."

"She needs all of us. But right now she's getting water and a compress and Mark."

"Gramps, I really think—"

"No, you don't sometimes, son. Go get the water and a cool compress. Mark, we have a nice guest room down here. Will that do?"

She felt the one who was probably the devil lift her, and she couldn't really complain, since she'd selected him, but she was suddenly questioning her pointer finger. And as he picked her up and carried her, she wondered if she'd just consigned herself to heartbreak hell.

Mark sat on the edge of the bed and wondered how he could possibly have done anything more wrong with this woman.

He scrubbed his face and rubbed his eyes and didn't have a clue what to do next. He'd just declared before God and Gramps—who were a little interchangeable at this point—that he loved her. And he was certain neither would ever let him forget it.

He loved her. He knew it. But he'd blown it.

Then again, she'd thought he was the bad one, and she'd picked him anyway. That was a point in his favor.

298

Nothing he'd put on his résumé if he ever applied for a dating service, but, still, it was something.

He wrung out the towel from a bowl of cool water and laid it on her forehead again. "Talk to me, Leah. Or are you ignoring me?"

She didn't move.

"Either you're in a coma, or you're avoiding looking at me. I don't like either option."

She still didn't move.

"I'll pour this bowl of water over your face."

Not a twitch.

He checked her pulse again, and it was strong. But nothing was working. She'd dropped like a stone and he was frankly scared.

It was really stupid, but he leaned down and kissed her. And her eyes fluttered open. They were foggy, and her face scrunched in a who-the-hell-are-you look, but her eyes opened.

"Leah?"

"Mark?"

"Now that we've introduced ourselves, hi."

"What's going on?" She tried to sit up, but he held her back.

"Where are we and why are you here?" she asked. "This is the guest room."

"Gramps made me take you here. He was afraid I'd compromise you otherwise." He touched her forehead, felt her pulse, and relaxed. "I think I shocked you. But you're a slugger."

She looked around. "The guest room. Where are Steve and Gramps?"

"Leaving us alone."

Her eyes cleared. "Wait a minute. Steve would never let you near me."

"Never underestimate the power of Gramps."

Real life suddenly hit her. "What time is it? I have to get ready."

"For what?"

She sat up in bed. "I have a job! Isn't that great?"

"That's terrific." He forced water down her throat while he figured out how to phrase what he wanted to say.

It wasn't working. He had no right to stop her. Telling her he loved her would make her run. She had a career ahead of her, wherever it took her.

She stared at him. "What is it, Mark?"

"May I have a few minutes to figure this out?"

"What's to figure?"

He took a breath. "Well, you accused me of not telling my secrets. I only have one. I mean only one that matters to you and me. The rest are work-related, and you don't care about those anyway."

"I care about everything that has to do with you."

"This would be story time."

She just stared at him as if he were the librarian from hell. "Mark, I don't have time for this. I only have a few hours before I fly to Georgia."

"Okay." He looked at her with effort. "I wish you all the best."

"That's not a story, Mark."

"I cut to the chase."

For a little thing, she had strength. She knocked him off the bed. "That's the best you can do?"

He picked himself up and rubbed his hurt rump. "What was I supposed to do? Help me, here, Leah, because I'm lost."

"I wasn't that out of it. I heard you. Why aren't you fighting for me?"

"Because you deserve to do what you want with your life?" he ventured.

"Try again."

Mark's immediate impulse was to pull away and tell her it was none of her business. But a stronger impulse told him to stay, to tell her the truth.

"Do you mind if I go get a glass of water first?" he asked.

"Is it that hard?"

"Yes."

"Then you never have to tell me."

"Oh, yes, I do. I'll be right back."

He made his way down to the kitchen, only to find Gramps sitting there.

"Is she okay?" Gramps asked.

"She's fine. She's being a pain."

"Oh, then she's okay."

Leah stayed on the bed in the guest room, because it was the safest place away from Steve. And her heart was pounding. She didn't know if she really wanted to hear Mark's "terrible" secret. But she didn't know if she could live not knowing it either, if it was awful.

When he came back she looked into his eyes and couldn't believe they'd ever lie. But something was terribly wrong. "Are you a murderer?" she asked.

"Not yet, but your brother's at the top of my list."

She smiled. "Scratch him off. I'll be done with him before you can load your gun. Anyone else? Like me?"

He sat down on the edge of the bed and made her drink water until she could substitute as a fountain. "What is going on, Leah?"

"What do you mean?"

"Why are you leaving?"

"Hello! Because I found a job?"

"Away from here."

"I go where they ask me."

"I don't want you to go."

She pushed him away and jumped up. "How can you even say that?"

"Because I'm a selfish jerk."

"You want me to forget I have a purpose?"

"Of course not! But couldn't you have a purpose here?"

She got up and dragged him down to the parlor. Along the way she yelled, "Go away, Steve! Go away, Gramps!" and they heard muffled, "Okays."

They sat down and Leah, whose heart was killing her, said, "Mark, I want one sentence from you about what you want from me."

"You're doing this sociologist thing, aren't you?"

"Just answer the question."

He sat there for a long time, thinking. Leah almost wanted to clunk him.

He took a breath. "I want you to love me."

Leah stopped wanting to clunk him, but wasn't sure how to deal with the uncertainty. "I do love you."

He glared at her. "Then you wouldn't leave."

She glared back. "I'm supposed to give up my work for you?"

"No. Just do it here."

"How about you give up your work to be with me?"

"Okay."

Leah stared at him. "You're kidding, right?"

"Not at all. Do you want me there, Leah?"

"Would you really do that?"

"In a heartbeat. Do you want me there?"

"In a heartbeat."

"About time!" they heard from the hall.

"Go to bed, Gramps!" Leah yelled back.

"Treat her right or you're toast."

"Good night, Steve."

They smiled as they grabbed on to each other.

"One other thing I need to cover, sweetheart."

"If you don't want to tell me your secret, I'll understand," Leah said.

"Just listen. When I was training in Quantico, I met a woman also going through the program. Her name was Heather. I fell pretty hard for her. She was smart and beautiful and ambitious. I was fairly certain that once we finished training, I'd ask her to marry me."

"You loved her that much?" she whispered.

"I thought so at the time. But now I realize what a mistake it was. One weekend she said she was going home to visit her folks before the final push. I called her there one night and they didn't know what I was talking about. She never had plans to go there."

"Where'd she go?"

"I didn't find out until she got back. She'd learned she was pregnant."

"Uh-oh."

"So without telling me, asking me, talking to me, she 'got rid of the problem.'"

"Oh. My. God."

"She basically told me her career came first, and nothing was going to stand in her way."

"Oh, Mark! I'm so sorry."

"The point being, I felt utterly betrayed. And heartsick. I would have taken our baby in a heartbeat, and never asked her for a thing. But she didn't give me that choice."

"I'm so sorry," she said again.

"So you see why I was so hurt by . . . everything that happened here."

"Of course I do."

"But you aren't Heather. You're nothing like Heather."

"Well, I do want to have a career, Mark. I can't deny that."

"As well you should. You've worked hard."

"And I did lie to you."

"To protect your brother. Not to betray me, but to keep from betraying him. Trust me, you are *nothing* like Heather. You and I are the real thing, baby. I love you. See you in Georgia."

Epilogue

The entire clan gathered at Gramps's house for Thanksgiving. Leah and Mark, Kate and Steve, Jake and LeAnne—who was due in a week—and, of course, Shelley and Gramps, who were squabbling again, this time over who made the better candied yams.

Leah had been busy settling into her new apartment and her new job, but she'd still managed to miss her brother and grandfather like crazy. She began bawling the moment Gramps had opened the door, and an hour later she was still sniffling.

It had taken Mark a few months to open an office in Georgia, but he'd come down nearly every weekend since Leah had moved. And he'd learned so many creative ways to show her—no matter how busy he was—that she was never far from his thoughts.

Flowers arrived at least twice a week. Once he sent a singing telegram to her apartment. She was sure his secretary was coordinating it all, because Leah received e-mails from her several times a week with his itinerary, so she basically knew where Mark was almost all the time.

She'd been jealous for a while there when he had taken to having supper with her family Wednesday nights, but the results had been worth it. Steve was beginning to trust Mark again, and Gramps had all but adopted both Shelley and Mark.

Steve and Kate couldn't take their eyes off each other, and Jake couldn't take his hands off of LeAnne. All in all, they'd come a long way from a few months ago.

Mark backed Leah into a corner. "So tell me, miss, what are you thankful for this year?"

"Well, let's see. I'm thankful for the new no-run panty hose that came out."

"And?"

"And the Skins are playing well."

"And?"

"Hmm, I love my new apartment."

"Keep going."

"Those aren't enough for you?"

"No. Dig deep. Think harder."

"Steve and Kate seem happy."

"They're actually almost sickening."

"Unlike us, huh?"

He bent and kissed her. "Right. We're very discreet."

She laughed. "Oh, I almost forgot!"

"Yes?"

"LeAnne and Jake asked me to be J.J.'s godmother."

He gave her an indignant look. "You're not trying hard enough."

"Oh! You mean you? Yeah, I guess you're okay."

"Such a ringing endorsement."

She laughed, but then sobered. "I'm so glad you'll be near me almost permanently soon."

"Right after the holidays."

"I still don't understand why you're holding out on moving in with me," she said.

"I told you."

"Right. No marriage, no cohabitation. You sure have a strange sense of ethics."

"Maybe so, but I'm standing firm on that one."

Right then, Gramps and Shelley put out the call for everyone to gather at the table. It was so crammed with food, they could probably feed a third-world nation.

Once everyone's plate was full, Gramps held up his champagne glass, and everyone followed suit, even though LeAnne's was filled with lemon water.

"To friends old and new," Gramps said.

"To friends."

"And now a Smith family tradition. We go around the room and everyone mentions what they're most grateful for. Let's begin with Shelley, who I personally think should be grateful for my cooking lessons."

Shelley snorted. "That'll be the day. Well, of course, all the great new friends. But I'm most grateful I'm getting a new roommate."

Mark said, "Huh?"

Shelley shrugged. "You're moving to Atlanta. I don't want to stay in that house all by myself."

"Who's moving in with you?" Mark asked suspiciously.

"No one. I'm moving in here."

"What?"

"Gramps has graciously offered me a room."

"Oh, Shelley, that's wonderful!" Leah said, who thought it was a perfect solution. She'd been so worried about Gramps the last few months. She looked at Mark. "See, your sister has no problem with cohabitation."

Gramps cleared his throat. "Jake?"

"That's easy. My gorgeous wife and our baby. And, of course, my new career, thanks to Mark."

"LeAnne?"

"A healthy baby and a grounded husband," LeAnne said.

"Kate?"

"So many things I can't even name them all. I'm grateful for newfound happiness."

"Steve?"

"To second chances," he said, smiling at Kate, who blushed.

"Leah?" Gramps said.

"I'm grateful to be getting a new roommate shortly, too." And she smiled at a suddenly gaping Mark.

"Mark?"

"I'm grateful to be able to accept Leah's marriage proposal."

Everyone laughed, because they all knew the significance of Leah's invitation and Mark's acceptance. The negotiations over their future living arrangements—and marital status—had been an ongoing battle.

"And now you, Gramps," Leah said, squeezing Mark's hand.

"That's easy. I'm grateful for love."

"Hear, hear."

And then they dug in.

Turn the page
for a special sneak
preview of

TO KISS
A FROG

by
ELLE JAMES

Coming this March!

Chapter One

Bound to a cypress tree, Craig Thibodeaux struggled to free his hands, the coarse rope rubbing his wrists raw with the effort. A fat bayou mosquito buzzed past his ear to feast on his unprotected skin. The bulging insect had plenty of blood in its belly, much more and the flying menace would be grounded.

What I wouldn't give for a can of bug repellent.

Craig shook his head violently in hopes of discouraging the little scavenger from landing.

The dark-skinned Cajuns who'd kidnapped him stood guard on either side of him, their legs planted wide and arms crossed over bare muscular chests. They looked like rejected cast from a low-budget barbarian movie, and they didn't appear affected by the blood-sucking mosquitoes, in the least.

"Hey, Mo, don't you think you guys are taking this a little too far?" Craig aimed a sharp blast of breath at a bug crawling along his shoulder. "I swear I won that card game fair and square."

The man on his right didn't turn his way or flick an eyelid.

Craig looked to his left. "Come on, Larry, we've been friends since you and I got caught snitching apples from Old Lady Reneau's orchard. Let me go."

Larry didn't twitch a muscle. He stared straight ahead, as if Craig hadn't uttered a word.

"If it will make you feel any better, I'll give you back your money," Craig offered, although he'd really won that game.

He'd known Maurice Saulnier and Lawrence Ezell since he was a snot-nosed kid spending his summer vacations with his Uncle Joe in Bayou Miste of southern Louisiana. He had considered them friends. Until now.

Granted, Craig had only been back for less than a week after an eight-year sojourn into the legal jungles of the New Orleans court system. But his absence shouldn't be a reason for them to act the way they were. An odd sensation tickled his senses, as if foreshadowing something unpleasant waiting to happen. Sweat dripped off his brow, the heat and humidity of the swamp oppressive.

"Look guys, whatever you're planning, you won't get away with." Craig strained against the bonds holding him tight to the rough bark of the cypress tree.

"Ah, *chere*, but we will." A low musical voice reached out of the darkness preceding the appearance of a woman. She wore a flowing, bright red caftan with a sash tied around her ample girth and a matching handkerchief covering her hair. Although large, she floated into the firelight, her bone necklace rattling in time to a steady drumbeat building in the shadows. Her skin was a light brown, almost mocha, weathered by the elements and age. But her dark brown eyes shined brightly, the flames of a nearby fire danced in their depths.

Despite the weighty warmth of the swamp, a chill

crept down Craig's spine. "Who's the lady in the muumuu?"

The silent wonder next to him deigned to speak in a reverent whisper, "Madame LeBieu."

Craig frowned and mentally scratched his head. Madame LeBieu . . . Madame LeBieu . . . oh, yes. The infamous Bayou Miste Voodoo Priestess. He studied her with more interest and a touch of unease. Was he to be a sacrifice in some wacky Voodoo ceremony?

"Are you in charge of these two thugs?" Craig feigned a cockiness he didn't feel.

"It be I who called upon dem." She dipped her head in a regal nod.

"Then call them off and untie me." Craig shot an angry look at the men on either side of him. "You've obviously got the wrong guy."

"Were you not de man what be goin' out with de sweet Lisa LeBieu earlier dis very evening?"

"Yes," Craig said, caution stretching his answer, as dread pooled in his stomach. He didn't go into the fact that Lisa wasn't so sweet. "Why?"

"I am Madame LeBieu and Lisa be my granddaughter. She say you dally with her heart and cast it aside." The woman's rich, melodious voice held a thread of steel.

Craig frowned in confusion. "You mean this isn't about the card game? This is about Lisa?"

"No, dis be 'bout you mistreatment of de women."

"I don't get it. I didn't touch her. She came on to me, and I took her home."

"Abuse not always takes de physical form. You shunned her love and damage her chakras. For dis, you pay."

Craig cocked an eyebrow in disbelief. "You mean I was conked on the head and dragged from my bed all

because I refused to sleep with your granddaughter?"
He snorted. "This is a new one on me."

"Craig Thibodeaux, I know your kind." Madame
LeBieu shook a thick, brown finger in his face. "You
break hearts wherever you go, dating one woman after
another and no love to show for it. You've wielded your
loveless way for de last time." Madame LeBieu flicked
her fingers, and the flames behind her leaped higher.
Then, reaching inside the voluminous sleeves of the
caftan, she whipped out an atomizer and sprayed a
light floral scent all around him. The aroma mixed and
mingled with the dark musty smells of the swamp's
stagnant pools and decaying leaves.

"So you're going to douse me in perfume to unman
me?" Craig's bark of laughter clashed with the rising
beat of the drums. The humor of the situation was
short-lived when the mosquitoes decided they liked
him even more with the added scent. Craig shook all
over to discourage the beggars from landing.

"Ezili Freda Daome, Goddess of love and all that is
beautiful, listen to our prayers, accept our offerings,
and enter into our arms, legs and hearts." Madame
LeBieu's head dropped back, and she spread her arms
wide. The drumbeat increased in intensity, reverberat-
ing off the canopy of trees shrouded in low-hanging
Spanish moss.

The pounding emphasized the throbbing ache in the
back of Craig's head from where Madame LeBieu's
henchmen had beaned him in his room at the bait shop
prior to dragging him here. The combined smells of perfume and swamp, along with the jungle beat and chanting nut case made his stomach churn. The darkness of
the night surrounded him, pushing fear into his soul.

Craig had a sudden premonition that whatever was
about to happen, he was not going to like and had the

potential to change his life entirely. Half of him wished they would just get on with it, whatever it was, the other half quaked in apprehension.

The Voodoo priestess's arms and head dropped, the drums crashing to a halt. Silence descended. Not a single cricket, frog, or bird interrupted the eerie stillness.

Craig broke the trance, fighting his growing fear with false bravado. "And I'm supposed to believe all this mumbo jumbo?" He snorted. "Give me a break. Next thing, you'll be waving a fairy wand and saying bibbity-bobbity-boo."

Madame LeBieu leveled a cold, hard stare at him.

Another shiver snaked down Craig's spine. With the sweat dripping off his brow and chills racing down his back, he thought he might be ill. Maybe even hallucinating.

A small girl appeared at Madame LeBieu's side, handing her an ornate cup. She waited silently for the woman to drink. Craig noticed that his two former friends bowed their heads as the Voodoo lady sipped from the cup then handed it back to the girl. The child clutched the cup as if it were her dearest possession and bowed at the waist, backing into the shadows.

With a flourishing sweep of her wrist, Madame LeBieu pulled a pastel pink, blue and white scarf from the sleeve of her caftan, and waved it in Craig's face.

"Mistress of Love, hear my plea.
Help dis shameless man to see."

"You know I have family in high places, don't you?" Craig said. Not that they were there to help him now.

Madame LeBieu continued as though he hadn't spoken.

"Though he's strong, his actions bold, his heart is loveless, empty cold.
By day a frog, by night a man,

315

'til de next full moon, dis curse will span."

Craig stopped shaking his head, mosquitoes be damned. What was the old lady saying? "Hey, what's this about frogs?"

"A woman will answer Ezili's call, one who'll love him, warts and all."

"Who, the frog or me?" He chuckled nervously at the woman's fanatical words, downplaying his rising uneasiness. His next sarcastic statement was cut off when Mo's heavily muscled forearm crashed into his stomach. "Oomph!"

"Silence!" Mo's command warned of further retribution should Craig dare to interrupt again.

Which worked out great, since Craig was too busy sucking wind to restore air to his lungs. All he could do was glare at his former friend. If only looks could kill, he'd have Mo six feet under in a New Orleans minute.

Madame LeBieu continued,

"He'll watch by day and woo by night, to gain her love, he'll have to fight, to break de curse, be whole again, transformed into a caring man."

"You didn't have to knock the wind out of *my* sails." Craig wheezed and jerked his head in Madame LeBieu's direction. "*She's* the one making all the noise, talking nonsense about frogs and warts."

Mo's face could have been etched in stone.

The old witch held her finger in Craig's face, forcing him to stare at it. Then she drew the finger to her nose and his gaze followed until he noticed her eyes. A strange glow, having nothing to do with fire, burned in their brown-black centers. Madame LeBieu's voice dropped to a low, threatening rumble.

"Should he deny dis gift from you, a frog he'll remain in de blackest bayou."

With a flourishing spray of perfume and one last

wave of the frothy scarf, Madame LeBieu backed away from Craig, disappearing into the darkness from whence she'd come.

Craig's stomach churned and a tingling sensation spread throughout his body. He attributed his discomfort to the nauseating smells and the ropes cutting off his circulation. "Hey, you're not going to leave me here trussed up like a pig on a spit, are you?" Craig called out to the departing Priestess.

A faint response carried to him from deep in the shadows. "Don't tempt me, boy."

As soon as Madame LeBieu was gone, the men who'd stood motionless at his side throughout the Voodoo ceremony moved. They untied his bonds, grabbed him beneath the arms and hauled him back to the small canoe-like pirogue they'd brought him in.

Forced to step into the craft, Craig fell to the hard wooden seat in the middle. When the other two men climbed in, the boat rocked violently, slinging him from side to side. One man sat in front, the other at the rear. Both lifted paddles and struck out across the bayou, away from the rickety pier.

"So what's it to be now?" Craig rubbed his midsection. "Are you two going to take me out into the middle of the swamp and feed me to the alligators?" He knew these swamps as well as anyone, and the threat was real, although he didn't think Mo and Larry would do it. Would they?

"No harm will come to you what hasn't already been levied by Madame LeBieu," Mo said. Dropping his macho facade, he gave Craig a pitying look. "Man, I feel sorry for you."

"Why? Because a crazy lady chanted a little mumbo jumbo and sprayed perfume in my face?" He could handle chanting crazy people. He'd represented a few of the harmless ones in the courtroom. "Don't worry about me. If I were you, I'd worry more about the monster law suit I could file against the two of you for false imprisonment."

"Going to jail would be easy compared to what you be in for." Larry's normally cheerful face wore a woeful expression.

The pale light of the half moon shimmered between the boughs of overhanging trees. Craig could see they were headed back to his uncle's marina. Perhaps they weren't going to kill him after all. Madame LeBieu was probably just trying to scare him into leaving her granddaughter alone. No problem there. With relatives like that, he didn't need the hassle.

Besides, he'd been bored with Lisa within the first five minutes of their date. Most of the women who agreed to go out with him, were only interested in what his money could buy them. Lisa had been no different.

The big Cajuns pulled up to the dock at the Thibodeaux Marina. As soon as Craig got out, they turned the boat back into the swamp, disappearing into the darkness like a fading dream.

Tired and achy, Craig trudged to his little room behind the shop, wondering if the night had been just that. A dream. He grimaced. Dream, hell! What had happened was the stuff nightmares were made of. The abrasions on his wrist confirmed it wasn't a dream, but it was over now. He would heed the warning and stay away from Madame LeBieu's granddaughter from now on.

He let himself in through the back door and stared around the place while flexing his sore muscles. The room was a mess from the earlier scuffle, short-lived though it was. Craig righted the nightstand and fished the alarm clock out from underneath the bed.

Without straightening the covers he flopped onto the mattress in the tiny bedroom. It was a far cry from his suite back home, but he'd spent so many summers here as a boy, the cramped quarters didn't bother him. He was bone tired from a full day's work, a late night date gone sour, and his encounter with Madame LeBieu. What did it matter whether the sheets were of the finest linen or the cheapest cotton? A bed was a bed.

"Just another day at the office." Craig yawned and stared at the ceiling. It would be dawn soon and his uncle expected him up bright and early to help prepare bait and fill gas tanks in the boats they rented to visiting fishermen.

Craig closed his eyes and drifted into a troubled sleep where drums beat, witches wove spells, and frogs littered the ground. A chant echoed throughout the dream, "By day a frog, by night a man, 'til the next full moon, this curse will span."

What a crock!

Professor and research scientist, Elaine Smith, moaned for the tenth time. How the staff must be laughing. Brainiac, Elaine Smith, member of Mensa, Valedictorian of her High School, Undergraduate and Masters programs, with an IQ completely off the scale and she hadn't had a clue. Until she'd opened the door to the stairwell in the science building to find her fiancé, Brian, with his hands up the shirt of a bossomy blond department secretary, while sucking out her tonsils.

The woman saw her first, broke contact and tapped Brian's shoulder. "Uh, this is a little awkward." She twittered her fingers at Elaine. "Hi, Dr. Smith."

"Elaine, I can explain," Brian said, his hands springing free of the double-D breasts.

Without a word, Elaine marched back to the lab.

She'd only been away for a moment. If the drink machine on the second floor had worked, she wouldn't have opened that door. Thank God, she'd made this discovery before she'd been even more idiotic and married the creep.

She crossed the shiny white floor to her desk and ran her hand over her favorite microscope, letting the coolness seep into her flushed skin. With careful precision, she poured a drop from the glass jar marked Bayou Miste onto a slide. With another clean slide, she smeared the sample across the glass, and slid it beneath the scope.

The routine process of studying microorganisms calmed her like no other tonic. Her heartbeat slowed and she lost herself in the beauty of microbiology. She didn't have to think about the world outside the science department. Many times in her life, she'd escaped behind lab doors to avoid the ugly side of society.

"Elaine the brain! Elaine the brain!" Echoes of childrens' taunts from long ago plagued her attempts at serenity.

Elaine snorted. Wouldn't they laugh, now? Elaine-the-brain, too stupid to live.

A tear dropped onto the lens of the microscope, blurring her viewfinder, and the lab door burst open. Elaine scrubbed her hand across her eyes before she looked up. She'd be damned if she'd let the jerk see her cry.

"Elaine, let me explain." Brian strode in, a sufficiently contrite expression on his face.

He'd probably practiced the expression in the mirror to make it look so real. Elaine wasn't buying it. She forced her voice to be flat and disinterested. "Brian, I'm busy."

"We have to talk."

"No . . . we don't." She turned her back to him, her chest tightened and her stomach clenched.

"Look, I'm sorry." Brian's voice didn't sound convincing. "It's just . . . well . . . ah hell. I needed more."

Elaine's mouth dropped open, and she spun to face him. "More what? More women? More conquests? More sex in the hallways?"

He dug his hands in his pocket and scuffed his black leather shoe on the white tile. When he looked up, a corner of his mouth lifted and his gray eyes appeared sad. "I needed to know I was more important than a specimen, that I was wanted for more than just a convenient companion."

"So you made out with a secretary in the stairwell?"

"She at least pays attention to me." He shook his head. "I should have broken our engagement first, but every time I tried, you'd bury yourself in this lab." He ran a hand through his hair and stepped closer. "It would never have worked between us. I couldn't compete with your first love."

"What are you talking about?"

"Your obsession with science." He inhaled deeply and looked at the corner ceiling, before his gaze came back to her. "Face it, Elaine, you love science more than you ever loved me."

"No, I don't!" Her denial was swift, followed closely by the thought, "Did she?"

He crossed he" arms over his chest and stood with his feet spread slightly. "Then say it."

"Say what?"

"Say, I love you," Brian stood still waiting for her response.

Elaine summoned righteous indignation, puffed out her chest and prepared to say the words he'd asked for.

321

She opened her mouth, but the words stuck in her throat like a nasty-tasting wad of guilt. Instead of saying anything, she exhaled.

Had she ever really loved Brian? She stared across at his rounded face and curly blond hair. He had the geek-boy-next-door look, and he'd made her smile on occasion. She'd enjoyed the feeling of having someone to call her own, and to fill the lonely gap in her everyday existence.

But, did she love him? After all the years of living in relative isolation from any meaningful relationships, was she capable of feeling love?

Her chest felt as empty as her roiling stomach. He was right. She couldn't say she loved him when she knew those words were a lie. And as much as she didn't like conflict, she disliked lying more. How long had she been deluding herself into thinking they were the perfect couple?

"It's no use, Elaine. Our marriage would be a huge mistake. The only way you'd look at me is if I were a specimen under your microscope. It's not enough. I need more. I need someone who isn't afraid to get out and experience the world beyond this lab."

Brian turned and walked out, leaving a quiet room full of scientific equipment and one confused woman.

Afraid to get out? Elaine glanced around the stark clean walls of the laboratory, the one place she could escape to when she wanted to feel safe.

Dear God, why can't I be like normal people? Brian was right. She felt more comfortable behind the lab door than in the world outside.

When she stared down at the litter of items on the table, blinking to clear the tears from her eyes, she spied the jar labeled Bayou Miste. The container had come to her in the mail, an anonymous sample of

Louisiana swamp water. She stood, momentarily transfixed by the sight of the plain mason jar, a strange thrumming sound echoing in her subconscious, almost like drums beating. Probably some punk with his woofers too loud in the parking lot.

With an odd sense of fate, she leaned over the microscope, dried her tear from the lens with a tissue, and studied the slide. Her skin tingled and her heartbeat amplified. Here was her opportunity to get away from the lab. If she couldn't solve the microcosm of her love life, she could help solve the pollution problems of an ecosystem.

Chapter Two

Light glinted off the mirror on the eastern wall of the tiny bedroom, nudging Craig out of a deep sleep. He cracked an eyelid and stared at the persistent glare. Sunlight on the mirror? The sun never shown directly into this room in the morning, only in the late afternoon. Glancing at the clock on the nightstand, he jerked awake—groggy, but awake.

Six-thirty? As in six-thirty in the evening? He squinted at the clock. Yes, the little red light indicating PM glowed and the sun only shone into his room on its way to the western horizon. Damn. His uncle knew he had a meeting with Jason Littington at one o'clock this afternoon. Why didn't he wake him earlier?

Craig stretched and flexed his muscles, surprised how agile he felt after being tied to a tree. He felt woozy, not like a concussion, but more like a hangover from too much alcohol and not enough water to replenish his brain cells. But, all in all, no harm had been done in last night's fracas.

Fuzzyheaded, but definitely hungry, he rolled out of bed—and fell a long way down to the floor. Too late, he realized he should have put his feet down first. As he fell, his body tensed, and his muscles braced for impact.

Craig landed on all fours, the wind temporarily knocked out of him. When breathing returned to normal, he looked around.

Huh? He hadn't been drunk when he went to sleep the previous night. But here he was, crouched on the floor looking up. The bed he'd just vacated and the wooden nightstand towered over him. He shook his head to clear the haze. Something wasn't right. Perhaps it was because he was squatting.

Squatting? Why am I squatting?

He attempted to straighten, his muscles bunching in an unfamiliar way. When he tried to stand, he only leaped to another squatting position, and he was no taller than before. The nightstand and bed still loomed next to him.

Noises from the front of the store alerted him to his uncle's presence, and he crawled for the door, forcing his arms and legs to propel him. He'd never noticed how dusty and bumpy the wooden planks were. The going was slow and tedious, but eventually he made it to the doorway leading from the back room into the bait shop.

Craig opened his mouth to cry, "Uncle Joe!" but his voice croaked.

"I don't know where that boy gets off, leaving me here to answer to Littington," the old man muttered.

Craig forced air past his vocal chords, only to emit another croak. *I'm here, Uncle Joe,* he thought, willing his uncle to turn his way. *I was here all day. Why didn't you wake me up?*

Joe Thibodeaux had his back to him, rooting around behind the counter, shifting small boxes of weights and hooks, searching for something.

"Damn!" Uncle Joe pulled back his hand. A hook protruded from his thumb, blood oozing around the gold metal. "This place needs a good cleaning. Couldn't find a snake if it stuck its head out and bit my ass."

He gingerly eased the hook from the digit and dabbed the blood against his T-shirt. Then, he turned and circled the counter, practically stepping on Craig. "What the heck—" Uncle Joe used the tip of his sneaker to push Craig out of his way. "You don't belong in here. Go on. Get on out of here. I ain't got time to mess with you." His uncle strode for the door leading out to the dock.

A fly buzzed past Craig's head and he froze, his gaze tracking the insect's flight. An urge so powerful, a primal instinct older than time, erupted in his brain. He struggled to control it, fought to stop it, but he couldn't help himself. How could he deny what his body insisted on doing? He watched in horror as his tongue snaked out to snatch the fly from the air, and he swallowed it whole.

His eyes bulged. *Was that my tongue*? *I saw my tongue out in front of my face*? Making the next logical connection, Craig gagged. Bluck! He'd swallowed a fly! He stuck his tongue out and pawed at it with his hand to remove the bug guts and germs. It was then he noticed his skin.

The room spun and Craig sat down on the floor. He blinked his eyes several times, and then held out his arm again. It wasn't tanned and sprinkled with manly black hairs, like it had the night before. His skin was smooth, shiny and—and—green!

Numb with shock, he crawled to the glass display cabinet with the expensive fishing reels. He bunched the muscles in his legs and jumped high enough to peer at his reflection in the glass. A mottled green water frog looked back at him.

No way!

He jumped again. The frog came into view again.

This couldn't be happening. He was still asleep and this was just a continuation of the whole Voodoo thing—one long crazy nightmare. People just didn't change into frogs overnight—no matter what that Voodoo witch would have him believe. He was asleep right? He bunched his legs to take another look. Propelling himself off the ground, he realized he'd miscalculated a little too late and whacked his head into the glass.

Damn!

Not only did he see the frog again but, based on the pain in his head, he wasn't asleep either.

His legs trembled, and he leaned against the cabinet, feeling his miniscule frog heart pounding against his slick white chest. A chest like the one on the frog he'd dissected in high school. Not a chest a man could pound his fist against.

Holy shit. Now, what was he supposed to do? Somehow, he had to find that Voodoo witch and get her to undo what she'd done.

Shadows lengthened in the bait shop. The sun was setting and Uncle Joe hadn't turned on the inside lights.

Craig's skin tightened, stretching and pulling. He trembled with the force of every cell in his body splitting and changing in a miraculous metamorphosis. A roaring sound filled his ears and he watched as everything around him shrank.

Focus, Elaine. She had a mission to accomplish come hell or high water. By the looks of the long causeways she'd crossed getting here, high water it was. If she concentrated on her mission, she wouldn't keep thinking of Brian's betrayal nor the millions of gallons of water surrounding her.

With a shiver coursing down her spine, she sent a fervent prayer to the heavens that she wouldn't have to get in it. Hopefully, everything she had to do, she could do from a boat or dry land. Egad, a boat. Another shiver shook her body.

Elaine had inherited her mother's cursed fear of water. No one incident could be blamed for her irrational panic in regard to getting in over her head, much to her chagrin. There was no logic in this crippling fear. Ever since she was a child, she'd been deathly afraid of entering water deeper than her bathtub, much preferring to shower.

Then why the hell didn't she send a graduate student to the bayous instead of coming herself? She sighed. She'd face a thousand miles of swamp filled with water just to get away from the university and the disaster of her love life.

Elaine had spent the entire trip from Tulane to Bayou Miste fuming and berating her blind stupidity. Why hadn't she seen through Brian's lies? Throughout their four-month courtship and ultimate engagement, he'd been kind, attentive and accommodating of her need for space to do her work. What more could she want?

Passion, gut-wrenching love, and most of all fidelity? Was that too much to ask? They'd been engaged, for heaven's sake.

She slammed her palm against the steering wheel. If she hadn't seen it with her own eyes, she'd never have believed Brian was having an affair. Right under her nose!

No matter. She was much better off without him.

When Elaine pulled into the little town of Bayou

Miste, Louisiana, on the edge of the Atchafalaya Basin, she had completed her self-coaching session. She was a worthy and intelligent scientist whose work was important to the protection of a fragile ecosystem. She would locate the source of pollution killing the creatures that lived in the swamps. Once her research was complete, she would document her findings and take whatever action was necessary to close down the source and force them to clean up the mess they'd made.

But, as much as she tried to use logic and reason, Brian's rejection still stung. Was something wrong with her? Would she ever feel more passionate about a man than science?

The trip had taken longer than Elaine had anticipated. She hoped the marina was still open. She wanted to move in to her rental cottage and set up her lab as soon as possible.

Bayou Miste could barely be called a town. Main Street ended in the parking lot of Thibodeaux Marina, beyond which, spread endless miles of swamp. Dilapidated houses lined both sides of the street for the equivalent of one city block. It was a good thing she'd made her arrangements before she came. Only one rental house existed in the entire town and it was all hers for the next three weeks.

An unsettling thought struck her and she glanced up breathing a sigh of relief when she saw electrical lines. By the looks of the buildings, the town had to have been built over seventy years ago, maybe a hundred. Peeling paint curled off the sides of a few houses. Weather and the swamp humidity had done their job to try to convert the structures into recycled compost.

The marina's bait shop was in the same condition, except where someone had applied a fresh coat of white paint to a square patch about seven feet tall and seven feet wide. The bright white contrasted sharply to the graying boards. The can and paint brush stood against the wall, waiting for the painter to pick up where he'd left off.

The dock stretched to the side and behind the bait shop located at the center of the marina. No one stirred in the lingering heat of the late evening. She understood why. She flipped her visor down and checked her appearance attempting to smooth the frizz her hair had become in the moist air. It was no use. Her hair knew no boundaries with one hundred percent humidity. She gave up.

Much as she hated to admit it, Brian had a point. She hadn't been out of the laboratory in a while. Mixing with people, and being sociable was not easy for her in the best of circumstances. Invariably, she clammed up and stood like a lump or, on occasion, she blurted out her opinions and alienated everyone within earshot. She preferred to read or walk alone. Sometimes she talked with other scientists, sharing information on past experiment or theories.

She felt like a fish out of water when she was outside the university environment. What did normal people talk about? What could she find in common with them? Hopefully, it wouldn't be an issue while she was in Bayou Miste. She would find her specimens, conduct her studies and not be bothered by social obligations.

Elaine pushed her glasses up her nose, gathered her purse and her courage and climbed out of her practical, four-door sedan. After a few deep breaths of thick swamp air, she almost gagged. The rank smell of fish and stagnant water permeated the air. She squared her shoulders and marched up to the door of the bait shop, pointedly ignoring the water beyond.

Mr. Thibodeaux said she could find him here. Not

only did he own the marina, dilapidated as it was, but he was also the landlord of the house she'd be living in during her stay. She hoped the house was in better shape.

She pulled at the rusty handle on the screen door, hoping the inside of the bait shop didn't smell as bad as the outside. When the door swung wide, she stepped into the dark interior and inhaled deeply. Again, she choked. A combination of earthy, fishy, musty odors assailed her nostrils.

Her eyes adjusted to the darkness after the waning light from the setting sun. Soft thumping noises emanated from the far end of the store, but she couldn't see well enough in the dim interior to make out a person. Why hadn't anyone turned on the lights?

"Excuse me," she called softly.

More thumping and scuffling ensued. Elaine thought she heard a faint moan, but nobody appeared.

She cleared her throat and tried again. "Excuse me." Her voice echoed off the walls, and she cringed.

Still no response.

What was wrong with these people? She knew she'd spoken loud enough this time to wake half the town. Perhaps the person behind the counter wasn't a person. Maybe it was a dog or cat.

A frown settled between her brows. Whatever it was might be trapped or hurt and needed her help. She strode across the room and had almost reached the other end of the building when a man rose from behind the counter, his back to her.

Elaine stopped so fast she almost tipped over. Her eyes widened and her mouth fell open.

Wow!

She'd never seen such a beautiful specimen of the male of her species in all her twenty-six years. His broad, bare shoulders were solid and tanned, each muscle neatly defined and precisely curved. His back tapered down to a trim waistline, disappearing below the top of the counter to what promised to be sexy buttocks of firm proportions.

With his back still to her, he cleared his throat. "Am I . . . ?" He held his hands up to the meager light from the windows and flexed his fingers. Then, holding his arms in front of him, he plucked a hair. "Ouch!" He laughed out loud and shouted, "Thank God!"

Elaine stood in a silent stupor as the muscles in his shoulders flexed and extended with each movement. Her mouth went dry and not a single coherent thought surfaced.

He turned and treated her to the full force of his ice-blue stare. Ebony hair hung long around his ears and curled down the nape of his neck in dark waves. A single lock fell across his forehead and he pushed it back with a broad hand.

Elaine's fingers itched to pull the curl back down on his forehead. Her stomach turned flip-flops at the expanse of hard-muscled chest only a few feet away.

Startled by her reaction to the half-naked man standing in front of her, her eyes widened and she licked her lips. At least she *thought* he was half naked. Was that a bare leg she could see through the glass case standing between them? Her gaze slid downward.

The man glanced down, his eyes widening. A faint red stained his cheeks. He folded his arms across his chest and quickly leaned against the counter. "Can I help you?"

It took her several seconds to locate her tongue before she could reply. "I need you," she stammered.

The man smiled and a wicked eyebrow rose up under the stray lock of hair that had fallen back over his forehead. He didn't comment, nor did he move, staying firmly in place, the counter covering him from the waist down. "You want me?"

Heat crept up her neck and into her face, when Elaine realized what she'd said and what she'd tried to see. "I mean I'm here about the bed."

His smile broadened.

Elaine pressed her hands to her cheeks, her mortification complete. Where had her intellectual vocabulary and scientific mind gone? She felt like a giddy, hormonal teenager instead of a revered scientist with numerous research articles and a book under her belt. "Oh, good grief, let me start over."

"Perhaps you should." His words seeped into every pore of her skin like butter on a hot potato. He could have mocked her sudden inability to articulate. Instead, he graced her with an encouraging grin.

Elaine's mouth opened, but her brain refused to engage. She had the overwhelming urge to run her tongue over his lips to taste his next sentence.

He cleared his throat. "Are you, or are you not, going to start over?"

Elaine gulped, then stammered, "I'm Elaine Smith." Wiping the sweat from her palm, she stuck her hand out.

"Craig Thibodeaux." His rough hand enveloped hers. The simple gesture sent tingles through her digits, reminding every cell in her body she was female, single and over twenty-one.

The myriad of sensations raced from her fingertips to her lower extremities, moistening places that had no business being wet in the company of a strange man . . . a sexy-as-hell, strange man. Maybe shaking hands with him wasn't such a good idea after all.

When her senses returned, she jerked her hand back and rubbed it against her khaki slacks to still the spread of electrical impulses triggering an entirely chemical response throughout her body. Her reaction was pure physics and chemistry, nothing more, nothing less, she told herself. Besides, hadn't she just broken off an engagement? Get a grip.

"Mr. Thibodeaux, I spoke with you on the phone about renting a cottage for three weeks." She chose her words carefully, rather than uttering embarrassing nonsense like she had earlier.

"You must have spoken to my Uncle Joe. He owns the place."

"Oh, I see." She dragged her gaze from the vicinity of his chest and scanned the interior again. "Where can I find him?"

"I think he's out on the dock. Why don't you go see?" Craig didn't make a move from behind the counter. "I'd take you out there, but I have something I need to do first."

The thought of the dock paralyzed her. Docks were generally built around water. "I can wait," she said, quickly. "Go ahead and finish what you were doing."

Craig frowned and glanced away. "No really, I don't want to hold you up. Just go on outside. He's sure to be within shouting distance. I'll be out in just a minute."

"Okay." Elaine stared at the door he indicated with all the anticipation of one heading for a guillotine. "Are you sure you don't want me to wait?"

"Positive. Please, go on."

Geez. He was in a hurry to get rid of her.

Good. She didn't have time for men. Remember? Besides, she couldn't possibly have anything in common with an uneducated fish boy like Craig Thibodeaux. She was better off sticking with her scientific studies. She could have much more interesting conversations talking to herself. At least with her own company, she knew where she stood. A little voice popped into her head, yeah, hiding behind a microscope.

Elaine liked to think she was moving at a swift walk toward the door. If she was honest, it was more like a snail's pace. But she didn't stop, she kept right on going. Even though the dock was scary, the marina owner's nephew left her more unsettled than the murky swamp around her. She reminded herself that she'd come to study frogs, not the mating habits of the Cajun swamp people. The less she saw of Craig Thibodeaux, the better off she'd be.

AGAINST HIS WILL

TRISH JENSEN

Get Ready For . . . The Time of Your Life!

FBI agent Jake Donnelly is not a happy camper. His favorite aunt is gone and he's gained . . . not the childhood retreat he loves, but custody of a bulldog. Worse still, the terms of the will require him and Muffin to spend two weeks at a dog spa owned by a quack canine shrink named LeAnne.

But after one look at the luscious LeAnne, Jake knows the dogs aren't going to be the only ones drooling at the Hound Dog Hotel. At a place where doggie astrologers talk about the Puppy Love dating service and breakfast is eaten at the Chow Chow diner, it is easy for desires to be unleashed. Private therapy sessions with the lovely doctor soon have Jake eating out of her hand and deciding maybe Muffin *is* man's best friend if he can bring his owner and his trainer together for good.

___52377-9 $5.99 US/$6.99 CAN

TRISH JENSEN
Stuck
with
You

Paige Hart and Ross Bennett can't stand each other. There has been nothing but bad blood between these two lawyers . . . until a courthouse bombing throws them together. Exposed to the same rare and little-understood Tibetan Concupiscence Virus, the two archenemies are quarantined for seven days in one hospital room. As if that isn't bad enough, the virus's main side effect is to wreak havoc on human hormones. Paige and Ross find themselves irresistibly drawn to one another. Succumbing to their wildest desires, they swear it must be a temporary and bug-induced attraction, but even after they part ways, they can't seem to forget each other. Which begs the question: Did the lustful litigators contract the disease after all? Or have they been acting under the influence of another fever altogether—the love bug?

___52442-8 $5.99 US/$6.99 CAN

ROBIN WELLS

THE
BABE
Magnet

Holt Landen is in trouble. He's been left with a six-month-old child he never knew he had, and while he's attracted plenty of babes in the past, they were always the kind in high heels and garters.

Stevie Stedquest dispenses parenting advice on a radio talk show, but she doesn't have kids. And though she wants a child of her own, Mr. Right is nowhere on the horizon.

Baby Isabelle needs a mother in the worst way. A temporary marriage between her newfound father and Stevie would solve the problem, but they seem terribly mismatched. Fortunately, Isabelle has two aces up her diaper: opposites attract, and her daddy isn't the only babe magnet in the family.

- -